CW00494029

Radical Love

Also by Neil Blackmore

Soho Blues

Split My Heart

The Intoxicating Mr Lavelle

The Dangerous Kingdom of Love

Radical Love

NEIL BLACKMORE

HUTCHINSON
HEINEMANN

1 3 5 7 9 10 8 6 4 2

Hutchinson Heinemann
20 Vauxhall Bridge Road
London SW1V 2SA

Hutchinson Heinemann is part of the Penguin Random House group of
companies whose addresses can be found at global.penguinrandomhouse.com.

Penguin
Random House
UK

Copyright © Neil Blackmore 2023

Neil Blackmore has asserted his right to be identified as the author of this
Work in accordance with the Copyright, Designs and Patents Act 1988.

First published by Hutchinson Heinemann in 2023

www.penguin.co.uk

A CIP catalogue record for this book is available from the British Library.

ISBN 9781529152074 (hardback)
ISBN 9781529152081 (trade paperback)

Typeset in 12/14.75pt Dante MT Std by Jouve (UK), Milton Keynes.
Printed and bound in Great Britain by Clays Ltd, Elcograf S.p.A.

The authorised representative in the EEA is Penguin Random House Ireland,
Morrison Chambers, 32 Nassau Street, Dublin D02 YH68

www.greenpenguin.co.uk

MIX
Paper from
responsible sources
FSC® C018179

Penguin Random House is committed to a
sustainable future for our business, our readers
and our planet. This book is made from Forest
Stewardship Council® certified paper.

AUTHOR'S NOTE

This is a true story. All named characters at Vere Street were real people, as revealed in both pseudonyms and actual names in the press and in legal reports of the time.

Newspaper reports, published pamphlets, fragments of letters from John Church to Ned, and cited popular poems are all real. The trial transcripts are, for the most part, verbatim from the record.

'The story of this man who had killed a messenger and hanged himself would make interesting reading. One could almost write a whole chapter on him. Perhaps not a whole chapter but a reasonable paragraph, at any rate.'

Chinua Achebe, *Things Fall Apart*

'The most sublime act is to set another before you.'

William Blake, 'Proverbs of Hell'

PART ONE

The Place Being London
(well, sort of . . .),
And The Year Being
Eighteen Hundred And Nine

Chapter One

or

Fuck You, Napoleon!

Know this of me: I was born to be Nothing, but I have turned myself into Something. When I say I was born to be Nothing, I mean that when I was two or three years old, I was found – by whom, I was never told – wandering in the street, clapping my hands outside a church. I was yelling – to no one, to myself perhaps – at the top of my lungs a word sounding like 'John'. That was why they named me John Church – it was no deeper than that.

I spent most of my childhood in the Foundling Hospital in Bloomsbury, where London leaves its abandoned children to rot. There, the wardens, both male and female, showed me emphatically my worth: 'Ooh, look at him, he is a Mary-Ann from the very ground up!' – *whack!* – 'What a filthy little thing, all filled up with a pervert's nature!' – *thump!* – 'O, no wonder his mother chucked him, look at him, the pathetic little runt!'

What does the clever orphan know? That love is not for every child. Yet, once, I did know love. One day, when I was very young, a woman came to the Foundling Hospital. The wardens said that she was my mother now. I do not know if she was my native mother, or some other person, it was never explained. She took my small hand in hers, leading me through the city to the public coach station. We rode out into the country in a shared carriage to a place named Tunbridge Wells. The other travellers told her what a pretty son she had. My black hair, my blue eyes: my new mother said thank you so politely. I sat in silence, astonished.

Even now that I am thirty years of age, I remember that sumptuous summer. Her tiny country house, nestled down a hedgerowed lane. How it felt for me, raised against cold, dripping stones and daily punches of the Hospital, to play in country fields. How bright was the sun – unadulterated by city smoke – on my skin. How the church bells and the bird-song patterned the redolent air. At dinnertime, my mother's voice would call to me: *John! John! John!* I would lift from whatever outdoor mischief I was at and feel love emanating towards me.

Then, one day, she took me back. We caught the public coach back to London. My mother did not tell me where we were going. I didn't realise until the Foundling Hospital appeared in the distance. 'No!' I cried, starting to yank away from her. She just tightened her grip on my hand: 'Come on, John! *Come on!*' I would have run away if I could, bit her hand, kicked her shin, but she was too strong. Standing on the Hospital steps, she explained to the warden: 'He's too much. He's just . . . too much.' Her voice was flinty with irritation; that irritation, of course, was for me. I could not understand; hadn't it been the same sumptuous summer for her? I remember watching her walking away, vanishing down to a black speck in the street. All I was thinking was: turn back and look at me. Mother, *turn back and look at me.* TURN BACK AND LOOK AT ME! But she did not turn back.

So, what is the nature of my achievement, and of my self? If you were to see me in the din and throng of a London street, you might notice me. I am a fellow above six feet tall, broad of shoulder, positive of disposition, handsome of face. Do you raise an eyebrow? Don't – it's true. I am not in the habit of understatement, you'll find. Though I wear a good black suit, unfussy but well made, you might not expect that my profession is that of preacher. To most folk I am not 'John Church' but

4

'The Reverend Church'. Mine might not seem that impressive a journey, but to me, from where I began, I as good as flew to the moon. My hopeful and positive spirit has profited me. My adult nature retains its mischief and its confidence. If all this renders me an uncommon sort of priest, then that is not a matter of regret; for I do not regret very much.

The chapel where I preach, which – through miraculous effect on my part – I bought a few years before the start of this story, is named the Obelisk. It is a severe, puritanical type of building: granite walls cold to the touch, vaulted undecorated ceilings from which pigeons shit. You'll find it in Kennington, the very last part of Southwark before open Surrey fields turn marshy underfoot. On fine, cloudless days, you can walk not ten minutes from the Obelisk into arbours of country lanes, hawthorn blossom bewitching in springtime, fully sunlit in summer. But Southwark is no bucolic vision. Everyone knows that London's mirror city, on the other side of the Thames, is a shithole – metaphorical, literal and moral. It is a centre not of trade, politics and polite society, but of fucking and drinking. If the river rises, the sewers bubble grey-brown water out through people's cobbled floors, popping strangers' farts into your kitchen's air. Factory owners and brothel madams lock workers in secret attics, tell no one if the building catches fire and those inside burn to death. But there are two wonderful things about Southwark. First, it is full of radicals; second, it is marvellously cheap!

Four distinct categories of person come to the Obelisk: common or garden Southwark radicals who have heard of 'Reverend Church' and his teachings; those who live round and about and just want to hear a preacher on Sundays; modest bluestockings who come to glance up and down at a handsome priest, eyes darting with desire, bibles on their laps; and lastly, smallest in number, a group of African abolitionists. It is this last group we shall presently come to consider. It is they who matter most, in how everything would change.

It was a Sunday morning, late in the year. Not yet wintry: London stays mild whilst the rest of Britain freezes. Sunday morning is my main service of the week; I do not hold an evening Sabbath. Standing above my chapel's worshippers in the plain stone pulpit, I gazed out at the crowd; the pews were full. I was more than halfway through my sermon, and I was coming to the crux.

'We must love radically,' I was saying to my congregation. 'Ordinary folk, when they are encouraged to practise hate in the name of religious bigotry and intolerance, serve not Christ. They serve priests, perhaps, and bigots. And kings.' A round of approving murmurs. What I teach is very simple. That people should love was Christ's only real instruction. In faith, we need a revolution as we have had in recent decades in politics and thinking. We need a revolution of love, acceptance and tolerance, in remembrance of Christ's simple instruction, and to set aside the religion of old authorities – cruel, bigoted, judgemental laws and punishments. In freeing themselves to love, ordinary folk will free themselves in more profound a way, in recognising their interest is with one another, and not with princes. And so I continued: 'Our chapels and churches should be radical spaces, not fortresses from which our enemies can oppress us. Our mission is to say that bigotry and violence serve no one but those enemies who wish to oppress us. The next great revolution, my friends, will be the revolution of tolerance!'

A man in rags leapt to his feet. 'Praise Jesus!' he cried. 'And praise Reverend Church! He is the bringer of a revolution of tolerance! He is a prophet of love!' Hear this now. I may at times be immodest, and my enthusiasm for what I preach bursts out of me, *but* I will confirm to you: I am not a prophet. I pinched most of my ideas from the Antinomian teaching (don't worry: I'll explain later). Of Jacobins and Girondists, of the Popular Radicals and the Philosophic ones, ask me nothing! All I know is this: people want to be saved. They want it more than any other thing. And most of all, they want to feel like they are good enough to be saved. My belief is so very simple, it stuns me that no Christian ever seems to have thought of it before, or at least since Christ's day: love so that you yourself can be loved; tolerate so that you will be tolerated; give up hatred and violence; embrace your fellow man. Truly, there is nothing else to know in faith. All else is just violence and bitterness and judgement; a self-damnation.

There was an air of levity in the moments after the man had shouted, and it is good in preaching to allow a few seconds for the room to breathe. I let my eyes scan my congregation. Row after row, face after face: different faces every time yet somehow always the same. It was then that I first saw him. He was looking straight at me, his eyes intelligently watchful, alert to the moment, a hint of shyness. His face was long and angular with high, severe cheekbones. A young African man, he was younger than me, in his twenties. I studied him closer. I could write a list of descriptions, if that's what's required: his chin almost unshaven, a light black fuzz across his jaw; his throat, long and slim; prominent collarbones revealed by his open-necked white shirt. But more than that, there was a softness to him, something you might call feminine, a prettiness as much as a handsomeness, a hazy kind of beauty, one that is not sure of its own existence. Looking at him, I felt that sensuous crackle of seeing someone for the first time; perhaps the only time, you never know. My throat clenched, my eyelids flickered. Just as suddenly, he seemed aware that I was looking at him. Some embarrassment entered him; his gaze fell away, as if to read a pamphlet on his lap. Clearing my throat, I looked back down at my hands, spread on the pulpit lectern. And that was it: nothing more.

When the service was done, people came forwards to exchange words with me, to shake hands. Among the first was my friend, Mrs Caesar, one of the Africans who came to the chapel, a marvellous person for whom I held the highest respect. I knew little of her history save that she had been born in her native land, a country in Guinea, then was enslaved in the West Indies. She emancipated herself in London – through what efforts I do not know. She then became a campaigner for the end first of the Slave Trade, achieved two years past, and now of Slavery in its entirety, still to be achieved. Always, a troop of smart, scholarly young men followed her around, a line of starch-shirted ducklings following their mother. But she was not their mother. She was their leader.

I shall confess straightaway. I know only a little of abolition-ism, only what any person knows: that in the last century there were cases in which ordinary African folk sued their masters for their freedom, proving that Slavery was not legal in England but only in its colonies; that a great number of liberal English-men began to agitate for the end of the Trade, holding huge meetings, writing massive letter campaigns; that the struggle for Emancipation was now decades old, allegedly delayed by the war, but really by what people called 'The Interest', a group comprising White West Indians, merchants and politicians in London, Bristol and Liverpool, and the Royal Family. I wish heartily to see the end of the evil practice, but again, I must tell you: of the subject, I am no expert!

'Ah, Reverend Church,' Mrs Caesar began, 'your sermon was most thought-provoking and insightful.' She let out a knowing laugh. Her eyes were quick like mercury, full of good humour. 'As always, O!' she added, as if correcting an oversight. She

8

beckoned forwards her young men to greet me and introduced them by name, as they stopped in a line: a Josiah, a Joseph, a Jebediah. But then there was the sole female follower she seemed to possess: her daughter, Miss Lydia Caesar, whom I already knew. An austere person, of high intelligence, well read on radical and revolutionary subjects, far beyond my own knowledge, she was not the friendliest soul. She had a habit of keeping her gaze to the ground whilst speaking, then suddenly looking up at one piercingly, often saying quite stark things. I always felt Miss Lydia did not like me, though I never understood why, for am I not a perfectly charming fellow?

'How are you today, Miss Lydia?' I asked.

Eyes down: 'Most well, thank you, Reverend Church.'

'Did you enjoy the sermon?'

Eyes up: 'Somewhat, Reverend.' *Somewhat?* 'Your ideas are quite interesting.' *Quite* interesting? 'I just don't know how applicable they are.' Eyes back down.

'Applicable, Miss Caesar?'

Eyes up: 'Realistic is perhaps a better word.'

Before I had a chance to respond, her mother spoke: 'Reverend Church, my Lydia is a preacher too! You will come to see her speaking one day. Then you could give your impressions to her. She will surely value your advice.' Lydia's eyes fell to the chapel flagstones. She did not want my advice. O, but I would *gladly* give it, to annoy her, to enjoy it. The thought passed through me, so trivial. I looked along the straight line of her mother's followers. It was then I saw him again. He gave me the very smallest of smiles and nodded, almost imperceptibly: the young man from the pews. Mrs Caesar did not introduce us. Sensing her daughter's irritation, she said good day. There were no more introductions.

Presently the chapel emptied. Sweeping along pews to check for forgotten hats, dropped gloves, I found myself distracted. I had a horrific duty to perform that afternoon and it was weighing heavily on my mind. I dreaded it; but I would do it. That is the nature of 'the duty', the responsibility on men like me. Lost in my thoughts, I heard a voice behind: 'Reverend Church . . . ?' I turned. It was the young man again; he had come back. Standing in the chapel's great doorway, left open, he held a felt hat in front of his body. The way he fiddled with it – fingering and turning the brim in his hand – made him seem nervous. He took a step forwards and moved into a pool of sifted light falling from the high chapel windows. It gilded him; but its haze made him seem diaphanous. 'Reverend, I . . . I just wanted to say how I enjoyed your sermon. I hope you don't mind me coming back to say so.'

He had this curious stillness about him, his form long and elegant. Obscured somewhat by the light, he was simultaneously there and not there; that would turn out to be his whole quality, in fact.

'Not at all,' I replied. 'Thank you. Did you not leave with Mrs Caesar and your fellow Society members?'

He shook his head. 'No, I am not truly part of her group. I just know one of the members.'

'Ah,' I said. 'I thought I had never seen you here before.'

He smiled and gave a small shake of his head as if to confirm I had not. 'I just wanted to say that I find your ideas most interesting. I am not sure I understand how all of it works in practice' – just as Miss Lydia had said – 'but I would appreciate the opportunity to talk of them more.' His voice was clear, deep but light, a trace of a northern accent, a soft sibilance barely discernible unless you listened closely. He turned his face hesitantly to one side. Falling at an angle, the light from the windows brushed his face, revealing the contours of his cheek and jaw. His lips pursed momentarily in thought. 'Do you have time to talk now about your ideas, Reverend?'

Every part of me wanted to say yes. But still I had my duty to perform. I had to commit myself to doing the right thing. 'I cannot today, I am sorry.'

'O, I see . . .' He seemed sincerely disappointed.

'Will you come to the service next week?'

'I'm not sure,' he said.

Know this: I am driven by impulses, by my urges in the moment. Come what may, they rule me; I do not rule them. 'Well, if you do, we could go for a walk after service then and talk about my ideas. I could give you as much time as you like another day.'

He weighed up the possibility of doing this. Those lips that had closed thoughtfully a moment before now parted to reveal a luminous smile. 'All right,' he said. *All right*, he would often say, just like that, neutral, mysterious.

'What's your name?'

'Ned.'

'Ned,' I repeated.

He said nothing else, not even good day. He just gently raised his hand, his fingers separating – in a soft, feminine gesture – in mid-air. Walking away, he was swallowed up by the daylight outside the Obelisk's doors.

So that was it: the start of everything.

The same afternoon . . .

It is twenty years since the Revolution in France. The war between our countries started then and has continued ever since. Twenty years of war: what does it do to a country? What happens to a nation that has forgotten what it's like not to be at war? Old Boney Napoleon has sucked Englishmen away to fight him in such huge numbers that everything we once knew is altered. (In fact, I hardly remember a time when we were not at war: killing Frenchmen, killing Americans, killing Indians.) Young men go to fight, get press-ganged, are ripped violently away, and do not come back. Their womenfolk – young and with hopes for shared futures – wait and wait for their return, until they accept they are waiting for nothing. Europe's fields and plains lie thick with the corpses of its boys – British, French, Austrian, Prussian – and London – and I suppose Paris, Vienna, Berlin too – is transformed into a city of ghosts: the ghosts of men lost in battle, the ghosts of those women's dreams and shattered futures.

But war brings more urgent concerns than that routine of grief and death. Rocketing inflation has turned buying food into a reckless, ever-changing game of guess-the-price. The cost of flour rises vertiginously but then wages fall. People lose their jobs; landlords, too scared or too hard-hearted to give a person a chance, kick them out. They don't care that those people have nowhere to go and now their rooms lie empty. It's London; there's always someone else to pay the rent. People are frightened and they endlessly, compulsively ask when the war will end, when things will get back to normal; then the worst question of all: what if things *never* get back to normal?

Anxious times are rarely kind times. The French-owned eating houses have had to close. Foreigners get beaten up in the street by men shouting 'God save our English King!' even though we all know he is 99 per cent German. But those who have had it worst in these times are Sodomites – mollies – men like me. In the past, they say, few people cared about us, or sought to trap us and kill us for our crimes. Once upon a time, those among our number who dressed as ladies went to the Vauxhall Pleasure Gardens to offer gentlemen a dance for a shilling, and people thought it the funniest thing. Things get worse and worse. My friend, James Bartlett, was hanged just months before, one of so very many who have been arrested, pilloried, gaoled and executed, as the war's ill mood has poisoned one English person against another. The press loves to recount the stories of our discovery, our disgustingness, our destructions. Let me amend: anxious times are *never* kind times. And yet in these times, at never such a great phase since the revolutions in America and France, people have turned towards radicalism, and they talk long of their great and liberal convictions. Some of these people are the same people who clamour for the mass execution of Sodomites: they write articles in newspapers on liberal causes; they see no contradiction. That is the true spirit of our dark age, perhaps. People hold fast to their convictions, and there is nothing that can shake them, not even goodness or truth.

That afternoon, I walked all the way along the Borough High Street up towards the Bridge, to take me over the river. Crossing to the northern bank, into London itself, I pushed through the throng on Fish Street Hill. Every inch of pavement had feet standing on it: traders and hawkers, costermongers and coal heavers, entertainers holding monkeys on leashes, listlessly strumming guitars, or hedgehogs seated at tiny tables, dressed in tiny, prickling bonnets and jackets, hard-mouthed street children selling and stealing, other children in velvet suits stepping quietly behind their mothers' eyes, watching the urchins, fairground-mirror versions of each other; your life went this way, and mine this. Tough shit, comes the city's reply; this is London, get over it.

Approaching Newgate, I could hear the crowd before I could see it: that eerie sound, the faraway roar of people pressed together, all shouting for the same thing. I held my breath in trepidation and pushed ahead, towards it. A young woman, her body green and scrawny with gin and syphilis, asked, 'Any business, dearie?' Her pincer hand grabbed my arm sharply, cruelly, but she smiled like we were lovers true. The incongruity of such a touch made me pull away. I saw the hurt flash in her eyes, then the smirking self-protection: 'Suit yerself.' She kept her eyes on me a second longer: 'Go on then, *fuck off!*'

I turned onto Old Bailey and only then saw the crowd in all its awful multiplicity. Hundreds had come: hundreds of bodies, a great marine tide of people, pushing and swaying and baying for blood; lethal, frivolous and righteous all at once. In front of the Prison was a scaffold, and under its swinging nooses stood three men. Behind them stood priests and Patrol officers, the arbiters of law. The men on the scaffold's hands were all tied behind their backs. One of the men was Richard Oakden, whom I knew, even if I would not quite call him a friend. I knew him from the molly houses, the secret places where men like us go to meet and drink and fuck.

Consider what kind of person was there that day: rough sorts, people who came only to see the entertainment of a man destroyed, but also many good Christians, who came, with bags of fried pork rind to share with their neighbours, to pronounce God's work was being done. And then there were radicals too, preachers and pamphleteers, who came to say that the city must be cleansed and the first to die must be the Sodomites. O, rapists are two a penny, but to see a Sodomite hang, that is the finest, most righteous kind of day out.

A bailiff started reading the crimes and sentences. The crowd tried to fall silent, but there was still laughter and boisterousness all around. The bailiff stood, legs astride on the platform, bellowing like a town crier reading out a royal proclamation. 'Dennis Fitzgerald . . . for the crime of rape.' *Ooh!* went the crowd. 'Cornelius Sullivan . . . also for the crime of rape.' *Ooh!* 'And finally, Richard Oakden . . .' He had been made to stand a little away from the other two prisoners, who glared at him, even in the proximity of death, to distinguish themselves: *we are not like him!* The bailiff took a long actor's breath. 'For the crime of sodomy.' At once it broke, appalling and deafening, a single massed scream splitting the air. Hundreds of hands lunged upwards, fingers curled into claws.

'Fuck you, faggot!' a man yelled at my side, with such bone-deep fury, all the while sloshing a jug of ale in his hand. At his side was another man: 'And *fuck you*, Napoleon! God save our English King!' People around began to cheer and raise their jugs of ale.

Did you laugh? 'Fuck you, Napoleon!' I said it as a joke, to lessen the horror of what was about to happen. What is it like to die on a scaffold facing a hurricane of such hatred? This is the purpose, then, of the duty. Once convicted, the day you die, your family will not come. Your parents, your children, will disown you as soon as you are charged. Your friends will say they have never heard of you. I do not blame anyone; they are right to be afraid. When James Bartlett's widow came to claim her husband's body earlier that year, the crowd tried to put out her eyes. What was her failing? *Being a bad wife.*

The duty says you will not die alone. It says someone will remember you as a friend, or as a lover, or someone who just did not deserve to die like this. It is not solely an act of charity. It is a kind of contract between all of us of our nature. One day, it might be us up on that scaffold, standing only inches from the noose. In a moment, it will be us staring at the curve of the rope, wondering how it will feel as it razors our, no, *my* skin, how it will feel as the lever is pulled, the noose suddenly tightens, the neck snaps. We come and count out our remaining time, and hope that one day someone will come to perform the duty for us.

What was about to happen was Richard Oakden was going to be killed for being like me. *O, John Church!* you might cry. *Doesn't that make you stop and think?* But let me tell you this. To stand among a crowd shrieking for a man's death – a man like me, no less – does not undermine my beliefs. I am not discouraged in my ideas about men and their native goodness. I feel only the urgency of my work. None of these people were born feeling this hatred. It was planted in them, a seeded poison. I feel only more certain that if they understand the practice of tolerance, they will be freed. And who does not want to be free?

I turned to see if anyone else had come. I looked right and then left, my eyes rushing across the mass of faces, recognising no one. Then I saw her, her eyes already hard on me. How long had she been watching? That day, Sally Fox was dressed as a man, brimmed hat and heavy greatcoat, but she is not just a man. She is also a queen: the queen of queens at London's molly houses. Sally is the funniest, sharpest-mouthed, toughest queen in all of London, and I love her. Sometimes she goes by another name, Kitty Cambric, but I always call her Sally, or Sal. I do not even know what her masculine name is. That is deliberate. A name known is a name revealed, the day the Patrol takes you.

The truth is that I fucked Sally once – only once – a very long time ago; that's how we met. It's important I confess this to you now: I don't want any misunderstandings. We met under cover of dark on the city's rough, marshy boundaries around Moorfields, which they call – once in jest, now brutally – the Sodomites' Walk. Sal was dressed as a man that night too. In the dark, we circled each other, just the age-old signals of smiles and eyes, until we drifted over soft soil to some bushes, where I fucked her from behind in the darkness. We did not kiss, hardly looked at each other. All she said to me that night as I slipped out of her body was: 'O, that sorted me out.' She pulled up her breeches and sauntered away into the night, no doubt, on to the next cock. I expected never to see her again. Two weeks later, I spotted her crossing Cornhill. I turned away, hoping that she had not seen me – just another random figure, another random fuck. Walking away, though, I heard a shriek cracking the air in two: '*Oi, you!* Do you dare ignore me? O, I can't believe the *living cheek* of it!' And that was it: Sally Fox and I were friends.

Now, years later, outside Newgate Prison, the bailiff started shouting the instructions for the execution; the crowd was lurching forwards; my body jolted with the tide but I kept looking at Sally. Usually her manner was funny, ferocious, fearless, but now her gaze was terrible, knowing, merciless; I had to break away from it, I could not bear it. Oakden and his companions stepped forwards, towards their nooses. Eggs and rocks and potatoes began flying, part of the ancient ritual. Instantly blood was streaming down the men's faces, but none more than Oakden's; people were aiming at him. The impacts made Richard Oakden glance up, and immediately we were looking at each other.

Our eyes connected. We were never friends, but we knew each other, in the way that men who go to molly houses do. Shall I tell you that in that moment he looked comforted to see me there? He did not. He looked ashamed and afraid, in the knowledge that he was utterly debased, in front of the whole city, about to die. He glanced down at the scaffold floor, and I was relieved to be released from our hollow, haunting connection.

The bailiff was shouting for the levers to be readied. The moment of killing was here. Quickly hoods were wrestled over heads, the men started protesting, the priests started mumbling blank words about salvation, nooses were slipped around necks, ropes on gibbets creaked, and bang, it was time. The bodies fell fast, one, two, three: each, a loud, hard thump. Necks snapped like branches stepped on in a forest; strange death screams; then silence. Oakden's legs kicked wildly, though I am sure he was already dead. There was wild, happy, pious cheering everywhere. 'Kill the sinner!' men and women were chanting. 'Kill the sinner! Kill the sinner!'

I turned; Sally was still staring straight at me. She nodded once, summoning me to follow her. I began to push through bodies in the direction of the Cathedral; she did the same, moving in parallel in the crowd. In less than a minute, we were walking one in front of the other, a dozen yards apart, all the way down Ludgate Hill. London's constant file of people pushed against us, summoned to see the killings, not yet knowing they had missed the fun. In front of me, in the gap between me and Sally, a woman repeatedly glanced back in my direction. I would not have noticed her usually. She was of an unremarkable type: forty years old, or so, white cap covering her hair, its loose strands blowing around in the breeze, skin bright and pink with a life of hard work. But she kept looking back again and again, with such intent, that I could not help but see her. Had she been with Sally all along? Almost on the corner with Farringdon Street, Sally stopped and turned abruptly, forcing the woman and me to do the same, so that we stood in a loose triangle, three bodies.

'This is my friend, Johnny boy,' Sally said, as if we had been talking all along. 'She wants to meet you. They call her Mrs Cook.'

Sally always spoke in this way, imperious but risen from the gutter. 'Is that because it is her name?' I asked, teasing her. Her friend laughed a little; I sensed at once that she knew Sal well, knew what she was like.

'Good day, Reverend,' the woman said. 'A very great sadness performed today, another cruel death.' Her accent was Irish, faded with time.

'Did you know Mr Oakden?' I asked, and she nodded yes.

Sally never had time for sad reflections: 'I told you he was good-looking, didn't I?' She was talking about me. 'O, and he's clever, and awful charming, and well' – she pointed directly at my crotch – 'down there, hung like an ironmonger's dray horse!'

Mrs Cook's eyes went wide with shock. 'Sally!' I cried, and she laughed at her own salaciousness. This is how queens talk; if you don't like it, it doesn't matter. They'll talk that way, regardless. Sally cocked her thumb at the woman. '*She* has a proposal for you.'

'What proposal?' I asked.

Mrs Cook leaned in towards me: 'I keep a tavern on Long Acre, Reverend, but my husband is opening his own tavern on Clare Market.' She dropped her voice so no passer-by might hear. 'The tavern on Clare Market is to be a molly house, Reverend.' She blinked and paused. 'I need someone to perform the weddings.'

I was surprised. In the past, at molly houses, there were mock weddings – performed to raucous, drunken laughter – between men who were almost too half-cut to stand, before they crept off to some dingy room where one of them would try to thumb his gin-killed cock inside the other. But they had been a joke, nothing more, and that had been years before. I had never once seen it in any of the houses I visited, in half a lifetime of going. Mrs Cook said quite breathlessly: 'We *will* pay you, Reverend Church.'

And so that, I suppose, was another kind of start.

FROM *THE MORNING POST* NEWSPAPER
(Published widely at this time – I keep these things secreted
away, and I am not sure why)

Yesterday, Cornelius Sullivan, Denis Fitzgerald, and Richard Oakden,
were executed, pursuant to their sentence, in the Old Bailey. They
appeared to meet their awful fate with firmness and resignation. Sul-
livan and Fitzgerald were attended on this melancholy occasion by
a Roman Catholic Clergyman, and Oakden by the Ordinary. None
of the prisoners uttered a word on the fatal platform, except to the
Clergymen by whom they were respectively attended.

But it was clearly observable, that Sullivan and Fitzgerald, during
the awful ceremony, regarded, with seeming horror and indigna-
tion, their fellow sufferer Oakden, who was tied up at some distance
from them, until the signal for suspension terminated all feeling upon
the contrast of their crimes. Oakden suffered for an unnatural crime.

Chapter Two

or

Erections Under Evening Gowns

During the week following . . .

A few days later, a barefooted runner-boy appeared at the Obelisk. He fetched me a note from Mrs Cook. She asked me to come to meet her at her husband's new establishment in Clare Market. The tavern, she wrote, was named the White Swan. The house was opening on the Friday and she wanted me to see it before. 'Got an answer, mister?' the boy cried, loudly. I had just ended a regular midweek prayer meeting; the last straggling worshippers turned to listen. He asked it that noticeably so that I would feel pressured to pay him something more.

I crumpled the note slowly in my hand and muttered no. The boy looked dejected, having lost a farthing. Of course, I used to be a boy not so different to him; I know the tricks and the wounds that go with a child's street life. I smiled, told him to hang on, and I fetched a coin from the collection plate. 'Most Christian of you,' one of my worshippers observed. I handed the boy the farthing and ruffled his hair. For his part, he called me a cunt and then stalked off.

Clare Market lies on the south-eastern edge of Covent Garden, that famously chaotic nest of whores and pickpockets. The two areas are ugly sisters, but the former is the meaner, concealing a knife she is not afraid to use. By day, it is on first appearance just an ordinary London market: busy, dishevelled, a warren of concealed walkways and twisting lanes. Open stalls sell every kind of meat, cheap trinkets, under-the-counter grogs that can blind a man, stolen goods robbed from houses both fancy and plain. But by night, Clare Market turns into a boiling hell. Everywhere there are drunkards and thieves, and eyes roam the street looking for victims. An army of brutes takes over, waiting to prey on those brave enough to come there; a whore leads a man with too urgent a cock down a dark alley and shoves him with a knife, or has a partner waiting in a shadow with a claw hammer ready to crack a skull like a walnut. A popular story ran about a young man who disappeared in its heartless warrens, and all that was found of him were his bones and shoes. Children are still told not to go to Clare Market lest they see his ghost.

Molly houses are in every part of London: the plushest streets of St James, the roughest parts of the City or, Lord love us, Whitechapel. Somehow word of them always spreads, and it is not long till they become busy. 'Have you heard?' 'Did you know?' 'Have you been?' The house briefly flowers for a few months, even a few years, until the owner winds it up before they are exposed; or else they *are* exposed and all hell breaks loose. There is such danger in going, of arrest by the Patrol, of suspicion from neighbours, of attack, of blackmail, and ultimately of the heartbreak that comes from them closing and you being left alone again. Despite the risk, still men go to the houses. They go because not to go, not to make contact, not to feel their desires, not to touch, not to be touched, is to ensure a life of feeling like you are drowning. Which do you choose: the certainty of one kind of death, or the possibility of another?

The law does not set foot in Clare Market, if it can help it. It is not unknown for Patrol officers to go missing in its streets and be found days later, face down in the open sewers that flood silty shit out into the Thames. Who's looking for trouble in

Clare Market? The law isn't. Let the fuckers inside rot, is the view. That made it an excellent place to set up a molly house.

The White Swan tavern was on Vere Street, in that filthy, vicious tangle of streets south of Lincoln's Inn: Portugal Street, Sheffield Street, Clements Inn. There, the poor are at their poorest and the desperate their most desperate. When I arrived, the White Swan looked a solid, unremarkable London public house. As I stepped through the front door, the place was not too busy, though. It was still only the middle of the day, the day I first went. Behind the bar, I saw Mrs Cook was chatting to a customer. She looked over and waved, sticking up a finger in the air to tell me to wait. She finished up her conversation and quickly wiped down the bar as she walked around it towards me.

'Reverend Church!' she said, and I heard her voice again: sweet, with a levity. She turned to a young man behind the counter. (This was Philip Kett, the waiter.) 'Oi, Philip, are you all right for half an hour? I got some business to talk through here.' The fellow did not give much answer; Philip Kett was always as sour as a puss – save, memorably, when he was drunk. Mrs Cook smiled at me in a charming, open way. 'Shall we go upstairs, Reverend?' Her hand touched my elbow, and she leaned in to whisper: '*To see the rooms . . .*'

Molly houses always hide in plain sight. Having one above a noisy, rough public house was clever: the boisterousness downstairs would obscure any sound from above. Mrs Cook now led me round to a separate, discreet side door. The stairs up had a slight turn in them, so what lay beyond was visible neither from the street nor from the main tavern. Again, clever: different entrances to each establishment. At either end of the staircase were not one but three very heavy curtains, which killed any sound travelling. The molly house was on the second floor, leaving a whole floor between it and the tavern to ensure sound wouldn't travel. Twice there were signs that read 'PRIVATE – NASTY DOGS AHEAD'. Only those who knew about the house would know to ignore the warnings and to enjoy the joke. Even those who ignored the signs would still find a bolted door with a spyhole ahead, far too sturdy to be kicked in. Usually, a password was required to enter. Mrs Cook had thought of everything, it seemed. All she needed was for no one to betray her to the Patrol.

Beyond the bolted door was the main room, a bar in one corner from which drinks would be served. She said it was beer, wine, rum, but no gin. Gin makes folk do lunatic things, she said. Every window had heavy shutters and drapes; no treacherous shards of light could be cast out over the streets, for people to wonder what was 'going on up there'. For now, in daytime, the drapes and shutters were pinned back, letting a wan light in. A great ocean of dust, trapped in mid-air, gilded by the sunshine, moved in sudden, sparkling tides as we entered. All around the room were stacked chairs. The sunlight cast shadows through their pyramids of legs. Without sitters, it only amplified the eerie emptiness of the place. Mrs Cook took me down corridors, up stairs, revealing a maze of rooms. Several had beds in – two at a time, undressed – and nothing else but jugs to be filled with water and piles of the cheapest towels. 'Will there be no blankets on the beds?' I asked.

'That will be *extra*, Reverend.' She looked as if she did not know whether to say the next thing to a man of God. 'Forgive me, Reverend, but some of these men, well . . .' She laughed briefly, nervously. 'They don't know how to be clean.' She gave me a most meaningful look. 'What I mean is, Reverend . . . I don't want no shit on my sheets.'

She said it so seriously but I began to laugh, and seeing me do it, her face cracked too. 'You have thought of everything, Mrs Cook.'

'O, I know how to turn a coin, Reverend, and I am not

ashamed of that. Couples can have a room to themselves or a room to be shared. Shared costs less, of course. And some want to retire in threes or fours. Some want to *marry* in threes or fours.' She shrugged. 'I make no judgement, Reverend.' Her eyes flicked to mine, a knowing smile on her lips. 'Only . . .' she said cautiously.

I leaned in. '*Only*, Mrs Cook?'

'Only who wants two blooming husbands, Reverend?'

She was funny; I liked her. I always like funny people. I could see why she and Sal were friends. We came to a pretty room, unexpectedly lushly decorated: mirrors, padded stools, hooks on the wall to hang clothing, mannequin heads for wigs. The other rooms were so ruthlessly bare. 'This is where the girls can dress,' she said. Mollies often referred to themselves as 'girls', whether dressed female or not. I would never call Sally 'he', no matter how she was dressed; she'd probably punch me in the eye.

'You know the molly-house business very well,' I said.

'My mother was in the trade, Reverend. She kept a house here in town after we came over from Dublin. I know a lot of girls from back then, or through my mother. The girls trust me, so . . .'

'But why are you doing it now, Mrs Cook?'

She paused for a moment, as if it were a puzzling question. 'I like the girls, Reverend.' She meant the queens. 'I like their company. They are sisters. They consider me their sister too. I am proud of that, to be their sister. They live in a dream, these girls. Downstairs' – she pointed downwards as if through floors – 'I see men as they truly are, but up here, I can help these girls live in a dream.'

'A dream of what?'

'A dream of being a woman, Reverend. If only for an evening.'

She smiled and directed me onwards. We came to a last room,

the most lavishly decorated of all. It was festooned with cheaply painted pictures of pans piping and naked Greek gods, all rippling torsos, tumbling golden curls; the ceiling billowed with gaudy golden drapes. 'What room is this?' I asked.

'It is the Wedding Chapel.'

I laughed with shock. 'It does not seem very chapel-like to me.'

She shook her head. 'It is only a bit of fun, Reverend Church, for everyone to have a laugh and a giggle. They are not truly getting married, are they?'

'I thought people did not want weddings any more, Mrs Cook. I thought it was something from years ago. I've never seen it in all my days going to them.'

She seemed a little confused by this, not too comforted. 'I don't know if they do or don't, Reverend Church. My mother used to offer them, so I thought . . .' She shrugged again. 'I mentioned it to Sally, and she said that she reckoned girls might want it. It's only a bit of fun, ain't it, Reverend?'

She said I would need to come every Sunday evening, the busiest night, when we would perform the weddings. This was fine for me. As I have already told you, I never give Sunday evening service at the Obelisk. She said I could come and drink for free, 'within reason, of course, Reverend,' any night I liked. However, the opening night of the molly house would be that coming Friday and she wanted me there for that. 'To show you off, Reverend,' she said.

She asked if I wanted to go and meet her husband, and so I first laid eyes on James Cook that afternoon, down in the main tavern of the White Swan. He was one of those broodingly dark and handsome men, powerfully built with an edge of unexpressed menace; a man to whose face I might turn in the street – just momentarily – to see if he would, perhaps, look back. (You never know who will; *truly*, you never know.)

Mrs Cook and I sat down to await his joining us, which – quite artfully – took several minutes.

When in time he did come, James Cook yanked a chair from another table towards him, spun it around backwards and sat down with his large arms and huge hands splayed over its back. His thighs, almost splitting his tight breeches, pressed around the back of the seat. He stared at me for several seconds. Of course he knew the erotic effect he had; men like him always do.

'This is him, is it?' he growled at her. 'This is your priest?'

His wife spoke deferentially. 'Reverend Church, Jimmy.'

He snapped a hard, male, bantering laugh. 'A priest named *Church*?'

I smiled, to show willing. 'You have done a great deal of work, Mr Cook,' I said. 'The rooms upstairs are well furnished.'

He nodded towards his wife. 'She's done most of it. I let her decide what to do, and I just go along. She is a man, sometimes, my wife, in how she acts and thinks.' He said it unkindly. I did not ask him: *Are you then the woman?*

We chatted awkwardly for two minutes, the three of us. Then a meat-hauler came in with half a pig on his back. Mrs Cook quickly got to her feet to go off and deal with him, saying, 'Excuse me, Reverend.' Mr Cook and I were left together alone. I was about to say something sociable, when he lunged forwards and grabbed my thigh with his hand. 'I am not one of them, you know!' he spat.

The suddenness and force of his action made me rock backwards a moment. He'd caught me unawares: the confidence of his aggression, the stab of my shame. In situations such as these, sometimes I can lash out, strike. Sometimes I can do impetuous things, but in this particular moment, I was able to hold on to my best senses. Carefully, I picked his hand up from my leg, looked at him calmly and stood up. 'Mr Cook, even if you were, I would not be interested in you.'

His face fell a little. Normal men are sure that every Sodomite secretly lusts after them, no matter how decrepit or distasteful they are. James Cook was the very opposite of decrepit in his physicality, yet he was not at all attractive to me. The sort of man I like has a delicacy in his soul – and a mind worth spending time with. I thought of that young man in the chapel, who had waited for me, ringed with light. His name was Ned, I remembered then. And as I slipped away, out into the day, I could hear Mrs Cook's voice behind me: 'Reverend Church? Reverend Church?' But like my erstwhile mother, I did not turn around and look back.

The Friday . . .

I returned to Vere Street then for the opening night of the molly house. In the main room on the second floor, Mrs Cook and I clinked glasses and wished ourselves well. About eight o'clock, bodies began to arrive, and by half past, a dozen or so people were there. By nine, there were twenty customers; it surprised me, such a large number on a first night. Mrs Cook had certainly got the word out.

Every type of man goes to a molly house. Perhaps more than in any other place in London, there you will see Noble next to Nothing. As long as you have money to buy drinks, and a desire that outweighs the danger, every rank is the same in the molly house. The waiter, Philip Kett, poured drinks; people eased into chatter and flirtation. Whenever anyone knocked at the main door upstairs, Kett or Mrs Cook went up and pressed their face to the spyhole. 'Who is it?' they'd yell. The password would be delivered in a male voice: 'Your sister, come to attend your wedding.' Then we'd hear the bolt slide back. Only one voice diverted from this password: 'It's Sally! Fucking open up! I'm freezing my balls off out here!'

Hearing this, Mrs Cook opened the door: 'I thought that would suit you very well, Sal.'

'*Oi!*' Sally cried as she breezed inside. 'The living cheek!' She arrived with a hessian sack over her shoulder. Inside it was her other self, waiting to be unveiled: a crumpled dress, a raggedy wig, half a ton of white-lead face powder. Sally was the queen of queens, but she was as rough as a butcher's dog.

Less than half of those present retired to the cocoon of the dressing room, all a-giggle and a-flutter, to begin their transformations. These were the queens. Mrs Cook went in and out too, so that at times only the 'men' like me stayed in the main room. The day Mrs Cook showed me around, the house had seemed such a vast, empty space. Now, filled with warm bodies, all chattering and drinking, it felt hot and cramped. Men moved around each other with a sensual buzz of static, hands in the smalls of backs, on biceps or shoulders, to ask someone to move or else to catch their attention. Quickly the air grew fetid. People called for drinks – and more drinks. 'Hang on!' Philip Kett would groan. People would call again. '*Fucking – hang – on!*' A young man named Tommy White introduced himself to me. He was pretty and dewy-skinned, polite and charming. He was with another young lad, named James Mann, who gave me the sort of look that the young and beautiful will: *How lovely and fascinating I am, how lucky you are that I am speaking to you.* I smiled; it may be lovely for the young to be young, but it is far less fascinating than they imagine. Only with time do people understand how brief that youth is, how inevitably its leaves fall. We talked for a short while, and I did not know their intention: to speak to a man like me for I was their preference, or to ask me for some money for 'entry'. Some molly houses allow lads who rent, take a cut of the monies, but some do not; I did not sense that Mrs

Cook would not brook trade. An older man joined us, a big gruff fellow with no art to him but a soft, pleasant demeanour nonetheless. The man's presence immediately excited White, who introduced me to him, gazing at him with shining eyes. His name was John Hepburn. It was then I realised that this strange, odd-matched pair, Hepburn and White, were lovers. Nothing about Hepburn was what you might imagine Tommy White wanted. He did not look rich, or even that smart, and yet Tommy gazed at him as if he were the moon on a clear night.

Mrs Cook appeared in the main room, striding into its centre and clapping her hands. 'Gentlemen! The ladies are *finally* ready!' she cried with a wink. As one, the men there began to whoop and cheer – but an odd, quiet cheer, to avoid detection from the regular world two floors below. A flutter of fans and perfume, a volcano's ash of wig and face powder, and half a dozen queens burst in on us. They were in full – *full* – make-up with wigs piled up high. Their dresses – just simple maids' dresses, bought third – or fourth – hand from Thames Street market stalls – ballooned around them, transformed with carefully stitched-on bows and flowers made of fabric. It was years since any Mayfair lady of fashion had worn such clothes. Dresses were all billowing simplicity these days. I heard one queen groan: 'O, this corset is so tight, my balls are throbbing!'

'Quit moaning!' Sally shot back. 'This is what we ladies have to suffer!'

She sashayed fearlessly into the centre of the room, swinging her hips and winking and calling to every man around her: 'Hello, sweetie! Hello, my dear!' Sally was not beautiful – that was not her magnificence. She was short and stocky; her face was as masculine as mine. She had a misshapen arm, which, in her mid-sleeved dress, she wore quite openly, unconcealed. No, Sally's magnificence was precisely in her glowing knowledge of herself, of what she was not and what she was. She flirted with

30

everyone, half a joke, half a celebration of her authority. She bought drinks for those who could not afford it, and brazenly snatched drinks from those who clearly could. But everyone forgave Sally. There was nothing to do but to forgive her.

Other queens followed her into the room's centre. Here they were, painted beauties, things of splendour, some bold and flirtatious, some nervous and blushing. Some looked just like real girls and some looked nothing like. There was no rule that said one was higher than the other. All you needed to do was to *believe* what you were was real.

Sally came up to me: 'Oi, Johnny boy, do you know my friend Leonora?' She turned, pointing to a small, neat African queen. Her lips were painted deeply, suggestively red; she pursed them now. She had a doll-like quality, dainty and detailed, her clothing so precise, so deliberate, that she seemed more like a figurine seen in a Mayfair curiosity shop. She bowed to me very elegantly: 'Reverend . . .'

'Black Leonora, we call her,' Sally said.

Leonora turned sharply to her sister. 'Black-*Eyed* Leonora!'

Sally did not even blink. I did not yet know what close sisters they were; that each would have died for the other. Did I understand the distinction she drew? Leonora would always insist on 'black-*eyed*'. Next Sally introduced me to a tall, heavy-shouldered queen, who nodded to me with rehearsed poise. 'This is the Duchess of Gloucester.'

'A very great pleasure, Reverend,' she said with an almost comical reverence.

Sally sighed and told her to stop making a tit of herself. 'You're not at the palace now, dearie,' she said. At this, the Duchess cast her a warning look, but Sally was not to be put off. 'Our Duchess is a very, very fine gentleman's servant who works in one of the' – she began to whisper theatrically – '*royal palaces.*' The Duchess shushed her – the rule at the molly house is no names, no secrets, remember. Sally waved her hand in the air, unperturbed. 'I ain't said which one, have I?' She looked back at me and hooted: 'She probably don't fucking know herself, silly sod!'

More bodies arrived, more grog was drunk; the air grew hotter, then hotter still. People's foreheads began to shine; they had to loosen their cravats for fear they might faint in the heat. I was introduced to a queen who went by the name of Miss Sweet Lips. Never in my life have I met a creature quite like her. Beneath a white wig, the lacquer of chalky powder and red-rouge cheeks was a strikingly handsome man. Miss Sweet Lips did not seek to erase her masculinity, though. She wore her stubble openly, did not shave it and cover it with thick lead paint as all the other queens save Black-Eyed Leonora did. Dark chest hair grew like ivy above her décolletage. Even her dress was cut so that her athletic male legs were daringly revealed. Queens usually aimed for feminine authenticity, and they hit or they missed. Miss Sweet Lips was not like them; she wrote the rules of a different game. She was accompanied by three men, who each tried to hand her drinks. She accepted them like a pagan goddess accepts human sacrifices: utterly certain that she deserves them, beguilingly ungrateful. After Sally introduced us, it was several moments before Miss Sweet Lips even acknowledged I was there. She said without looking at me, grinning libidinously at one or other of her admirers: 'Oi, Father! Are you marrying us this evening or are you fucking us?'

Sally gasped like Sarah Siddons. 'I *must* apologise, *Reverend*, some of these whores, well, they are just *as common as shit.*'

I laughed. Sally's eyes were all mesmerising false outrage. For her part, Miss Sweet Lips pursed her mouth and snorted a contemptuous laugh. 'Sally Fox, don't pretend you haven't talked like a whore about this one.' She pointed straight at my crotch. 'You already said he could roll that thing halfway down his leg.'

Sally shrieked, in bright outrage: 'O, *you evil bitch*, I said no such thing!' I had not a single doubt that Sally had said exactly that.

Pfft, Miss Sweet Lips went. 'What kind of holy spirit did he leave inside you, Sally Fox? The sort that dribbles down your inner leg the rest of the evening?'

At this, Sally burst into laughter and leaned forwards, her good hand touching my arm: 'Johnny boy, as I remember, it was at least two cupfuls!' The queens screeched with laughter.

The mood began to quicken; men's minds turned to more sensual pursuits. There was canoodling, kisses offered and refused, hands brushed away once, twice, and then a sharp 'Yeah, all right, pal, *enough!*' Here and there, girls' make-up began to slide in the heat and with too much drink. But the more grog was consumed, the more entrancing men found them. Soon there were discussions of retiring to one of the bedrooms and fingers were fiddling with swelling members in breeches. In turns, the queens would go, 'Mmm, you're a naughty boy,' and then, 'If that thing squirts on this silk, I'll fucking gut you!'

Always, Mrs Cook was watching the room. She wiped down tops, spoke to customers, went over to whisper in someone's ear that her wig had started to slip. 'You can see your real hair, dearie,' I heard her say. The queen told that would quickly grab at her wig, and cry out loud, and run to the dressing room. 'Go and touch up your powder,' she might say another time, a code for: *Slip away with me, I can see this fellow's bothering you.* Presently she came and stood above me, where I was sitting with my beer.

'You are kind with the girls,' I said. She waved my words away, but it was true, she was. She didn't need to be like that, so kind with them. 'What does it hurt me to help them with their hair, or show them how better to do their rouge? It doesn't hurt me a lick. What kind of person would it hurt so much that they wouldn't accept it?'

'All sorts of people, Mrs Cook.'

She gave a small, sad smile. 'A man like you may pass in the street unmolested, but look at these queens. You only need take one look at some of them to know what they are. What does it cost me to give them this? O, I need to get paid but that's not why I do it, or not just why I do it. These girls are in my heart. Their lives can be so hard. Look at Sally.'

'Sally?'

'Don't you know?' She seemed surprised. 'Sally has been taken before.'

'Taken?'

'Yes, she was arrested for sodomy. That's why she changes her name, Kitty Cambric, Sally Fox, other names besides.' I did not know there were other names. 'Because it is not safe for her to have only one. She cannot be connected to her own past if she gets done again. That was how her arm got hurt. Didn't you know? She doesn't keep it a secret.'

Truly, I hadn't a clue; we had never discussed it. I felt my mind go blank, felt sweat pearl cold on my skin. I thought of funny, smart-mouthed, fearless Sally. I thought of her in moments when death must have seemed so close. I thought of all the things that were so awful and wonderful about Sally, then marvelled that the world believed the right and moral thing to do was to strap her to a stage, tie her hands into holes and let the city attack her; all for who she was. The day that Richard Oakden was hanged rushed back at me, but not just that; the weight of having to suppress this fear I feel all the time; the risk, the proximity, perhaps even the inevitability, of violence against us.

'Right,' Mrs Cook said, smiling calmly. 'Do you think it's time to do some marrying, Reverend Church?' Without waiting for my answer, she clapped her hands. The chatter did not immediately die down. My thoughts had not entirely shifted from what had happened to Sally, yet the noise and commotion of the house swept me up. 'Ladies, please! *Ladies!*' Finally everyone

34

fell silent and turned to the mother of the house. 'Now, do we have any brides?'

Miss Sweet Lips put her hand in the air. 'Me, Mrs Cook, I am feeling *awful* nuptial tonight.'

'Who, pray, is your husband, dearie?' Mrs Cook asked.

Miss Sweet Lips was still standing between her three admirers. She looked at one and then the other and then the other. 'O, I don't mind as long as someone sticks it in me.'

Everyone was laughing. Sweet Lips was as funny as she was deadly, as winking as she was terrifying. We all laughed because what else could we do, knowing that two floors below was the normal world that would at any moment, if we were revealed, kick down the doors and tear us limb from limb. I thought of what William Webster – William, my first true love – and I had believed, years before, about the goodness of people, and the possibility of change in the world. But I was not yet ready to see that the crucible of change would be a few rooms above a pub on Vere Street.

Chapter Three
or
Boys

When I was eleven or so (though nobody knew for sure, of course, thanks to my dubious origins), the wardens of the Foundling Hospital sold me. (Yes, *sold me*.) It was into a bonded apprenticeship to a gilder on the Blackfriars Road. I remember the Hospital warden counting out the guineas he was paid, licking his lips like it was Christmas.

*

Once again, I was led away, but this time, to a very different fate. After a period of great struggle and many humiliations, I found work for a composition-ornament maker on the Tottenham Court Road. I made small resin moulds of cherubim, figures from the Bible, members of the Royal Family, all kinds of useless tat. One day, a strange young man of a similar age to me came in and said he was looking for a gift, which he bought. He came back the next day and the next. As he spoke to me, his eyes glowed with attention and excitement, and I understood that those eyes were for me. He was the most beautiful, sensitive, good-natured creature I had ever met. He said his name was William Webster.

*

It is in my nature to swan-dive into what I feel, without fear, without caution, and I fell in love with him so quickly and so completely. Knowing that I was in love with him, I determined that he should love me in return. I can be very determined in matters of the heart, because a man like me must be. Love, for the Sodomite, is the most ephemeral, the most transient of things; you must grab it before it floats away. He suggested I should come to his chapel with him, and when I told him I had grown tired of all the rules and condemnations of the Nonconformists, he grinned in the most beautiful manner and said: 'But we are Antinomians. We don't have any rules. All we do is love.'

★

On my breaks at work, William would bring some pieces of pie or bread and cheese wrapped in waxed paper. He would sit with me in the sunshine around the newly built streets of Bloomsbury, unwrapping and proffering them to me. I went with him to his chapel, and for the first time heard the Antinomian message: the rejection of all and any laws, in favour of prioritising Christ's instruction to love. I did not know it then but it was the first step on my path to the Something I am today. When he and I met, we talked about what it might mean: a moral world based not on rules, and violence, but on love and tolerance. We imagined a new kingdom of mercy and acceptance, and how it would benefit the lives of ordinary folk, to love and so to be loved, to accept and so to be accepted. Once I said to him it would be the ultimate revolutionary act: a world predicated on love. His eyes were shining with admiration.

★

The composition-ornament maker grew tired of this strange boy forever coming into his shop, asking when my break was. After a goodly time, he told me I had to make a choice: either my friend had to keep away or I would lose my job. I will never forget the look of amazement on the man's face when I told him to stick his *fucking job*. But I would never not have chosen William. Cut out my lungs, cut off my limbs; I would *never* not have chosen him.

*

Madly, with hardly a farthing to our names (God's teeth, we were poor), William and I decided to become full-time preachers in the Tottenham Court Road Sunday School. We held wild-eyed sermons, eschewing all rules, decrying every parish priest, demanding only that men and women should love each other. In the end, we had to leave – they said we were too much – ending up at the Fitzroy Sabbath Sunday School on Cleveland Street, but we were sacked from there as well. Undeterred, we preached wherever we could. We wrote and printed inky pamphlets right on my rented room's bare floor. Sitting next to him, scribbling our words, reading them aloud to each other, praising and helping each other, I felt so very happy.

*

There was an erotic, a sensuous connection between us from the very start, of course; I knew it from the off. I remember the first time we kissed, in fact. It was late afternoon, spreading into evening, and we had been out walking all day, this way and that, for I have always, compulsively, loved to walk, having spent most of my childhood locked up in one place or the other.

We ended up in the cemetery on Bunhill Fields, and as boys do, for effect, we lay between the graves, just talking and talking and talking. It was too late for mourners to come with flowers. Some gang might rob them among the stones, in that heavily wooded cemetery. If anyone saw us then, so confident as to lie flat out among all the carved names and dates, they might think us robbers too. We were lying next to each other and, eyes shining, he was listening to me talk; I don't remember what I was saying but he was laughing and laughing. He turned to me, caught my hand in friendship (perhaps) and said: 'I like you, John, I like you so much.' And there with the light changing through the trees, I leaned across and kissed him, and as I kissed him, he caught his breath and pulled away.

'What are you doing, John?' he cried, but I was too far in to be fearful now. My impulsiveness is my master, as I have told you.

'I am in love with you,' I said with that certainty that walks with impulsiveness; you don't have to regret it till later, that way.

His eyes were so wide and so pale in that light. He blinked once. He began to smile, and I kissed him again. This time, he let me, opening his mouth to mine, there, hidden by the gravestones.

*

We moved into a flatlet on Orange Street just below Leicester Square, rented to us by an infamous madam named Mrs Barr, and we preached there too. I followed William's example as a sermoniser, used his ideas and what scraps of opinions I could harvest from the Antinomians. One day, Mrs Barr made her girls come in from the brothel 'to hear the word of the Lord from them nice boys'. 'It might do you some *facking* good!' she yelled at them as they piled in through the door. William was not there. They sat before me looking so bored. I watched their bitten-up faces, their folded arms, their scratched knuckles, how their eyes rolled across the ceiling and out of the grubby windows, anything but to hear the word of the Lord. They meant to reject me, but O, Lord, I am not easily dissuaded.

I knew how to reach these girls: for I had once been the same as them, a tough kid from the streets. I got down from my fruit-crate pulpit and walked up to the toughest one of all. She had not been looking at me, but as I approached her, she glanced up with sharp contempt. 'What is your name?' I asked.

'Katherine,' she said.

'Katherine, I have something to tell you.'

'And what's that?'

I gazed at her fearsomely, the same way I now gaze at the pews at the Obelisk every Sunday morning. It was on Orange Street that I learned many tricks.

'The Lord does not care how many men you've fucked, Katherine.' Her eyes went round; she had surely never heard the Anglican vicar at St Martin-in-the-Fields talk like this. 'He does not care about how you make your living. I am come to tell you that the Lord only cares that you love. All else is not a cause for your damnation. Perhaps there is no damnation at all. All I know is that if you love, and bring kindness to people, and accept them as they are, the Lord will love you. And perhaps you, a prostitute, do bring kindness to people. For all I know, you are the one doing the Lord's work and not me . . .'

She looked quite profoundly shocked. 'I beg pardon, Reverend?'

I smiled at her, a small, conspiratorial smile. 'You heard me, Katherine. You heard every word.'

I turned to another girl and asked her name. 'Mary,' she said, chastened and intrigued now. Then another: 'Arabel.' I told them the same: that God loved them, he cared nothing for their sins, he cared only about their goodness, their openness to other people, the tolerance and love they showed to others.

'Fucking hell,' Arabel muttered, and Mary burst into tears.

*

Our ministry grew apace. By day, we preached in that tiny, dingy room, in turn standing on a chair and reciting from our annotated New Testaments, passages and paragraphs that pointed towards the revolutionary aspects of Christ's teaching. At night, we slept in the same bed. Now and then, naked under sheets save for a nightgown, we kissed and touched each other's bodies, until William whispered, 'No more, John, please, I am afraid of the Lord.' One night, I said to him, 'But, William, I thought there were no rules, so why are we afraid of expressing love?' He turned his face to mine, his eyes a-wonder, his lips parted. 'I am a virgin,' he said. 'I do not know what to do.'

'Me too,' I said. This was not true, of course. From sixteen years old, I had rented on the London streets, and fucked more men than I could count. But he needed to believe that about me then.

*

This was the happiest time of my life. Love had found me after all, found that abandoned, unwanted child. O, I do not say that it was always easy. William sometimes complained that I was too intense and that I expected too much. I think he was just frightened of what we were feeling, of the intensity of what he felt for me. How can one expect too much of love? It is not possible. But all I had to do was lie quietly in our makeshift bed on the floor, his head against my bare chest, my fingers running through the ends of his hair, and I knew that there was nothing else I wanted, and that he surely felt the same.

*

Then, one day, William's brother arrived from their village out in Essex. Someone had written to tell him that his younger brother was shaming himself all over Soho with some preacher, and there were all sorts of detestable rumours circling us. I was amazed to hear this, and never heard it again from any quarter. The brother smashed up our rooms, tore pages from our annotated bibles, punched and kicked William, calling us filthy Mary-Anns, foul degenerates. I started to punch the brother back, and he seemed amazed that violence might be a two-way street, but it was William who finally restrained me. Covered in his blood or mine or perhaps his brother's, he told me to stop. He said he had to go, he had no choice. 'Or you could stay!' I cried. 'Or you could stay! You could stay! *You could stay!*'

But he did not stay.

*

I never heard from, or of, William ever again. After he had gone, I lay on the floor of our flatlet for a very long time. I remember my head hard against the floorboards, staring up through the tiny top-floor attic window, at the stars twinkling above the river. I remember thinking: *I am destroyed.* I remember thinking: *I am abandoned again, rejected again.* Love did not save me: *it killed me.* The wardens at the Hospital had been right. *No wonder his mother chucked him, look at him, the pathetic little runt.* Perhaps I lay there all night, I don't remember; perhaps it was several days, paralysed by grief, thinking I would die.

A thought appeared in my head: *No, I have been loved.* And that thought spiralled and swelled and budded flowers, unfurled whole branches out into the air: *However briefly, someone loved me; no matter their behaviour after, I know they loved me.* I might not be someone who had received much love, but now I knew about it; truly I did, and I understood its potential in people's lives. I had told another human being that that was what I wanted; maybe I could tell another person that again.

I got up and walked to the tiny window of that room above Orange Street, which looked out over the hill and down towards the river. The moon was high in the dark sky; I blinked and smiled to myself. I decided there and then to begin again.

The Sunday, the second of this story . . .

I was standing in the pulpit at the Obelisk, looking at him. Ned was standing with Mrs Caesar. She was talking to him brightly, on some serious subject, and he nodded attentively. Idly, without consequence, I was drawn back into the strangeness of his beauty: the angles and planes of his face, a hazy, elegant, painterly quantity to his form and its movements. Now and then, as Mrs Caesar made one of her humorous observations, he pursed his lips in a half-smile and then suddenly, sunlit, his lips revealed a beautiful, generous smile.

It was time to begin the sermon. I tapped the lectern on top of the pulpit although I had brought no notes. I never bring notes; I do not need them any more. 'Today I want to talk to you about how hard tolerance is. We like to think it is easy, so natural, to be tolerant, but that is not true. Tolerance can be difficult, demanding.' A little buzz passed around the congregation. 'Tolerance is the acceptance of the views and being of others, of their inalienable right to hold those views, even though they might appal or offend you. I see many people in the world say they are tolerant, but when asked to tolerate views that differ from their own, they absolutely refuse. They mark their refusal as a badge of honour. Their intolerance is a mark of their tolerance, in fact! And why? Because tolerance is hard, demanding. Tolerance means we must listen to others, and accept that our version of events, no matter how sincerely held, may not be an absolute truth. It means we cannot insist on the implementation of it as such. It means accepting the right of others to be different, to think differently to what we think or who we are. It means accepting the right of others to hold views, do things even, which we find offensive. Allowing people to do and think these things threatens our views of the

43

world, even of ourselves. So why should we do such a thing, given how much tolerance requires of us, without personal benefit?'

I paused. It's good to pause. 'But for me, tolerance's difficulty is also its gift, for it does in fact offer benefits, and pleasures. First of all, tolerance renders the incurious person curious. It forces him or her to engage with ideas or with people that are not like them or theirs. A curious life is better than an incurious life. Secondly, I believe tolerance frees folk. I do not mean the tolerated – who are of course freed by it – but the tolerant. To hate, to be suspicious, to root out difference, to be intolerant, does not just make us incurious, it is' – I shrugged – 'exhausting.' Laughter. 'To persecute is exhausting. To be intolerant requires bitter, angry vigilance. Whose life is improved by bitterness and anger? So to tolerate frees us because it frees us from the exhaustion of hatred. And lastly, it reminds us that human beings are good, that their goodness is divinely created and any diversion from that acceptance of others is man-made. In tolerance, we remind ourselves that people who are not like us can still be good, even if they are different to us. We are reminded of the universal native goodness of human beings, that evil is an exception not a rule, and that our differences are dwarfed by our shared humanity.' It was this thought that drove me on, in my beliefs, the day they hanged Richard Oakden; this certainty that people can, and will, change.

When the service was done, Mrs Caesar came to speak to me. She had a folded piece of paper in her fingers. I looked at the line of followers behind her. Her daughter, Lydia, was at her side, but Ned was not with them. 'Mrs Caesar,' I said. 'Your group is different every week.'

'Only two new ones today, Reverend Church.' She looked back at the troop of followers. 'Emmanuel! Frederick! Come!' Two young men stepped forwards. The first, Emmanuel, was round and respectful, nodding and smiling sweetly. I saw the other – Frederick, who was very handsome – tilting his chin proudly upwards.

'Did you enjoy the sermon?' I asked them, as I ask probably forty people every Sunday morning. It was Emmanuel who answered.

'Very much, thank you, sir,' he said. 'I am most interested in your subject.'

'Tolerance?'

The young man nodded. 'I have just read Kant, sir—' he said meaningfully, as if *I* should know anything about such a thing.

'Who shares your name,' I said brightly. The young men, as one, furrowed their brows. I was afraid that I sounded stupid.

Emmanuel tried to clarify: 'He states that we must practise toleration, for whilst we may be certain of our own moral values, we cannot be certain of God's.'

Mrs Caesar let out a long, slow breath. 'So we cannot persecute if we are not entirely certain of God's intention, then.'

Emmanuel nodded to her respectfully. 'Precisely so, madam.'

'I think that is a very narrow definition of tolerance,' I ventured. 'It does not account for tolerance having its own benefits and pleasures, as I have explained. But I do not wish to debate Kant with you, Emmanuel.'

The young man shook his head emphatically. 'O, I cannot acclaim him, Reverend, for he bitterly hates Africans.'

Lydia Caesar said to Emmanuel: 'Then he is a hypocrite! Like all these fellows who blather on about Reason whilst forcing our faces into the gutter. They all announce their goodness, but half of them enslave us yet.' The young woman looked at me. 'The one thing you did not account for in your speech, Reverend Church, is that people *enjoy* their intolerance. Or when they feel the limits of their tolerance are stretched, for example by the recipients of it who are not *grateful* enough' – her eyes flicked to some of her companions – 'then they will revert to intolerance and feel safe there. Safe and right.'

Mrs Caesar began to speak: 'Reverend, I have forgotten, O! Lydia is doing her talk this week. I am sure you will give her many useful pointers if you come along and review her performance. You will come, of course, Reverend, as you promised?' Now she handed me the folded piece of paper in her fingers. She had written it out before, with every intention of giving it to me.

THE ANGEL TAVERN
FLEET STREET
ON SATURDAY EVENING
AT HALFWAY PAST SEVEN O' CLOCK

'Will you come, Reverend?' Mrs Caesar asked.

I took the slip of paper and smiled at her, to let her believe whatever she wished. But I did not care for Miss Lydia, her views or her speeches. I was only thinking about one thing, one person: 'Did Master Ned go home? I was expecting to see him after service. He asked me to talk with him about my ideas.'

Mrs Caesar smiled, turning towards the chapel entrance. 'He is waiting for you, Reverend.'

She pointed and there he was, in the chapel doorway, where, the week before, I had seen him vanishing into the light. He had reappeared, re-formed, lifting his hand – his fingers loose in mid-air – to show me he was there. He had come back, as he had said he would.

★

As Ned and I walked from Kennington to the Bridge, a half-hour even moving quickly, we talked about life at the Obelisk.

He called me Reverend Church several times, and eventually I told him just to call me John. He said he had never met a preacher who asked to be called by his Christian name before. 'I am not like other preachers,' I said, and his eyes lingered on me, looking for meaning.

The top of Tooley Street was its native maddening crush of Bridge business. I asked him where he lived. He told me that he had taken new lodgings on Mint Street, a notoriously awful part of Southwark where only the poorest live. He laughed a little as soon as he said it: 'Don't judge me, John, it is all I can afford.' I smiled. 'I have very little money. I have to share with a fellow I hardly know. We sleep in the same room, like boys in a dormitory.' He paused as if about to make a confession, I thought, about boys in dormitories, but in fact, it was not. 'I used to live on Old Broad Street north of the river, and had a room of my own with my job, but I lost my position. I worked as a junior clerk but the company sacked me.'

'Why?'

He shrugged yet looked at me most directly. 'They gave my job to an English lad, told me to leave.'

'You did nothing wrong? They just sacked you?'

'Of course I did nothing wrong. Yes, they just sacked me.' He did not explain any further. 'You work all alone at the Obelisk Chapel, John?' he asked.

'Yes, and it's become a lot of work. I am not very good at keeping accounts or records. It runs away from me sometimes.'

'Do you need someone to do your accounts?' He laughed merrily. 'I know a very reliable fellow just out of work. He only lives on the Mint. Very handy.' He was funny; I was not sure I had expected that he would be. I had assumed he might be another of Mrs Caesar's austere ducklings, but he was not; he was both soft and teasing, gentle but sharp.

Crossing the Bridge, we moved into the old City. There,

the press and chaos did not let up. London is unintentionally a sensual place. Endless is the proximity of strangers' bodies. They touch briefly, by accident, by design, seduction or attack. Men push into men, and against women who push back – *Oi, hands off, mush!* – or shrink away, invaded.

The noise around us then was relentless: trundling cart-wheels, animal noises, church bells, hammering and sawing from workshops, and everywhere, *everywhere*, people were shouting: to children, to customers, to those that had stepped on their foot or in the way of their cart. The commotion and the press of bodies was such that it made it hard for us to continue to talk; all people could do was march in single file in swirling rivulets. Now and then I felt his body in front of mine, the crowd forcing him to step back and touch me. More than once, as he bumped back into me, he turned and gave me a small, shy smile: 'I'm sorry, John, I'm sorry.' I laughed and told him it was fine, then he bumped back into me again. London, in all its crush and chaos, was conspiring to make us touch.

Clearing the Monument, we moved into broader, calmer streets. We fell into walking side by side and could talk easily at last. I asked him how he knew Mrs Caesar. He said he had known her daughter from radical meetings around. It was only when he had moved to Southwark, though, that he got to know them more. 'I am a great admirer of her mother's polit-ical work,' I said.

'Everyone admires the Caesars,' he replied.

I asked him how he had become interested in political radicalism. 'Through abolition,' he said quite neutrally. He spoke about the Government's abandonment of Abolitionism during the war in favour of protecting trade routes, and the interference of 'The Interest'. I asked him if he was himself a revolutionary. He said he was inspired by revolution – America, France, Haiti. He told me how he had become an active

48

abolitionist some years before, as the British Government was 'dragging out the end of the Slave Trade, using the war as an excuse to do so'. I asked him if he was a follower of Mr Wilberforce, widely credited in the press and the people's minds with ending the Trade, and he laughed quite airily, as if I was being ironic!

He spoke in hot, quick sentences about things of which I could see he cared; I liked that. He spoke confidently about books he had read, and the ideas in them which he seemed to understand. Letting him talk as we walked meant I could look at him uninhibited. Under his dark coat, he wore a thin white cotton shirt, of a cheap sort. Through the shirt – open at the neck, revealing the top of his chest, his collarbones, his throat – I was aware of his body beneath, slim, hard. The more animated he became, the more I saw that feminine quality I had noticed the first day, eyes twinkling, hands twirling, excitable rhythms, sudden flushed stops.

'And are you from London originally, John?' His question broke me from my thoughts.

'Yes, and you?'

'I was raised in the north, but came here ten years ago.'

'With your family?'

He stopped walking, forcing me to do the same. 'I don't know my family, John.'

'O, I am an orphan too, I never knew my parents either.' Those sparkling eyes again, held mysteriously on mine. 'Where in the north did you grow up?'

'In Yorkshire, in the countryside.'

I looked at him, but he revealed nothing more. 'Why did you move to London, Ned?'

He paused a moment. I could see him considering how he wished to answer – or rather, what. 'I am on a journey, John. I am trying to find something out about myself.'

That did not seem like an answer at all. It seemed like the avoidance of one. 'What are you trying to find out, Ned?'

'To find out who I am. I was raised not to know who I am, not to care, not to ask, and now I am free, I want to discover what it even means to be me. I came to London as part of that process of discovery.'

I understood what he was saying. 'You were a slave as a child, Ned.'

He nodded, his eyes falling to run across the ground. 'So I was not educated. I suppose I am educating myself by reading these books, going to these meetings. When you are enslaved, you are never encouraged to think beyond some small task to be completed under instruction. You are discouraged from thinking about the world, or ideas, or politics. *Firmly* discouraged.' I assumed he meant violence. 'Beyond that, you are told it is something you could *never* understand, that you do not have the capacity to understand, and you start to believe that lie. Such a lie is told about you, and the worst thing is that you come to believe the lie. But one day, if you are lucky, you come to understand that it is not true. Education is just a path anyone can walk, if they have permission. For me, that path did not start until I achieved my freedom.' Suddenly, unexpectedly, he smiled.

'How did you come to be free?' At once, I saw something change in him.

'Don't ask me to tell you the history of my enslavement, John, please.'

'Why not, Ned?'

He looked at me quite sadly. 'I am afraid I might grow to resent you.'

This shocked me. 'Why would it make you resent me?'

I could see that he was trying to explain himself, that he was not trying to provoke or insult me. 'Because you already know the story of Slavery. Every English person knows the story. They just pretend that they do not, that it is shocking to them. But it's not. Everyone knows the story.'

His eyes were on me, firm but not unkind. I had no clue what to say to him, and only hazily understood what he even meant, but I knew I wanted him to think I did. I smiled and he did the same. We had come close to the Old Street, beyond which was open country until lately. Now, of course, being London, they were draining the marshes and building houses. Only five minutes on from there was Moorfields, where once, on open ground, I had in darkness, and without names exchanged, fucked Sally Fox. I told Ned nothing of that, of course.

I asked him which writers he liked, for I find bookish sorts will always talk freely on that, and you can seem a bluestocking too, for having asked unbidden.

'Thomas Paine,' he said. 'The *Rights of Man* is the foundation, or rather, the consolidation after the Revolution in France. It is the blasting-away of all that soft liberalism, that we must be pragmatic and realistic. That is the thinking that excites me most, I think, the sort that sees the lie for what it is. I very much admire William Godwin. Not his silly novels. The *Enquiry Concerning Political Justice*. He looks to a time when all law will be replaced with a sort of radical anarchy. *You* must feel some sympathy with such a position.' *Did I? Must I?* 'And there is Mrs Godwin too. *A Vindication of the Rights of Woman*. What an incredible book, for those who want to see the world anew.'

He then asked me of my ideas, and further, how I had devised them. I told him of a young man, born Nothing, abandoned, but who also educated himself, also searched for meaning. He nodded, emphatically, showing our connection. I told him of my contact with the Antinomians and their radical rejection of law as a founding principle of religion, and yet, I told him, even as they said they did not judge, they judged all the time. Still, I pushed on with my ideas, I said, not by adding layers of theology and theory, but instead by stripping them away, back to the simplicity of Christ's instruction just to love. 'I believe that if people truly open their hearts to the radical instruction to love, to practise acceptance and tolerance, then all other things, like hate, bigotry, punishment, condemnation, will fall away.'

He considered this a moment. 'Have you thought how you will get people to change?'

'Through preaching about the radical possibilities of love, of tolerance, of winning people over, of getting them to perceive that they were deceived into hate, that it brings them, ordinary folk, no benefit.'

His eyes held mine. 'Do you think people will just magically give up their old ways?'

I realised he was not just asking me questions; he was questioning me. 'O, I see that you do not agree with me, Ned?' I asked, with some surprise.

His smile was so beautiful, so bewildering in its gentleness. 'Hatred and bigotry run very deep, John. People do not even recognise how much hatred they feel. I would like to say, if I think of where I agree with you, that tolerating the views of those we oppose at least allows us to keep open a dialogue, in hopes that we may persuade them to change, or at least reach a position better than that from which they started, but if I am honest, when I look at the world, that is not what I see. The risk of tolerance of that approach is abuse by the intolerant.'

'But ordinary folk would be only served by the acceptance of tolerance,' I said.

He shrugged. 'And ordinary folk act against their interests all the time. Politicians know it, priests know it, journalists, moneylenders, landlords, they all know it.'

I felt confused by him, not attacked, just his words made

me feel uncertain, not about my beliefs but about his view of them – and, I suppose, of me. 'So why are you here, Ned, walking with me, talking to me, if you do not admire my ideas?'

'O, but I do admire them! You are asking such interesting questions, John. Who is a radical, and what makes them so? And the thing that I think is most important: what is demanded of a radical, when radicals spend most of their time demanding things? Is a person radical simply because they say they are, or is it because of their actions and behaviours? These are the most interesting questions I have heard in a long time. They are questions at the very core of any moral philosophy, for anyone who thinks themselves radical.'

All this talk of 'moral philosophy' frightened me. I stopped dead; I had to tell him the truth, or else I risked becoming upset, and I did not want that.

'I must confess something to you, Ned,' I said sharply, turning to face him fully. 'I am not an intellectual. I am not well read like you. I was raised without education and I did not follow the path to erudition you did. I admire so much that you have done it, but I have not, and I don't want to pretend to you.'

He spoke, firmly but kindly. 'You should not pretend, John. You should never pretend. You never have to, at least with me. Look at what you have achieved already, what hope you give to ordinary folk. You have invented a new way of thinking, unlike any I have witnessed at first hand. Even if I do not fully agree, I admire you enormously.' He flustered, some embarrassment entered him, and his eyes went very round.

It was then that old impulsiveness grabbed me: 'Why don't you come and work for me, Ned?'

He looked so surprised. 'What, John . . . ?'

'We were joking of it a moment ago, but truly, why not?'

He laughed but he seemed so nervous. 'But what as?'

'My assistant. You are a clerk, and more educated than me,

and I need someone to help me with my bookkeeping. And you have all your radical connections, so I am sure that would be useful. I cannot pay you very much, but I can pay you something, and that must be better than nothing.' I paused; I had thought I was saying the right thing. The impulse hits me in a split second. Then I have all eternity to regret it after. 'At least until you find something more permanent.'

I was certain he was about to say no, even if he did like me. I go too fast; I act too wildly; people are driven away. 'I could,' he said instead. He let out a small, strange laugh, with some anxiety in it. 'Can I think about it?'

'You can tell me next Sunday, if you wish. You will have a week to decide.'

At this, his brow furrowed. 'Are you not going to see Miss Caesar speak on Saturday?' he asked.

I had had no intention at all of going. 'Yes,' I said.

He seemed happy when I said it. 'We should go together.'

'All right, Ned.' Any nerves left him, and all that remained in his smile was its spreading sweetness.

Chapter Four
or
Who's Afraid Of A Bit Of Faggotry?

The same evening, therefore remaining the Sunday . . .

The first regular Sunday night at the molly house was also the first night there would be weddings. After saying farewell to Ned on Great Surrey Street, from where he walked east to his home on the Mint, I walked west to mine on The Cut. Washing my face and changing my shirt, I made the journey across the Bridge to the north side, and on to Vere Street. It was night-time by then, and London was changed – more threatening in intent, more diffuse. In the darkness, the city's human press is transformed into something more spectral. Figures loom out at you, under lit oil-torches, or from around roaring, smoky bonfires that line the streets, burning up the day's rubbish. The night blinds you, then chokes you with fumes. The figures vanish again, swallowed nocturnally. Soon, they say, they will introduce the new gas lamps to the city. People imagine it will be like sunlight day and night; who knows what change brings? But it's hard to believe the city's threats will recede, just because the darkness has.

That evening, the air was crisp and cold; the next day there would be frost. An antic, whispery atmosphere infected the city, and gusts of icy wind whittled down sound. From the Bridge, I walked straight down Cannon Street, past the Cathedral and on to Ludgate Hill. On Fleet Street, the whorish buzz of Covent Garden felt more imminent. Just past the southern end of Chancery Lane, a throng of people became apparent, of that category in which London specialises: gawkers, ill-wishers, memorialisers of random, bloodied violence. Men and women were chattering excitedly and heartlessly, discussing whomever had suffered, relieved perhaps that it was not them – this time. I moved around the half-circle of people, not looking where they looked; I do not share this grim desire to see destruction. At the end of Bell Yard, I felt a tug at my arm, from someone at my side, out of view. 'Reverend Church! Why are ye here?'

Turning in the dark, I saw him appearing out of the gloom and shuddered. Mr Linehan was one of my worshippers at the Obelisk. Let me admit this openly: I did not like this man. He lived on the north side of the Bridge, far away up in the ward of Farringdon Within, but still he lumbered down to Kennington every Sunday. I did not like him on a visceral level – instinctively, almost vomitously. I sensed in him the hypocrisy – the fake moral rectitude – that I cannot abide. Yet he continued to come to hear me preach, week after week. 'I am going to a . . . religious meeting,' I said. 'In Soho.'

Mr Linehan had a bright red face much given to scowling, an angry mouth much given to spittle, eyes that assaulted in every direction. He swung round, pointing towards the circle of people. 'Are ye not going to try to see the body, Reverend?' He was almost licking his lips with cruel pleasure. 'It is in quite a state. Eyes plucked out, guts cut clean open.' He mimed a knife slitting open a stomach. I only wanted to pull away from him in disgust.

'Do you mean someone has been murdered, Mr Linehan?'

'Murdered?' He let out a sharp, nasty laugh. 'Punished, more like.' I didn't understand; he saw my incomprehension and hooted savagely. 'How can anyone murder *a molly*?' The word pulsed through me; like lightning hitting the ground. He moved closer to me as if to seek my confidence.

London is filled with murder. This is not just a city of meta-phorical ghosts, as I've said before, but of real ones, a patina of actual corpses: men old enough to know better, knifed in a pub fight; old ladies with their throats slit in their beds by burglars in the night; young women found in the Euston marshes, with newspapers reporting 'trussed up like chickens'; and children, endless children, murdered for pleasure or sport or by parents with too many mouths to feed. I do not have much to thank my native mother for, but at least she did not do me in. But in London, no one is considered more deserving of their murder than a molly. 'It's as much a Christian act to kill a faggot as it is a property owner's duty to kill a rat in your cellar,' Mr Linehan said. 'If you don't, it will soon attack your neighbours' houses too.'

'I don't think mollies attack property,' I said, trying to be dry, solely to hide my fear.

'O, they do attack!' he insisted. 'They attack women and chil-dren, 'tis well known. It has always been said, and good people should not deny it out of some well-meaning liberality!' It is in fact a curious thing held to be true that mollies are a danger to women. One would rather think that their husbands – for don't Normal men rape every day? – are the greater risk. But even good liberal women these days agree: *mollies* are their greatest danger.

I went to slip away from him; he caught my arm to pull me back closer. 'O, yes, Reverend, done up in a skirt with make-up. Disgusting! *Disgusting!*'

I tore my arm away from the vice of his grasp. 'Mr Linehan!' I yelled so loudly that folk turned. 'A human soul is dead!'

The man's face fell; he seemed quite bemused by my remark: 'Ye are a man of the Lord, Reverend Church. How can ye say such things? Even good people like thee and me, who are invested in the concept of tolerance, and the inherent nature of goodness in human beings, must understand God's laws.'

I heard him quoting my own ideas at me to justify his hate,

the very thing my teaching was supposed to deny. I blinked slowly, staring at him. Of course, he had no clue that he was speaking of me, and of the people I was about to go and see. 'I think, Mr Linehan, you should reflect on your Christian values if this is all you can say today!' The man was just staring back at me, uncomprehending. Briskly, I turned away, glad for the city's darkness eating me up.

I arrived at the White Swan early, going up the side stairs, concealed from the main tavern, and knocked at the bolted door. An eye appeared at its peephole: it was the waiter, Philip Kett. I heard him speak: 'O, it's you.' The eye disappeared; the door scraped open. 'Bolt the door behind you,' he said. 'The boss will be down in a minute.'

I sat alone in the main room, shivering with – I was not quite sure what – was it anger or rage or sadness? Philip Kett stood with his back to me behind the bar, turning a towel inside glasses. I thought of the girl who was taken, gutted, blinded, her body dumped for strangers to laugh and spit at. I have spoken of my own fear, but I wondered then at hers, in those last moments alive, knowing that certainly violence, and perhaps death, was coming. What were they like, those last moments? Did she die quickly, or slowly? Did she scream? Did she cry for help? Maybe someone came and, seeing the scene, joined in the slaughter.

'Reverend!' Mrs Cook appeared and broke my thoughts. 'Has Philip here offered you a drink yet?' Kett still did not turn from his task.

'No,' I said.

'Oi, Philip! Don't be such a blooming misery, get the Reverend a drink!'

Mrs Cook came to sit with me. Kett poured us a Madeira wine each and left the bottle with us. The wine's heavy sweetness revived me. 'Are you all right, dearie?' she asked me after a while. 'You don't seem yourself.'

I smiled and shook my head. I did not want to tell her what I had just seen; what good would it do? 'I am quite well.' She took a small sip from her glass then set it down. I watched her lick the Madeira from her lips.

That evening, we were a number of twenty perhaps, Sally and I, Black-Eyed Leonora, Sweet Lips and the Duchess of Gloucester among them. With the door safely bolted from within, several people carried large hessian sacks with them, tied very tightly, so nothing could be seen of their contents. Sally Fox cleared her throat theatrically. 'Will the ladies please prepare?'

The rush to the dressing room began, and I remained at the bar. At once, in the distance, was the riot of shouts and laughter and teasing: *Look at the state of her! O, my God, there are spiders in your wig! Put your back into it, it's only a fucking corset! Breathe in, for fuck's sake, how can you suck your balls UP THERE but not your gut IN THERE?*

Mrs Cook went in and out of the dressing room. I could hear her laughter joining theirs, sailing down the corridor, the sisterhood she had told me she shared with them. I heard her voice: 'No, like this, do you see?' or 'If you powder the wig more lightly, it will not shake off on your dress.'

We 'men' continued to sit outside as we had on the first night. I went to speak with Hepburn, who was on his own. I asked him where Tommy White was and he said that I would soon see. We chatted for a while, and he told me about his life as an ensign in a West India regiment, to which he would presently have to return. He said he was very concerned about Tommy being left alone in London, and I didn't wonder at that. Perhaps when he got back, someone as beautiful and sweet as Tommy would have found someone new. Young heads are easily turned.

A great bird-like chorus of giggling fluttered down from the dressing room. A few queens appeared in the main room, led by Sally. Then a vision appeared: Miss Sweet Lips, six feet tall, her handsomeness as a man held in erotic effect by the white powder on her skin, her scarlet lips, and the heart-shaped beauty spot on her cheek. Her bodice – breath-stoppingly tight around her muscular, masculine body – cut away not to a lady's gown but to a wrap of old damask, open at the front, revealing her long, athletic legs. All eyes were on Miss Sweet Lips, just as she liked it.

'Hmm,' she began, her eyes running over every man in there. 'I can see that some of you boys are already pointing in my direction.'

Mrs Cook slapped the end of the bar to call for attention. The *bang* drew all eyes away from Sweet Lips to her. 'Gentlemen, the ladies have decided tonight we will have a contest of pretty girls. They will parade before you and the prettiest of the lot will be chosen and acclaimed as our "fair maid".'

Sally looked around the room. 'But who is gonna be the poor fucking sod who gets to judge?'

Mrs Cook's eyes, glittering with the mischief that exists between friends, settled on me. 'Why, the Reverend!'

'O, no!' I cried, but people started to laugh and clap: *Reverend Church! Reverend Church! Reverend Church!*

One by one, the queens did a spin around the room, to be admired and judged. First came Sally, who – of course – played it for laughs, barrelling through the crowd like a docker. She stopped dead in front of me, looked right in my face and then smiled mock-sweetly. 'Johnny boy,' she purred.

Then came the Duchess of Gloucester, galumphing in a dark dress, with a very fashionable and probably expensive wide hat. After the Duchess came someone I did not recognise at first, a creature so pretty and delicate that if you did not know, you might have taken her for a real girl in the street. Dressed in a pretty cream gown with a low décolletage revealing a pale, hairless chest, her eyes shyly met mine: it was Tommy White! As a woman, he was genuinely, angelically beautiful.

Next was Tommy's friend, James Mann, in a wig of blonde hair that fell loose and long, wearing a curious milkmaid's dress. He was young and confident, lovely but with hard eyes. A few other girls appeared, and then last of all came Black-Eyed Leonora. She wore a turban as brightly red as her carefully painted lips. The dress she wore was almost like a *toilette* robe, in broad black and gold stripes that swept over her tiny frame down to the floor, only just about revealing her golden shoes. Her eyelids were also painted gold. She looked like some mysterious, imperial Sultana, all the way from Constantinople. She walked like a moving sculpture, and once in the middle of the room, turned in a complete circle for the viewers to admire her exquisiteness.

When the parade was finished, the girls gathered in the centre of the room. Mrs Cook called from behind the bar: 'Well, Reverend, who are you going to choose?' I looked along the line of girls. How ridiculous it seemed, and yet also so important: whom do you flatter / whom do you hurt? Should I choose the Duchess, whose win everyone – presumably even she – would know was only an act of mercy? Or should I choose Sweet Lips or James Mann, the obvious objects of lust in the room? Or Sally, who did not need it, or Tommy White, who wanted only Hepburn's eyes? The queens were all looking at me, hopeful and satirical, shy and brazen. I looked at Black-Eyed Leonora, and she bowed her head to me a little. I saw something in her then that I had not quite seen before: some sweet, hopeful sensitivity. I thought it interesting that, of all the girls, it might be she who wanted it most, to be acclaimed the prettiest. I made the deepest gentleman's bow to her; her gold-painted eyes grew wide. 'Leonora,' I said, rising out of the bow and extending my hand in her direction. 'She is the fair maid of the evening.'

She looked like she might burst. 'O, Reverend Church!' she kept saying. 'You've made me the happiest woman in the world!'

When the hour was coming close to ten, and it would soon be time to do some marrying, I saw Sally sitting alone in a corner on a banquette. She was rubbing her injured arm with her other hand. I went over to her; seeing me, she patted the spare cushion for me to sit next to her. Already I felt as if I had drunk too much, but my head was not quite swimming. One body was close to the other, with the familiarity of those who had once upon a time, very briefly, been lovers; a remembrance of intimacy. Her head fell against my shoulder, her horse-hair wig prickling my jaw. 'What you did for Leonora was so nice,' she said softly, with a sigh. 'You are a good man, Johnny boy.'

I liked that she said it about me. I liked it a great deal. 'She deserves it. She is like a work of art.'

Sally laughed to herself. 'You mean she costs a fortune and no one bothers to go and look at her.'

'Sal, you're terrible.'

'She is *my* sister! I shall say what *I* like about *my* sister!'

The queens can find a thousand ways to take offence.

'Did you hear about the girl who got killed on Bell Yard?' I asked her, and the mood changed.

'Do you know who?' I said no. 'If there is nowhere quiet nearby, the girls who work the mollies' walk on Covent Garden take their punters down there sometimes, or anywhere around the alleys in Clare Market after the shops shut. What happened?'

I told her I did not know, just that a girl got murdered. Sally listed names of girls she knew who worked the area, worrying who it might be, but again I said to her: 'Truly, Sal, I don't know.'

I could see how bothered she was: Sally Fox, who *never* showed fear, but she was also Sally Fox who had been to the pillory and knew all too well the violence that simmers in our city. She started slowly rubbing her arm again; she was unaware

rather God's love, just a law of nature – and then we came to this place where we had created such a vulnerable community. In that moment, I understood that what this place had to be was a place of transformation, of the radical possibilities of love in practice, in which people like Katherine, Mary and Arabel were freed by simple statements of love from the judgement of the world, to be able to see that we were not just equal, or free, but actually worth something; that we believed that about ourselves.

Every Sunday, I preached about love. I gave sermons about how we should rethink it, reimagine it: yes, its inevitability; yes, its universality. Mrs Cook had asked me to come to Vere Street to perform weddings – joke weddings – for those who thought that all they had – all they were worth – was joke weddings. I thought lastly of Mr Linehan, seeing our sister gutted by some man, likely with a wife, and children, and a good seat in church each Sunday. Linehan took his hate and insisted it was love, and it sickened me. We were not the worst of men. We were not Mr Linehan's disgusting rats.

I saw the truth. Our love was not a perversion. I saw that truth in Hepburn and White's love for each other, and Black-Eyed Leonora's happiness that evening. We deserved not just to love, but to be able to recognise the fact of our love before our friends. Everything here at Vere Street was said as a joke, but some things are not jokes. *Some things are true.* I saw that we were all worthy of love, and what we needed was someone to tell us that, for the first time. Suddenly, extraordinarily, I realised that person was me.

I knew what I must do. I got to my feet. Yes, it was my impulsiveness but it was also the moment that all my ideas came together. I had been asked how I could apply them in the real world. Well, here we were, in a world that was both play-acting and brutally, riskily real. I was facing the crowd in the main room. No one even noticed me standing up, except Sally and Mrs Cook, who were at my side.

'Quiet!' I cried at the crowd, but people kept chattering and laughing, all rolling in their cups, barely able to hear. '*Quiet!*' I yelled again, and people began to turn. It was Sally who finished it: '*Fucking shut up!*'

All eyes turned to me. I knew I was going to speak. I knew what I was going to say. And yet I was afraid, and I felt like I was faltering. 'We . . . we come here to perform joke weddings, but I want to ask you, is that all we are worth, men like us: jokes? Is that all we are: inversions of love? Do we think our love, our ability to love, is just a joke so all we deserve are joke weddings? But we are not a joke.'

Someone somewhere drunkenly called: 'What's he on about?'

'What am I on about?' I asked rhetorically. 'From next Sunday, for those who want it, I will not be performing joke weddings any more. I will be performing real weddings, marriages in the eyes of God. Any man who loves another man can come here, and I will marry them in the eyes of God, if that's what they both want. We are worth more than violence. We are worth love, and from next Sunday, those that want it, we'll mark your love. We'll marry each other, if that's what we want.'

The room remained pin-drop silent. Perhaps it was just shock. Perhaps it was the rustle of people thinking for the first time that this was even possible for them. The first time I came to Vere Street, Mrs Cook had said that she did not know if the girls wanted weddings any more. I hadn't known either, but now I did. Now I knew what I had to do – for my own kind, and perhaps even for myself.

Chapter Five

or

The Truth Comes Out . . .
But Not The One You're Expecting

The Saturday following . . .

That week, Ned had dropped a note to the Obelisk saying he would meet me at the location of the talk: the Angel Tavern, Fleet Street. About seven o'clock in the evening, I left my rooms on The Cut. I did not know this tavern at all – London has so many, one on every street corner and three more in between. When I got to the corner of Farringdon Street, I asked passers-by if they knew the place. But no one even seemed to have heard of it. 'Don't know it, pal.' 'Don't ask me, pal.' 'What, how should I know one of them places?' *Them* places? I did not understand.

Presently I found it, almost at the Strand, near the narrow lane down to the old Temple Church. The Angel Tavern was a tiny, battered sort of place. Its windows were cloaked in thick curtains, and no light – only the sound of music – emitted from within. As I pushed the heavy door, I noticed the wood nailed over its window and the broken glass panes beneath. Tavern noise hit me: chatter, laughter, glasses chinking, a fiddle and several drums playing at once. Eyes glanced up at me but, if I caught them, looked away. An old lady in bonnet and shawl, sitting alone, stared me up and down, without satisfaction. I realised that every other person within the Angel Tavern was

African. This was a Black tavern, of which there were several in the city. Was this why people did not seem to know one of 'them places', or at least affected not to? I looked around in hopes of seeing Ned, but he was not there.

The tavern-keep behind the counter nodded over at me. 'You all right there, pal? Know where you're going, do you?'

A second woman was standing at the bar, with a sack of onions slumped on top of it and a small beaker of stout at her lips. 'You looking for your holy friends, is it?' She arched an eyebrow then pointed at the ceiling. 'They're upstairs.' She grinned at the tavern-keep. 'Feeling the Lord move through them!' She took a sip of her stout and then crackled out a *ha!*

The keep pointed me to the staircase beyond the bar. Climbing to the first floor, in near-total dark, I walked down a crooked corridor. At its end I saw the glow of a large, open room with its door pinned back; candlelight and chatter within. Entering the room, again those inside were all African. Every sort of person was there: old and young, men and women, those dressed expensively and those most simply, almost in rags. A sea of heads, perhaps forty in number, sat in rows, facing a stage on which Mrs Caesar was standing. But where was Ned? In a queer sort of panic, I felt foolish, as if I had come here on no account at all. I quickly scanned the room. People turned to look at me, but eyes did not linger. I supposed they had seen a White fellow at one of their meetings before. Even so, the reversal of the world was clear to me.

Then I saw him on the far end of one row. He turned and smiled at me, shyly raising a hand in greeting; I felt such relief and pleasure. I pushed my way through the row on which he sat; he had kept a seat for me. People moved their knees and smiled or tutted. Ned picked up the hat he had placed on the seat. I laughed. 'Did you have to fight to keep a place for me?'

'I thought perhaps you had changed your mind,' he said then, gathering himself.

'Not at all. I've been looking forward to it. I was just late.'

This amused him; I did not know why. There was movement at the front and he turned his face to the stage; I looked too. Mrs Caesar was clapping her hands briskly and calling for quiet. Only then did I see Lydia Caesar sitting in the front row, chatting brightly with someone who looked like a dignitary of some kind. She laughed with him, enjoying herself, all easy company.

Mrs Caesar began to speak: 'Brothers and sisters, I am so happy to see so many of you here, for it reminds me how we must rely on our own brotherhood to win our war.' She spoke in a way I had not quite seen from her before; she spoke of war! 'I speak first to my brothers and sisters who are still illegally in chains, those few of you able to come here tonight, slipping away from your bondage. I want you to know that we never forget you, we free and freed Africans of this city. You are our brethren, and we work tirelessly to free you. Our day is coming, and we shall prevail. Some of you will not be able to stay because your gaolers will be wondering where you are. You must leave whenever you need to go, and know that we admire your courage and pray for your manumission.'

There was earnest applause. She said she would lead the meeting in a recitation of the 23rd Psalm: '"Yea, though I walk through the valley of the shadow of death, I will fear no evil: for thou art with me; thy rod and thy staff they comfort me. Thou preparest a table before me in the presence of mine enemies . . ."'

I was listening to the words, being murmured en masse with such intensity, her strong, clear voice the lead. When the psalm was over, with her face so serene, she looked over the crowd, took a small breath and said, quite peacefully: 'Death to the devil, King George!'

And all around came other voices: 'Death to King George!' 'Death to the devil!' 'Death to King George!' I knew that Africans despised the Royal Family, the heart of 'The Interest', but still it was quite bracing to hear such words said aloud, and by such a great number.

Mrs Caesar continued speaking: 'Now, tonight, I am very pleased to invite you to listen to my own estimable daughter, Lydia.' The mother applauded the daughter, who climbed up on to the stage; and all around us, others clapped too. It seemed as if she was well known in this political world.

'My brothers and sisters, one day soon, as my mother says, the Englishman is going to free us all and Slavery will end. I am not so sure he will, given he has for some years offered the excuse of the war with France to evade doing so, when we all know it is the placation of the slave-owner class that is his true intention.' There were murmurs of approval. 'So tonight, I have come to talk to you about forgiveness. Often I have heard our brethren talk about how we should feel after we are free. We perpetually ask ourselves: how are we going to forgive the White man, for all that he has done to us, three centuries of our murder, our dispossession and rape. Let me tell you, friends, I think this is the wrong question.' Folk watched her, and she let them. 'My question, brothers and sisters, is not whether we can forgive White people for Slavery. It is whether they will forgive *us* for it.'

At once, there was bright shock and plentiful calls for apology and explanation. I turned to look at Ned – who was staring at her, I noticed, quite intently. His eyes were warm and attentive. He was listening to her surprising words and, I could tell, admiring them. But I felt some brittle jealousy, I'll confess. I did not want him to admire Miss Lydia at all! She waved her hand to call the crowd to silence. 'Friends, I want to tell you a story I heard lately. It's about William Wilberforce, sainted White hero of our liberation. Now, Mr Wilberforce had a grand dinner at his house for all his friends in the House of Lords who voted for the passage of the Slave Trade Act, and many of the very sincere Church of England campaigners from all over the country. He even invited a number of Africans to come too, to prove his liberality. But do you know what happened next? The Africans arrived to sup at his house, dressed in their finest and ready to be part of a new world, but Mr Wilberforce made them sit behind a large curtain, so that White persons would not be offended by their presence.'

I noticed the entire room was silent; people seemed entirely unshocked and yet I was shocked! 'One day, in the future, Mr Wilberforce – or his descendants – will invite us – or ours – to sit at dinner, and they will not even ask us to sit behind a curtain. We will sit with White people, and we will all drink the same drink and eat the same food. And if one of us, or our descendants, says to him, "Do you remember when there used to be a curtain behind which you made us sit?" the White man will look with shock and say, "Beg pardon?" We will say, "Yes, there used to be a curtain you made us sit behind," and the White man will go, "No, I believe you are mistaken." If we say it again, he will become enraged and tell us to stop lying. Then his pretence will drop and he will say: "You are free now, why can't you be happy? You are free now, forget about the curtain! We freed you, so don't mention the curtain again." And we will say, "But you said you did not remember the curtain," and it will be then that the White man will know he can never forgive us. He will say: "You're lying. None of this happened. We did nothing to you." Or he will say it was some other White fellow who did it, but not him, and what he has, what he owns, the property and the investments, are nothing to do with what he did to us. All I can say to you is this. If the condition for freedom is to forgive and to forget what was done to us, then it is not a freedom worth having. One day, if we speak the truth, the White man will say he can no longer forgive us for speaking the truth of our history. It is then we shall be at the greatest risk, and the true evil of White folk will be revealed to us, again and again and again.'

She finished just like that. Usually, in such meetings, there is a prayer or at least a statement of faith in God that there might be change, but Lydia did none of that. Immediately there was great applause for her; she stood on the stage, basking in it. A preacher or proselytiser must enjoy acclaim, or else you are just an idiot dancing on a dais, making proclamations. Afterwards, there was much shaking of hands, in all directions. A collection plate was passed around, and new, still-inky pamphlets were sold at a brisk rate. Whilst Ned was in deep conversation with an older, clerical-looking fellow, Mrs Caesar came up to me and we chatted. She seemed very pleased that I had come, and I said I was full of admiration for her daughter. Presently, Lydia came and joined us. 'Miss Lydia,' I began enthusiastically, 'I can only congratulate you on your speech. I am not sure what I was antici-pating, but it was not such a talk of fire and accomplishment.'

I expected her to be full of thanks, but she regarded me coolly. 'Why did you not expect it of me, Reverend? Did you think I have insufficient intelligence for such a thing?'

Her chilliness should not have surprised me, but it did. 'O, not at all, but you are a young woman—'

Now she laughed satirically. 'It is only making speeches, Reverend Church. Where is the achievement in making pretty speeches?' Her eyes fixed on me very hard, as if to say: *You do it all the time!* 'Surely achievement lies in action.' She paused magisterially. 'Even "young women" can understand that.'

I gave her compliments and she gave me only insults back. I felt such anger towards her then; in another situation, I might have lashed out. Just then a fellow of some African heritage appeared at her side, a tall, rather handsome man, in a fitted jacket. It was the dignitary to whom Lydia had been speaking earlier. He bowed to us all, saying how much he had enjoyed her speech and how insightful he had found it. She greeted *him* effusively. Mrs Caesar introduced me to the fellow. 'Reverend Church, do you know Mr Robert Wedderburn?' I did not. Ned appeared at our side too, perhaps summoned by the man. 'And, Ned, you must surely know Mr Wedderburn.'

Ned's hand shot forwards and he was grinning broadly, obviously thrilled. 'Mr Wedderburn, what an honour!'

I understood then this man was notable in African circles. Suddenly Lydia was indicating towards me, though speaking to this Mr Wedderburn. 'Reverend Church was just stating his surprise that a young woman such as I might be a good preacher.' The Wedderburn fellow looked at me with searching, amused eyes. Did he know Miss Lydia's sharp teeth well? But that was not what I had meant at all. I faltered somewhat.

'Miss Caesar, you misrepresent me. You are a young woman, yes, in a world not filled with young women preaching, but my surprise was that your preaching was political in nature, not religious.'

'Is the radical in religion not the radical in politics?' Wedderburn asked.

Lydia's eyes were all harsh, bright amusement: 'Reverend Church preaches a form of worship in which he states all human beings are natively good and will accept tolerance and love in the end.' Her eyes held mine briefly, hot with contempt, flickering, jumping with her desire to harm me. 'What say you to that, Mr Wedderburn?'

I felt my annoyance; I did not let the man speak. 'No, what do you say, Miss Lydia? You seem to be full of meanings unexpressed!'

Her amusement was not abated by my obvious irritation; it was fed by it. 'O, Reverend, I am just a young woman at a political meeting, what know I of theology?' The other people were looking at me. The truth was I had no response to her. She was

73

cleverer than me, and nothing is more threatening than that. I felt Ned's eyes on me. Part of me wanted to react, wanted to lash my words against her, but in that moment, I knew that her words would be sharper than mine. A silence opened before us, with Lydia the cat who'd got the cream. It was this Mr Wedderburn who spoke instead, doing so kindly, yet dispassionately.

'Reverend Church, I hope sincerely you are right in your beliefs. How lovely would the world be if it in fact turned out to be filled with goodness and hope. It should be a most refreshing thing indeed.' He said this with the greatest possible levity, as if it were all a joke, and then said he had to go and speak with someone before he left for another meeting.

Afterwards, Ned and I walked away from the tavern, into the chaos of the London night. The mood could not have been more different than the meeting, the city's dark proposition. All along Fleet Street, the whores were on parade, making crude nocturnal suggestions to any male passer-by. Everywhere, people seemed goggle-eyed with grog. They railed around the outside of taverns, even though it was winter, or rushed towards the hawkers selling hot pies from carts. Meanwhile, Ned was talking excitedly of the speech we had just heard. He was saying that Lydia was mercilessly brilliant in her analysis of the realities both of abolitionism, as a force of action in law and community of Black folk, rather than a heroic narrative written by White folk about themselves. As he spoke so excitedly, I could only think of how harsh she had been towards me, on no good account. 'I think she is a new kind of person,' he was saying, 'unapologetic, brave, telling of the truth. She does not accept that old world of polite radicalism.'

I smiled and felt its tightness. 'And who was that Wetherby fellow?' I asked.

Ned's eyes bothered a little. 'Wedderburn. Robert Wedderburn. He is a great Abolitionist, an excellent radical. Have you never heard of him?' It was clear I had not. 'He is a very great radical and history will remember him,' Ned said confidently. I said nothing to that.

'Where did you first hear Miss Lydia speak?' I asked instead.

'I went to a Free & Easy Club, the one in Whitechapel.' The Free & Easy Clubs were well known in radical circles. They were not 'free and easy' in the sense the molly house was. They hosted events – usually held in a church hall or upstairs from a coffee house – where any kind of agitant or campaigner could go and address an audience, to expound their views on just about any liberal subject. Ned paused and looked at me meaningfully. 'Don't worry about Miss Lydia.'

'Worry?' I asked.

'She is ferocious and she is intellectual.'

I was going to pretend I did not know what he meant, but instead I decided to speak frankly: 'She does not like White folk, I think.'

'Perhaps not,' he said. Maybe I was expecting him to reassure me, but he did not. His eyes were on me, watchful but soft. 'Don't be sensitive, John. If she doesn't like you, then she doesn't like you. I don't think she cares if you are on our side, if that's what you are thinking. I don't think she believes that White folk can ever truly be on our side, and we must have faith only in ourselves, as African people. Perhaps she does not like you, John, but that's all right. White folk are well enough liked as it is.' He said this in a teasing way, which was not uncharming.

We decided to go down Kings Bench Walk and around the back of the Inner Temple, where the lawyers worked. Now it was late, the candles in the windows where solicitors scratched their quills were long since extinguished. We were on the edge of the gardens below the Inner Temple, a lush and quiet place in the middle of the City. There, in that dark calm, I felt my embarrassment cooling.

'Shall we sit here?' I said, indicating a small clear spot among the bushes. He looked around at the shapes and shadows of the garden, painted in night blue.

'Here, in the bushes?' he asked, as if it were quite ridiculous. I saw his genuine concern. It surprised me, another aspect of him. Did he think the place filled with robbers?

'We'll be fine,' I said, sitting down on the grass. 'We are both big, fit fellows.' He sat down too. We were silent a moment. The night was rather cold, and the grass under my arse was wet, seeping through the seat of my breeches. He tilted his head back to look up at the stars, visible above the river. 'How beautiful,' he murmured, then he looked back at me, grinning. I felt it so strongly then: not just his physical beauty, or his ethereal, feminine quality; not just that he was funny, intelligent, learned, curious.

'You are still without work, Ned?' I asked.

He pulled a comical/sad face. 'It is hard to get a position at the moment. I do not have enough contacts.'

'Then come and work for me,' I said, repeating my offer, but now more coolly, as if it was pure good sense that he might. 'You can keep accounts. I need someone to keep my books. I can hardly follow numbers at all.' He seemed uncertain. 'Won't we have a lark?'

His eyes were instantly on mine, glittering, mischievous, yet serious. 'A lark?'

He smiled, half laughed. Then, very abruptly, his mood changed. He was staring at me with such caution. His eyes were round with nerves. 'I don't want to do something that will harm me,' he said softly, mysteriously. I could hear his breathing. It seemed edgy. I looked into his eyes, then at his mouth, then back into his eyes.

'What could you possibly do that would harm you, Ned?' I

knew precisely what he meant. He was talking about our connection, and sex, and . . . whatever else.

'I like you, John. But I am not sure if I should work for you.'

'Why not?' He started fiddling with his fingers in his lap and did not reply. I would not let him slip away from me now, into his game of eyes and looks. '*Why not*, Ned?' Still no answer. He looked at me nakedly; his lips parted softly. I realised then that we were about to kiss. The moment felt so intense. I could hear my pulse thudding in my neck, my skin tingled with anticipation. But then he turned his face from mine.

'You are a mysterious person, John Church,' he said.

I moved towards him slightly but he did not look back at me. 'How am I mysterious, Ned?'

'I don't know.' He paused. 'I know nothing about you, not truly. All I know about is your ideas and your chapel.'

'What do you want to know, Ned?' I asked, keeping my body close to his.

Still he did not look back at me. 'Where do you live?'

'On The Cut, about ten minutes away from you.'

He nodded. 'Have you lived there a long time?' He asked the question in this flat way, suggesting not interest but rather some game that was being played.

'Not so long, Ned,' I replied.

And then he asked: 'Do you live alone?'

I drew back from him slightly, settling on one haunch. My withdrawal made him turn to look at me. Some suspicion passed over those starlit eyes. 'John . . . ?' Still I said nothing. 'John, answer me,' he said, more forcefully now. 'Do you live alone?'

'No,' I said. 'I live with someone.'

'With whom?' he asked.

I saw his face staring at me in expectation, and again, the game had turned against me . . . 'With my wife, Ned.'

There were a few seconds of complete silence, then suddenly he was on his feet, and stretching out his hand to shake mine, and he was gabbling: 'Th-thank you for inviting me this evening, John, I think . . . I think I should go home now,' and I was telling him to stay, I was saying to him, *don't leave, I can explain*, and he was saying, 'There is nothing to explain, John . . . What do you need to explain to me . . . ?'

'Wait!' I was calling as he fled. *Wait!* But he did not wait.

*

And you must wait too! Don't be angry! I have not misled you! I can explain everything.

*

I am not a liar. It's only a small deception. I don't want you to think I am manipulative in any way. Do you want me to start again? I can start again, if you need me to.

I promise you: I can *always* start again!

Chapter Six
or
O, Several *Explanations!*

Part one of the chapter

I would like to tell you the wardens of the Hospital were kind, but they were not. Kindness is not in the nature of those who care for orphans; how can a person feel compassion for children whom no one else wanted? What value has a thing everyone else has thrown away?

*

The wardens knew what we were fit and destined for; after all, they told us all the time. A question asked of us quite directly and often was: *What use to the world is someone like you?* When you are six, seven, eight, you don't have enough skin on you to wonder if that is a fair question to ask a child, so you ask it of yourself. *What use to the world is someone like me?* 'No use,' the wardens would hiss. 'You're of no use to the world, a piece of shit like you, John Church!' When you are six, seven, eight . . .

*

Most nights I dreamed of the woman in Tunbridge Wells, briefly my mother who had come to claim me and then rejected me, taking me back to the Foundling Hospital. I dreamed I would wake, in that luxurious knowledge of being loved, to the sounds of the country where I had spent that summer: bird-song, church bells, a tinkling stream perhaps.

In the dream, the Tunbridge Wells woman acknowledged that she was in fact my native mother, who had come back, not out of regret but out of never-doubted love. In the dream, we were no longer in the country but in a crowd, in London, in all the din and busyness of town. I was two or three, crushed, pushing through bodies, getting lost, my hand slipping out of hers. I can almost feel how it would feel in a child's hand, that moment after contact is lost, skin departing skin. For ever.

The image in the dream was her face white and sweaty with panic, as she ran madly to find me, shouting *John! John! John!* Now she was not the woman in Tunbridge Wells but my true, native mother, another person whose face I cannot recall. But, of course, my name was not John then; it was something else. I was a different child, the one who was thrown away.

*

For a very long time, I would dream of these women – my interchangeable lost mothers – just before waking, so that my first thoughts of the day were of love: the birdsong, the bells. I would hear the wardens' hobnailed boots clicking on the same cold stone floor. In time, I stopped dreaming of very much at all. A child like me learns it's better not to have dreams. Love is not for every child, I told you once. Or better yet: love is something you have to create. It does not come to you of its own accord and it abandons you at its pleasure, and there is no crueller feeling than that. So you have to find love. More than anything else, you have to pursue it, trap it, keep it with you, in hopes it does not leave you again. But you fear it will.

*

The wardens at the Foundling Hospital said that I was just bad to the bone. It only made sense that this was true, because I had been thrown away, by not one but *two* mothers, they said. Two different mothers had rejected me, so what was I worth? I blinked as they said these things and dug my nails into my hands, to make sure I did not cry. I wouldn't give them the pleasure. Then, before I was old enough to leave the Hospital on my own account, aged eleven or so, they sold me to that gilder on the Blackfriars Road, about whom I hinted to you before, and my adult life could begin.

*

That life was hard. The gilder told me that I was to expect no love, no softness, and O, I did not receive either! From the day I arrived, I was set to work, learning a little of the trade of gilding, but also blacking boots, cleaning grates and scrubbing sheets. The man – married with children who lived in splendid indolence at the house, whilst I toiled like a dog – allowed me to learn some letters, to help him with his work. But later, when he found out how well I taught myself to read, and how many of the books in his study-room I had secreted away to teach myself more, he yelled at me that I was a clever whore. He punched me so hard in the mouth that my lip split over my teeth. But I was so happy, with blood running down my face: *someone had called me clever!*

*

In the daytime, the gilder liked to curse and beat me and call me a 'stupid, filthy, ridiculous Mary-Ann', and at night, he liked to rape me.

*

This is the secret of all Sodomites, of course. They know the dark predations of Normal men on their bodies, which they keep like a sacred code from those men's wives and friends. Sodomites know too that Normal men will punish them for revealing these desires. They know the desires of the everyday man are as black as tar, and that they eat our hearts and bodies whole. They come to our beds and call us confessors and saviours, ask us never to tell their secrets, and we keep them, and then, with their friends, they drag us to the market square, to burn us as perverts. We die keeping their secrets, just like their wives do. All Sodomites learn to keep secrets. It's how we stay alive.

*

When I was fifteen years old, the gilder's wife found her husband and me in bed together, and he pretended – with his cock hard and waving about – that he had gone to use the po' and found me plotting to seduce one of their daughters, and that he was repri-manding me. I remember the look of bilious confusion on the wife's face as he started to punch and beat me, and said he would lock me in the coal cellar, with his cock still hard and pointing upwards. 'All right,' I heard her say, that bewitching neutral con-tract, as she twisted what she saw into what she could live with. She rushed to find a stick, and she beat me with it, as her husband kicked me whilst pulling up his long johns over his erection.

*

How many days did they lock me in their coal cellar? How they burned me with the things that they yelled through the door, the insults: molly, madge, sinner, foul invert, rapist, whore-son. How those words harmed even more than the hunger when they did not feed me. Days and nights passed. I was alone – afraid – in that darkness. The only sounds were those of the world above, continuing with me imprisoned (for how long I did not know, but I started to fear for ever, until I was dead), and those of the scuttling rats in the black. If ever I screamed or wept, the man upstairs yelled: 'Shut up, rapist! Seducer!' Once I heard their younger daughter asking, 'Papa, what do them words mean?'

★

Several days in, the mood of their incarceration of me had changed somehow, into something more desperate. By then I had stopped talking to the gilder and his wife, stopped begging them to release me, not knowing if doing so made them crueller or more frightened. They supplied me bread, and nothing else; there was a butt that collected the rainwater that leaked in from outside. One evening, I could hear the gilder and his wife whispering beyond the cellar door. 'He's been awful quiet today,' I heard the wife say, all nerves, 'you don't think he has some fever?' 'The pox from all his whoring!' the gilder snapped. 'What if he dies?' the wife asked. The gilder did not answer at first. 'There's no harm in that, maybe.' 'But we will have a corpse on our hands, husband.' 'We'd have to get rid of the body but there'd be no problem in that, just wrap it up and take it down to the river.' I heard the sound of hands clapping. 'Just throw it in. Throw it away, like rubbish.'

The wife's silence was awful. 'Maybe we should just starve him, husband, and wait till he slips into a torpor. And once he is no longer alert, we could do it, under cover of night.' Her words rang through me, so chilling: another mother – *she was not my fucking mother* – not caring if I lived or died.

The moment was like a revelation to me, and a pointer towards my future. For in that moment, I understood what I must do. I must show them my rage, to show them my power. I, who had all my childhood been so powerless in the abuse I had suffered, suddenly understood what was required of me to survive. Was that the *very first time* I went berserk, was that the first time I entirely let my impulsive, my impetuous, my fearless side overwhelm me? Then let me honour it. Lunatic, I flung my whole body at the cellar door, so that it banged as loud as a thunderclap right over our heads. Wildly, I started to kick the wood, with my bare knuckles punching the door, scraping the skin right off until my blood was flying like spittle, and I was screaming: 'Open up, you cunts! Let me go! I am going to kill you all! I am going to skin your little bitches of daughters alive and feed you their flesh! I will plunge my fingers into their eye sockets and rip out their sight, force their eyeballs down your fucking gullets! I will get a bread knife and fuck your throats and holes with it until you beg me to end it and slit your bellies open so you can bleed to death! *Let me go, you cunts!* You have five seconds to decide! In ten seconds, if you do not let me go, the carnage of you and your children's death begins!'

How sweet and nourishing were my words! A great peace came across my mind as I said them, understanding for the first time the power of my rage, to tell the truth to liars, to do whatever I must to protect myself, to keep myself safe from harm, to think only of myself for the first time, think what I wanted and needed to survive. Five seconds passed. One, two, three, four, five. I took a breath on every count. And then I heard it: the sound of them unlocking the door. 'Don't harm us,' the gilder, my rapist, begged with his hands up, in white-flag surrender. 'Show mercy to my girls, they are only children,' he pleaded.

I stared at him as if he were the madman. Hadn't I been just a child too? Why is one child more deserving of mercy than another? I think now of Ned and his stolen childhood.

*

I was free but I was in danger. I had no family. I had not finished my apprenticeship. I had no reference with which to find a job, an absolute disaster. No one will take you on without a reference from your father, your apprenticeship master, a gentleman who employed you. I told you I was born to be Nothing. But back then, I had no idea that I could become Something. At the end of my childhood, I found that I was Nothing again.

I confess what happened next: I turned to renting on the London streets. I was a handsome lad, with something between my legs that men wanted to buy. Money for fucking, is there nothing finer? You want to fuck a man in a world like ours, and they will pay you for the pleasure? Any boy's dream. Sometimes someone punches you, or does not pay you, or worse, hires you to go to a room and tells you to make love to them, and when you are inside them promises to take you away from this life, and give you a life of luxury, but then when the sex is over, throws you a couple of shillings and spits at you to *fuck off* and that sense of abandonment returns, and nothing can assuage or heal that, it feels, in the moment at least.

★

One day, something went wrong with a trick down a back alley off Austin Friars. I went with a man whose eye I had caught on Threadneedle Street, but when I got down the alley, he had a friend waiting with a knife. Even now I am not sure what the two wanted: to rob me or to murder a Sodomite, just for the pleasure of it. I remember punches and shouting, and the feel of my hand smashing into a man's face. And then I was running, running and running, until I was on Old Broad Street.

I clattered down into the cellar of a Nonconformist chapel, where I entered a small door which I slammed shut and bolted. As I turned, a man, dressed soberly in black, was staring at me. I realised that this was his chapel. 'You are bleeding, boy,' he said, and for some mad reason I cannot fathom now, I told him everything about the last years of my life and how I had ended up on the street. Like all priests, he licked his lips and tried to make me feel bad.

'Do you not fear for your soul?' he asked. I am cheeky. I

am naughty. But in that moment, I felt frozen before his stare. 'What is your name, young man?'

'Church,' I said. 'John Church.' And at this, the preacher burst out laughing, as if who I was were the funniest thing of all. I made some fast speech about the world, and how it was, and how I was going to be Something one day, even if I was Nothing now. Again, first moments, first times things were said and done as I became the man I am today.

'You should be a preacher, boy,' he said. 'You would talk round any congregation.' He patted my cheek and was looking at me so kindly. 'Now, if I give you a shilling, will you fuck me hard in my arse?'

And so the poison and hypocrisy of Normal men reveals itself, always, in the end. But I flashed him my handsomest smile. 'If I do, sir, can you write me an employer's reference?'

The priest laughed and laughed. 'If you fuck me good, boy, you can come and work for me here.' I stayed two months, and got myself a reference, and from there, I began to prosper. Weeds can grow in the cracks of city pavements, but that don't mean their blooms ain't beautiful!

*

Believe this of me: I do not lie. Sometimes I keep things secret. But I do not deceive. I just withhold the information that will harm me. This is what my childhood taught me, and it has carried me a long way, my secretive nature.

And yes, I know I haven't even mentioned my wife yet!

Part two of the chapter

I met Mrs Church at the Swedenborgian New Church on East-cheap. It was only a few years after I left the gilder, and now and then, I still rented if I needed to, but I had kept preaching. Sometimes I went to these churches to promote my beliefs, which I had honed and honed since those Orange Street days with William.

Mrs Church, whose maiden name was Miss Elliott, was older, educated and already set up alone in rooms off High Holborn, yet sought no work as a lady's companion or governess. She did not need money. Her father was a rich man in Hampshire. She lived on her own income. She was not a happy person.

We first spoke at a bible class, where I had made some grand speech on how men had to embody the teaching of the Lord in their daily lives in order to achieve salvation. I remember as I was talking, folk were listening and nodding primly, for I was already a good speaker. As I was starting to talk about love and tolerance – which the Swedenborgians, like most Christians, supported *in theory* – I saw a young woman in the class was watching me admiringly. I am a handsome man. I have told you that before. So I know what it means when people look at you in a certain way; and I am a Sodomite who used to rent – I am the master of the Meaningful Stare. But rarely do polite Englishwomen look at one with such *intent*.

At the end of the meeting, the young woman approached me. Her manner was unguarded and attractively direct, as she extended her hand to be kissed by a gentleman. (Her words, not mine.) 'I'm Miss Elliott,' she said. 'I've been meaning to speak with such a remarkable gentleman, sir.' I thanked her. We did not break our gazes. 'I think your ideas very exciting, sir. I think I should like to hear more of them. Much more.'

We were friends before we were lovers, and we were lovers before we were married. Our first confessions came when we said that we did not like the Swedenborgians and we wanted to leave. I told her I wanted to start my own chapel. I told her I needed to find the money. 'I have money,' she replied. We both confessed that we were sinners. She told me her father had sent her away because she was chaotic, and she drank too much, and could not fit in being a good Hampshire girl, but now she wanted to change. I admitted to her my nature, that I had laid with many men, but that now I wanted to be saved. She reacted with not a hint of shock or disgust, but by placing her hand on mine. 'Can't two sinners each try to heal each other of their sin?' For a while, we tried really fucking hard to heal each other's sins.

A few weeks later, we were married at the Swedenborgian New Church. It was the very last time either of us ever went there. For a long time, I was faithful to her, and did not go with men. I so wanted to believe that I was saveable; what sinner does not? I wanted the decency of Christian marriage to be enough; I wanted nothing more than for the world to be right, for it to save me from myself. But it did not. It was not enough. Feeling shame does not cure sin. What cures sin is to feel shame no more.

Eventually, I went back to the night and my wife clung recklessly to hopes we should not have indulged in the first place, and so, in time, gave herself up to her old vice, drinking – and cruelty, both to me and to herself.

The Sunday after he fled . . .

Morning service, the day after Ned had fled me on my admission of the truth. I waited at the pulpit, watching the congregation file in. Many regulars were there, but no Ned. Mrs Caesar was there, with Frederick and Emmanuel, but no Lydia either. Perhaps she had made her excuses to her mother; perhaps, given what Ned had said, she had told her mother she could not stand it any more; perhaps she preferred not to come, just as Ned had not, and went to some African chapel instead. I made my sermon. Now and then, people bustled in late, causing brief commotion. Each time, I looked up from my lectern: *Is it him? Is it him?* But it was not him. It was never him.

After I was finished at the Obelisk, as I walked across St George's Fields in the direction of the river, a fine drizzle began. Despite the rain, I did not rush. My coat spotted darker without ever quite becoming wet. I was thinking of Ned, and the fact he had not come. I had expected him to turn up with his breezy, strange smile, the flash of his eyes, and say something about how it didn't matter, not truly; or perhaps that he had thought about it and he still wanted to kiss me; or that he could not stay away; silly things, just drifting through my head. I corrected myself. I had no business to imagine such things. There was nothing between us; absolutely nothing, save that 'understanding' we had both described; and what was that worth truly? Why, nothing . . .

I knew my wife would be in our rooms; she hardly ever went out now. Her nature had changed so much in our recent years together, and I felt much compassion for that. But still it was hard. She never came to chapel but preferred to sit in our rooms and read books, novels by lady writers from other parts of the country. She was a learned woman, and consumed these books voraciously, saying that, through them, she lived lives she did not live herself. My wife liked to drink steadily through the day, and that affected her mood one way or the other. Occasionally, I persuaded her to go on walks and such, but those were rarities now. We were one of those couples who lived unhappily and who clung to what it meant to be a couple all at the same time. Or at least, she did; as I say, reckless hopes.

It was more than a year since my wife and I had taken the rooms above a cake shop on The Cut – the New Cut, to give it its proper name. This is the most eastern fringe of Southwark. There is not much city after The Cut, though of course, there are plans to build houses now on the open marshes at Lambeth and Vauxhall. But The Cut is not some pleasant bucolic suburb. The streets crawl with children too poor for school, muddy-footed and soot-faced, who rob and taunt with the brutish efficiency of rats. That is not to say they *are* rats; it is to say that they have been turned into them, in a country that likes to set rat traps for them: workhouses, Australia, the scaffold. Only lately there was a scandal when two Southwark kids, aged eight and ten, were hanged for stealing bread. Many people said that it was an illiberal outrage, in ours, the most liberal country in the world, and then others asked: *O, why do you hate England?*

Our landlords, Mr and Mrs Gee, owned the cake shop downstairs; the whole building, in fact. The poor folk of The Cut would come in to the cake shop, with money for some fine Dutch-cake or Welsh tea-bread for a high-tea Sunday, or just for a fresh egg waffle or gingerbread, if all they had was a farthing. The Gees served them all with patient smiles, whilst checking that no one's infant was stuffing egg custards into their pockets as their mother engaged them on the subject of the weather or the river flooding.

As I entered the shop – the bell above the door tinkling – the Gees were standing behind a counter festooned with cakes and pies. Mr and Mrs Gee looked identical, save for their clothing: short, round, white-haired, pink-cheeked, two smiling dumplings. (But smiles can hide sharp teeth, of course.)

'Good day, Reverend Church.' / 'Good day, Reverend Church,' they cooed in unison.

'Good day,' I replied.

'Busy, Reverend Church, at the chapel?' Mrs Gee asked.

'Yes,' I replied. 'You should come.'

'O, we will,' they said, in the same eerie unison. We all knew that they would not. People always feel they have to lie to priests.

'May I have a custard pudding to take up to my wife?'

'O, of course,' Mr Gee said. It was his wife who went to get the cake and handed it to me. 'Such a thoughtful husband you are, Reverend,' she sighed admiringly. I offered to pay, but she shook her head, to refuse a man of God's money.

'How *is* Mrs Church lately?' she asked 'kindly'. 'I haven't seen her for I don't know how many days.' Sometimes when my wife drank, she shouted, and I had to try to placate her. So Mrs Gee asked this question often, and always with a certain barely concealed but polite malice on her face, in which I was the victim and my wife the aggressor. But what can one ever say, except some bland reply? We three stood there for a moment of awkward silence, and when none of us could stand it any more, I relented and said good day.

'O, good day, Reverend Church!' / 'Good day, Reverend Church!'

Climbing one flight of the stairs at the back of the shop, I pushed the door to our two interconnecting rooms and walked inside. The door had been left open, which only meant my wife had forgotten to lock it after I went out. Sometimes she was greatly afraid for her safety, and sometimes she did not care a jot. Again, drink determined which. In the first room was the chaise on which I usually slept, and then, through a set of doors sometimes kept open, was the other a bed, on which my wife slept. I saw her there, dozing with a book on her lap. My wife's hair was loose and billowing flat over the pillows. I laid the custard pudding down. A bottle of port was left uncorked on a side table. I picked it up and held it to the window to let the light fall through the dark glass. The bottle was almost full; my wife was just sleeping, she was not drunk. That was good.

Walking back into the other room, I kicked off my shoes and stood in my stockinged feet, reading some notes I had scribbled down to myself for chapel business. My mind wandered, though; it would not hold on to anything. I started just to gaze out through the window, into the pale yellow air.

'You brought me a custard pudding?' came her voice. It made me start. I had thought she was asleep. Turning to look in her direction, I saw her sitting up in bed, gazing at me, not quite smiling.

'Yes,' I said.

'You were very deep in thought,' she said airily, but with an edge of suspicion.

'Just something at the chapel.' I almost said *someone* but pivoted at the last moment. She nodded uninterestedly.

'Was it a busy day at your chapel?'

Your chapel, she said. 'Yes, it is busy every week now. I keep telling you that if you came and saw it for yourself, you would know.' I saw annoyance flash across her eyes; I saw that for some reason she wanted to prick me. In the past, I'll confess it, we had lived off my wife's money, which she received from her father. But now we lived off mine. My wife did not always like that fact. She did not always like the success of the Obelisk, for it gave me financial independence.

'You would like that, husband, if I came and played the good parson's wife.'

This irritated me. 'Why wouldn't I like that? I would think you would like it.'

My wife found satisfaction in me sounding annoyed because then she could become the epitome of sweetness. 'What's wrong, husband?' she asked. My wife knew me very well, better than anyone. She knew what would rile me, knew what would provoke me. That was her cruelty towards me, as I must have had mine towards her, in that I did not love her and tragically she knew it. We bore the resentment of two bodies lashed together for ever. I gulped down my incipient anger.

'Nothing is wrong. What do you mean?'

'I have been married to you a long time. I know well when you are not coping—'

'*Coping?*' I snapped, and even as I did, still I knew what she was doing – 'coping' was a very carefully chosen word – she knew how to attack me. I felt like I was starting to lose control. 'I have just got in and already you begin at me!'

'Husband!' she cried, putting her hands in her loose hair. 'I am just trying to help—'

But she was not trying to do that, still lying on that bed. 'Help? How is this help?'

'By showing care for your well-being, husband.'

'Why are you provoking me?' I yelled. 'Why are you calling me "husband"? You know I hate it!'

'Does it ever occur to you that I call you "husband" because you are my husband, and I love you, despite everything? I love you, and you are my husband, and all I wish is for you to love me but you treat me appallingly—'

Suddenly I was all emotion and outrage, and she fake sweetness. My nature is impulsive and hot, and driven to extremes, but please, note the use of that verb: always, I am *driven* to react; and I react because someone else has *acted*. And so I do stupid things: I reached and grabbed the custard pudding and flung it through the air, not at her, away from her. But she let out a great shriek which might have sounded like '*WHY?*' if heard downstairs in the shop. I could imagine the Gees looking up at the ceiling and then at each other, tutting. The pudding slammed into the wall, then slid down it, the pearly primrose centre peeling open, falling with a sad slap to the floorboards.

Now my wife switched. She leapt out of bed, throwing the blankets across the room. 'Why do you have to do this, John? Why do you have to be like this? Why can't you be normal? I am so sick of your rages, and your fury, when I have done nothing at all!'

'I feel like you are drowning me!'

How ridiculous, you'll be thinking: why would a hero show

such a pathetic side to himself in the conduct of a narrative? But do you not think that those who are subject to rage don't know how ridiculous they are? It is the deepest source of their shame. My wife, I will tell you now, lest you let your finer feelings fly, is not a major character in this story. I do not propose to make her so. Do not expend your sorrows here; there is plenty enough sorrow ahead. My wife's and my tragedy is precisely that we are incidental characters in each other's lives, chained together by shame, and law, and fear. But if I were to ask for one ounce of compassion, it would be in what I said next to her, for in it was the true possibility of freedom both for myself and for Mrs Church:

'I don't understand you,' I said. 'I don't understand why you stay here! You could go back to Hampshire, meet a real man, some lusty country lad, tell everyone I was dead. No one would look for me! No one would care! Your family would be thrilled. You have your own money. Go, go back home, say you are widow, and find happiness!'

My wife's eyes went very wide, for what I said was terrible and true. Pretend I was dead. No one would look for me. Go back to the country, or some other city, start again, have all the things she wanted from her life. If she was a prisoner, her gaoler was not me. It was she herself.

Suddenly there was loud knocking at our door. Immediately – instinctively – the two of us froze. Two animals, startled in the moment the fox steps on a twig in the half-light. Through the door a voice, half brisk, half nervous: 'Reverend Church?' It was Mr Gee. He had come to complain before about the shouting. Steeling myself, feeling the flush of shame, I walked towards the door and opened it. 'Reverend Church . . . my wife and I don't wish to interfere but the shouting is awful loud.'

'I know. I am sorry, Mr Gee—'

'And the shouting has become most regular.'

'I do apologise, Mr Gee, and to Mrs Gee too.'

The man's earlier sweetness was replaced now by sharp judgement: 'Apologies are all well and good, Reverend Church, but if this does not cease, I shall have to ask you to leave this house.'

'Leave?' I cried, in great surprise. (I pretend that this was a great surprise, but my wife and I had strolled along this walk many times before, in other houses.)

'Yes, Reverend, and I am sure that it would not sit well with you to be wandering the streets of the city with nowhere to live, and your wife here' – his eyes flicked towards her, unseen beyond the door but now audibly weeping – 'a nice lady like her and a minister of the Lord, homeless on the Southwark streets.'

The landlord was glaring at me. I could feel him clocking up injustices against me and my wife.

The Sunday evening . . .

That night at Vere Street was busy. There were easily thirty-five, forty people, so that the main rooms quickly seemed full and the air hot and damp. I saw again how clever Mrs Cook had been in putting the house on the second floor of the tavern. The floor in between killed the noise from the molly house; the ordinary drinkers provided a counter-noise that hid ours from the world, windows shuttered and draped. A febrile mood enveloped us: of drinking, of the possibilities and actualities of sex. All the main girls were there – Sal, Black-Eyed Leonora, Sweet Lips, the Duchess – and plenty of new people. Young Tommy White and his older lover, Hepburn, arrived. Almost as soon as they came in, they asked if I would sit with them.

Even now that I knew them a little, how strange a pair they seemed: young and old, beautiful and drab. Yet Tommy White hardly let his gaze wander from Hepburn's face; the younger man's eyes glowed with love. Hepburn suggested I join him in drinking some Rhenish wine as his guest; an unexpected luxury. Kett brought a bottle and set it down. Hepburn said he would pour. My glass was first, but then as he poured a second for White, he looked up and gave his lover such a small smile, and White almost blushed with breathless pleasure; it was a beautiful sight to behold. They illuminated each other. 'Do you want to ask him, Johnny, or should I?' White said.

Hepburn smiled back. 'I shall ask him, Tommy, don't you worry.' I could see their nerves; I was beginning to wonder what they were about to propose. Hepburn began to speak: 'Reverend Church, sir, I told you that I am an ensign in a regiment, and I have to go back to my station on the South Coast presently for a period of duty.' He paused and then let out a long breath. 'Reverend Church, Tommy and me, we are very much in love, just like you said the other night, that we can be in love as much as any man and woman. Well, we were thinking about what you said, sir—'

He faltered, as if he could not quite believe what he was asking. Tommy, seeing his love flounder, laid a hand on his. 'I don't want no other men, Reverend Church. I only want Johnny.' He looked intently at Hepburn. 'When he is gone, if we was married and the men around here know I am married, then they won't come after me, will they? And I want to be married to my John, so he knows when he is away, that I am thinking only of him, I am keeping myself for him, if you see. And I want the world to know that I am his, and his only.'

Hepburn's eyes were pink with emotion. 'Reverend, I want to be married to Tommy, and he wants to be married to me. So . . . will you marry us, Reverend? A proper marriage, a service, the eyes of God, all of it.'

I felt my entire body swim with warmth and wonder. I leaned

forwards to pat both men on their arms. 'Of course . . .' I said. 'It would be an honour. An absolute honour.' They both broke into happy grins and stole glances at each other. 'But when do you want to marry?' I asked.

Hepburn looked at me as if here was the trick. 'Tonight, Reverend? 'Cos I go away next week.'

The mood at the house immediately turned joyous when the imminent wedding of John Hepburn and Tommy White was announced. Some of the queens, who considered him one of their sisters, stole Tommy away to get him ready in the dressing room, breathless with excitement. Meanwhile, the Duchess of Gloucester lumbered over to me. She was dressed in a long brown gown and white wig, and looked for all the world like a governess to a down-at-heel family in Berkshire. 'Reverend Church,' she began, indicating to a man at her side. 'This is my friend, Mr Sellis.'

As the 'mister' suggested, Sellis was dressed as a man. He had a foreign air to him, and was handsome and elegant. As soon as he greeted me, I could hear both his Italian accent and his sophistication. 'It is your first time here, Mr Sellis?' His eyes were on me quite intently – attractive, dark, liquid eyes.

'The . . . Duchess' – he said her name as if it were someone else's – 'has told me of it, yes.' I knew better than to ask how they knew each other; they would not want me to know. 'This is a wonderful thing you do tonight, Father,' he began to say. He called me 'Father' in the Romanist manner. Now he looked at me as if he were about to make a confession. 'I am in love myself. It would be my dream to have this.'

'Then why not come one night,' I said, 'and marry your love?'

There seemed such a tremendous sadness in him when I said that. 'I don't think . . . I don't think that would be possible for him and me.' Those handsome eyes ran fluidly over mine. 'Have you ever been in love, Father?' I did not answer; he did not seem to require me to. 'Nothing in life is the equal of love. No riches, no fame, no family, nothing. To have lived without love is to have lived without . . .'

'Without what?'

'Without sunlight.'

I took in a breath, remembering those days I had spent locked in that cellar, years before. The man spoke with such intensity that it simultaneously scared and ensnared me. Here it was: my instruction to love, not to just talk about it, but to do it, as I had once with William Webster, and I felt afraid. 'What does that mean if we have loved, or we could have loved, but love left us?' I was not speaking of Ned – *don't think that* – I am not even sure I was thinking of William Webster.

'It means we must do everything in our power to get it back, Father.'

'And what if it will not come back?'

'We must be radical in our commitment to getting it back,' he replied. 'We must be radical in our pursuit of it, have absolute faith in what we are doing, and then it will come back. Love will always come back, if we commit to getting it back.'

A radical love; I could hardly take my eyes off him. He was a handsome man, yes, but that was not it. It was rather as if this person – this perfect stranger – had seen some secret part of me, that I hid from everyone else. It was like he was saying: *I know who you are, John Church. I see straight through you!*

'O, here comes Mrs Hepburn!' I heard Sally cry. Turning, there was Tommy White with his sisters around him, dressed as a man but with his hair decorated with Christmas roses and mistletoe, his face lightly dusted with white powder and his lips softly pink with rouge. Black-Eyed Leonora led Tommy by the hand into the centre of the room, all eyes on him, the bride, and Hepburn positively puffed out with pride.

So, for the first time ever, not just at the White Swan but

ever in London, we all trooped into the Wedding Chapel, not as a joke, but for a real marriage between two men. When first I had seen this room, I had found it almost comical with its cheap paintings of pans piping and erotic male gods, some ironic joke. Now, in soft candlelight, and Tommy half-Apollo, half-Aphrodite, and Hepburn illuminated with love, it was transformed into somewhere else – somewhere of meaning.

I called the couple forwards. White and Hepburn were gazing at each other shyly, surrounded by their – my – friends. 'Dearly beloved . . .' I began, as I had so many times before.

At once Mrs Cook sobbed: 'O, Lord Jesus, I am going to cry!'

Folk fell into sweet laughter, including White and Hepburn. Sally handed Mrs Cook a dishcloth, and she dabbed at her eyes. 'Dearly beloved, we are gathered together here in the sight of God, and in the face of this congregation, to join together this man and this woman—'

'We all know which one of them's the woman,' I heard Sweet Lips say. I paused; I realised I had not thought of the words I was going to use. These words were not written for us; in fact, they were written in the express exclusion of us. I thought, to my amazement, of Lydia Caesar and her refusal to accept the rules and narratives of White folk. I saw then that, in this respect, she was correct. We must write our own words. We must not allow our own words, and our own selves, to be overwritten.

'My brothers and sisters,' I said, departing from the text. 'I will say the next part differently. I will say it differently because some things refer to us, and we should own what refers to us, and ignore what does not, for the hatred of others is theirs to own and not ours to accept. Now . . . it was ordained for the mutual society, help, and comfort, that the one ought to have of the other, both in prosperity and adversity.' I smiled at White and Hepburn and nervously they did the same to me. 'Into which holy estate these two persons present come now to be joined. Therefore if any man – if any*one* – can show any just cause, why they may not lawfully be joined together, let him – them – now speak, or else hereafter for ever hold their peace.'

We all knew the legal reason why they could not marry. We were bending the law – the law of the land, the law of God, most people would argue – to our own image. But again, we had to be brave; we had to write our own words. When I said that they could kiss, the room burst into applause. Mrs Cook gave up trying not to cry, and wept like a child, dabbing at her eyes with the dishcloth. Sally put her good arm around her, telling her not to be such a silly goose. Black-Eyed Leonora, usually so still and knowing, was laughing as happily as a drunkard. 'Tonight it is a wonderful world!' she kept saying loudly. 'Reverend Church has given us a wonderful world! Thank you, Reverend Church! Everyone, say thank you to Reverend Church! Today he has given us this wonderful world!'

People were applauding, and calling for three cheers for me, and I should have been swimming with their acclaim. But instead, I looked over at Mr Sellis, with his terrible, handsome eyes, and he was staring at me, unsmiling. Love must be radical, he had said, for what else was its purpose? I did not know the answer to that, but I did know that I should try to find it out. And my mind, and my body, hummed with Ned's running away from me. I knew then – I knew – what I wanted him to be, and I had let him slip away, because of – not my lies – my secrets.

PART TWO

The Following Spring,
The Year Being
Eighteen Hundred And Ten

Chapter Seven

or

A Twist!

That spring of 1810, so quite some time later . . .

It had been a curious winter in London, a season of long fogs
drifting in from the North Sea, binding the city for weeks at a
time. The fog crept like fingers walking along the street – visible,
eerie, invasive. People walked around white, spectral streets,
hands stretched in front of their bodies lest they bump into
strangers; in the kingdom of the blind. Forms appeared from the
milky mist, and looked at you in surprise, as you appeared just
as magically before them, then vanished again. The derelicts
who died on the open street were left to rot unburied, because
you could not see well enough which body was dead and which
was alive, in that strange, white weather.

*

The war ground into a quiet phase, not because of English suc-
cesses but because of a new, settled French imperium. Napoleon
came to peace with the Austrians, discarded the beautiful but
vulgar wife he famously loved, marrying a glum Habsburg
princess instead. The foggy air in London crackled with anxiety, as if hit with lightning. How long before the French finally
attacked our shores if they had no one else to fight now? How
long before a French emperor replaced our German king?
How terrible that would be!

I thought of what Ned had once said to me, about how ordinary people do not think of their own interest. Why should ordinary folk worry about such things; why do the gilded games of princes matter? But as some invisible vice tightened, people turned not to revolution but to mean, popular hostility, one to another. Enshrouded by fog, London talked endlessly of what would happen if the French finally invaded English shores. How long would England last; how long? We were taught it would last for ever! There was more and more violence on the streets; more mollies arrested; more foreigners attacked; but also more price rises; more people without a home; more children begging for food.

*

I did not see Ned once in all the time after he fled that night. London is small, a million souls poured into a few square miles. I wondered if I might bump into him, as I had Sally years before, two weeks after we fucked, but I did not. I thought about him a great deal, though. His going had not made him recede from my mind; far from it, in fact. I imagined things I would say to him if I saw him, sometimes light – *O, how nice to see you, you look very well, Ned* – sometimes true – *I want us to try again, to start again, Ned, more honestly this time* – sometimes vituperative.

I dared not ask Mrs Caesar about him. The Sodomite knows better than to risk that. Why should I ask about he who was nothing to me? But I wanted to ask her. I *longed* to ask her. In those first weeks, his leaving was a sad and silly regret, but then, long after the Hepburn and White wedding, I thought often of what Mr Sellis had said about love, about not letting it go. I was not in love with Ned, but over time, more and more intensely, I felt some loss creep into more: *What possibility have I lost, what chance have I allowed to slip away? Was this my chance, and did I let it go?* And whenever I thought of that, I saw Mr Sellis's dark, liquid eyes staring at me, in the molly-house candlelight.

★

Over time, I came to think of Ned more and more. He became the first thing of which I thought in the morning, and when I went to bed at night, the last. Things I might have done differently; things I should have said; things he should have done differently; things he should have been prepared to do. O, I did not imagine we were terribly in love, and he abandoned me. No, none of that. What grief I felt was not for him, not for us, it was for myself, my own lack of love. After all, what has my whole life been but a lack of love, and my grief at the knowledge of that lack? Absence makes the heart grow fonder; and, sometimes, madder.

★

Forgive me when I tell you this secret. I spent a whole afternoon walking up and down Mint Street, where he had told me he lived. I never intended to knock on any doors; I did not come close to doing so. How could I? I did not even know in which house he lived. I just wanted to breathe in the air where he lived. Mint Street is dominated by the workhouse there, one of London's most notoriously brutal. From within its barred windows, you hear the grind of charity's factory machines. But that's all you hear: there are no sounds besides the machines grinding. I was just innocently thinking: this is the street, and perhaps one of these is the house, and perhaps he is inside, in a room in one of these houses, on a bed, where his body lies. Will I lie beside it one day? Of course not. It was over before it had even begun.

★

By the end of March or start of April, London had tipped fully from winter into spring. The upstairs rooms at the White Swan had become even busier. Now there were nights when people had to be turned away because the house could not hold fifty or sixty bodies, and Mrs Cook worried that even a spare floor might not kill the noise. There were still the weddings of men together twenty minutes, but increasingly, they were of men together twenty years. The nature of the house began to change as its fame began to spread, and more and more people came, often just to stare at the sight of two men being married. Some people laughed and some wept. Sally, Black-Eyed Leonora and Miss Sweet Lips remained huge characters, but Mrs Cook confided to me that she was worried by too much change, too many newcomers. 'I have to look out for my original ladies,' she said, 'because one day, these fly-by-night feckers might be gone.' Soon hundreds of people in London seemed to know that code: 'Who is it?'/'Your sister, come to attend your wedding.' But others did not. When they were refused entry, they would shout, 'Let me in! I am come to the molly house! *Let me in!*' Were their voices loud enough to be heard on the street?

*

One Sunday, I was at the chapel. By that stage of springtime, the city's trees were pricking green again, birds were busy in their branches. There was the very first substantial sunshine and folk began to cast off their winter coats and bonnets. That day, after the main sermon, there was to be a bible meditation. I watched my congregation troop out after I had spoken: the radicals; the bluestockings; the Africans; the ordinary Kennington types. Mrs Caesar was there, with a line of starched-collar young men, but again, no Lydia. I did not grieve her absence so I did not ask after it. I had given a newly written sermon on the subject of practising acceptance, not just theorising about it.

People nodded and looked like the message was most important to them.

The bible meditation was to be led by Mrs Caesar, who wanted to consider a passage from the New Testament. If I gave Mrs Caesar the chance to speak, it guaranteed her little group would stay with her, so numbers would be good. She read from Romans 14: ' "As for the one who is weak in faith, welcome him, but not to quarrel over opinions." ' Her delivery was soft and steady and serious. ' "One person believes he may eat anything, while the weak person eats only vegetables. Let not the one who eats despise the one who abstains, and let not the one who abstains pass judgment on the one who eats, for God has welcomed him." '

My eyes ran across the people who had remained for the meditation. They gazed at Mrs Caesar speaking, all attentive faces. Then I saw Mr Linehan, the man I had encountered near Vere Street, when they found the body of the murdered molly. His face was different: he watched Mrs Caesar as she spoke, with the closeness of a cat watching a dove. While she was still reading – the passage 'Who are you to pass judgment on the servant of another? It is before his own master that he stands or falls' – he began speaking over her: 'Avoid judgement!' His voice was so grand, so vain, so intrusive, that Mrs Caesar faltered and looked up. When she returned her eyes to the text, she had lost her place. I had never quite seen her like that before. 'The very basis of that is Matthew 7:1,' he continued, taking the opportunity to interrupt her. ' "Judge not, that ye be judged." '

In that moment, I was swimming with anger, for my dislike of this man, for what had happened that night at Bell Yard, and now for his arrogance towards my friend. His saying 'Judge not, that ye be judged' sickened me. I could not stop myself from speaking too:

'Mr Linehan, do you not remember when we met at Bell Yard and you told me that a person had been murdered and that they had *deserved* to die.' Others at the meeting gasped in surprise. 'Was that not the most furious judgement? Setting aside your views of that person, did you not judge then? Now you say: judge not lest ye be judged.'

A vein popped in Mr Linehan's head. 'Sinners are inevitably judged, Reverend!'

'By whom or by what, though?'

His cheeks were pink with outrage. ''Tis written in the Bible!' he cried.

'Lots of things are written in the Bible, Mr Linehan. That we should not eat pork – but we all eat pork. That you should not suffer a witch to live – but we do not even believe in witches any more. That once a month, we should not allow a girl inside her father's house because she is unclean.' I smiled at him; he seemed appalled. 'Does your daughter sleep in the outhouse when her time of the month comes?'

He looked apoplectic with confusion; people started to snigger. 'I don't even have a daughter!' He sat back and crossed his arms, and his face went ever-more pink. I realised I needed to say no more. Might I dare hope that next Sunday, he would not return to Vere Street? (Sadly, he did.)

Afterwards, as I was saying farewell to the group, Mrs Caesar caught my arm and leaned in to murmur to me. 'Reverend Church,' she said, 'we have not seen you at another of our meetings.'

I shrugged. 'Well, Miss Lydia does not come here any more. I did not think she would appreciate my presence.'

Mrs Caesar said nothing to that. 'We meet on all sorts of subjects, with many speakers.' I was smiling at her blankly as she continued speaking: 'And some of my group go Thursday evenings to the Philosophical Institution, Reverend. At the

Corporation Hall, off Fetter Lane. It is a very good place, Thursday nights.'

I knew of it a little. I had once or twice, long before, been to see radical preachers at the nearby Moravian Chapel. Mrs Caesar laid her hand on my arm, in revelation. 'And your friend goes all the time. Every Thursday, I think.'

It did not even occur to me what she was saying. 'My friend . . . ?' I asked so very lightly, not hearing the tide roaring towards me at such speed.

She was smiling quite openly. 'Why, Master Ned,' she said.

I do not remember a word of what she said after that.

⋆

If I talk of twists, it is not on you that they are performed, but on me! At once, the possibility of going to see him felt like that second chance for which I had been secretly hoping. We Protestants are supposed to believe in our own fatedness. God knows from the beginning of time who shall be saved and who shall be damned. There is nothing you can do to alter your eternal fate. All you can do in this life is demonstrate your goodness, the fate towards which you are always walking; part of the elect. Only then shall you know that you are chosen; only by your actions are you known to be righteous. I knew what I must do, to be righteous. I would go to the Corporation Hall and act as if it was all inevitable, the two of us being back together; that would be part of the elect destiny – us meeting again.

⋆

You know enough of me now to know that my thoughts often take me over: glorious, happy, intense, racing, maddening, frightening. Sometimes I am in awe of my thoughts and sometimes I want to flee them; bewitching, pursuing things. Now my thoughts ruled me. From Sunday to Thursday, *they ruled me*. Waking each morning – Monday, Tuesday, Wednesday, yes, on and on – I thought of seeing him again. I shivered with the excitement of it; I was surely being thrown a second chance. But I don't believe in second chances, do I? *I believe in fate!*

THURSDAY!

The evening I would see him again, I found myself dressing smartly, in a freshly laundered shirt. I walked from home, across the river, and north-west to the Corporation Hall. I arrived and went within, finding my way to the meeting room. People sat in rows, facing forwards in solitary silence or leaning forwards into half-circle groups, restive and discursive. The light in the room was low and darkly golden, with a few candelabra spitting waxy flames. My eyes scanned the crowd just as they had the first time at the Angel Tavern. He was sitting quietly, near the front. My breath stopped, my pulse quickened to see him there, real not the ghost.

I crept to a seat several rows behind him, the very last seat on the row. Positioning myself in such a way that I could keep looking at him from behind, through the pattern of heads in front of me, I watched him talking briefly to the person next to him. It was clear they did not know each other, and he smiled shyly and laughed a little at whatever was being said, but then fell into a silence marked by a certain awkward embarrassment.

Suddenly people were clapping, as some fellow began to shuffle onto the stage. The applause felt like crows bickering above my head. 'My good brothers and sisters,' the man on the stage began to say. I did not care. I was neither his brother nor his sister; I was not here for speeches. My eyes flickered back towards Ned, who sat in perfect repose, gazing up at the man speaking to us from above. 'I have come to speak to you about the gathering might of forces in the country regions of this land, where in lately times, people have left the land and gone to work in factories and mines and such. Now, some fellows will tell you that these places are awful modern and are things of economic wonder, but I have come to tell you that they ain't that, but instead are the very furnaces of hell, where men and women no different to you—'

I was not listening. O, you can judge me all you like, and my radical credentials, but in that moment, I did not care about the factories, about the north, about the people and their revolutionary commitments. Sorry, but I did not. I cared about him and me. *In that moment, the whole world could be on fire, and I would care only about him and me.* So, I was staring at Ned with that intensity that starts to make your eyes swell, your throat ache. I was staring into the back of his head. *Turn and look*, I was thinking as I had that day, to the woman from Tunbridge Wells who had returned me to the Foundling Hospital. She had not turned; and he did not turn now.

The man on the stage continued: 'The working man is not going to tolerate their dispossession. They will rise up, find new leaders, and turn England on its head. Now you may think this means a great revolutionary movement, but look at France, look at Bonaparte—' *Turn and look*, I was thinking. And then, as if my wishing were some old-time love potion, some magick spell, he did it. He turned, and looked, and it was straight at me.

His eyes widened; I saw their bright shock. I was a ghost from his past, returning to his present. His brow knitted slightly for a moment then; his lips popped open, a breathless surprise. I felt sick, and I felt elated. I did not know what else to do – had I truly not thought this far ahead, such was my emotion? – so, stupidly, weakly, I raised my hand. He was perfectly still, watching me. Quickly, abruptly, without acknowledgement, he turned his face back to the front of the room. He did not look back again during the whole rest of the speech. I could sense his tension across the space. Did he mean to reject me?

The man from the north eventually finished speaking; applause. The clapping sounded like rain on a metal rooftop, immediately heavy, out of nowhere. Another man said there would be a short break; movement; the creaking of chairs and warm voices of appreciation. Ned looked around at me again. Our eyes connected a moment longer. I tried a smile. Something flickered over his face: acceptance, warmth. Without warning, he got to his feet and was walking towards me, until he was standing at the end of my row, above me.

'John,' he said. A pause. 'I thought I should come and speak to you.'

'I'm glad that you did, Ned.' Another pause – this time, mine. 'You look well.'

He did not thank me. He took a short, cautious breath. 'What are you doing here, John?'

'I came to hear the talk,' I dissembled. 'Mrs Caesar told me about it.'

'Mrs Caesar told you about it?' He considered this for a moment then relaxed. 'How goes life at the Obelisk, John?'

'O, very well, thank you. It gets busier and busier. It prospers.' We were silent briefly. 'I am sorry I no longer see you there.'

His eyes fell to the floor. When he looked back at me, they were soft and luminous in the room's low candlelight. 'We should talk, John,' he said. I had not expected that. 'Are you free to leave now?'

'Yes,' I murmured. *Yes, yes, of course yes.*

We left the Hall, tumbling down to Farringdon Street. The London night was in full effect. Shops were busy still, and taverns of course even busier, drinkers spilling out onto the pavement, in your way. Now and then they bumped into you and snarled a threat, and all you had to say was 'Don't worry, have a good evening', so that things didn't turn nasty. The gin-shops wore their ugly souls fearlessly. We swerved to avoid a woman, scrawny and haggard with grog before thirty, nursing an emaciated, blue-grey baby at her empty breast, all the while singing loudly an ancient song, waving a pewter jug in the air:

'As Oyster Nan stood by her tub
To show her in-clination!
She gave her noble Puss a scrub
And sighed for want o' cop-ulation!'

A young preacher stood on an upturned vegetable crate and screamed at no one from the Book of Revelations. ' "The beast was taken, and with him the false prophet that wrought miracles before him, with which he deceived them that had received the mark of the beast. Them that worshipped his image." ' And just as the young man bellowed at no one, no one listened to him either; only Ned and me. ' "These both were cast alive into a lake of fire burning with brimstone," ' the preacher railed, spittle flying from his lips. Beneath him were two sinners, whom he did not look at once, as if to do so might remind him of our humanity, and his own. ' "The devil that deceived them was cast into the lake of fire and brimstone, where the beast and the false prophet are, and shall be tormented day and night for ever and ever." '

I looked at this boy, so young and sweet-looking. He was a virgin, no doubt, or if not a virgin, that was because someone – like the gilder on the Blackfriars Road – had stripped that from him. Now he was all shame: shame for his desires, for men or for women, for his own body, for those of others. I wanted only to remove that shame from him. I wanted to wash it from his skin, his mouth, his eyes, and to replace it with happiness, with joy; but of course, I could not. I turned and smiled at Ned, who was not smiling now. 'Shall we go?' he asked.

Presently we were walking up Ludgate Hill towards the Cathedral, past the spot where Sally Fox had made me follow her after Richard Oakden was hanged. A light breeze had picked up, cold, coming in from the east. Ned put the collar of his jacket up. He was telling me of his life in the last months. He had found another job and lost it.

'You were sacked again?' I asked.

I did not mean my words to sound critical – 'again' – but he looked at me quite hard. 'Yes. I told you: Africans get sacked all the time. Why do English people find that so difficult to accept?'

He called White folk English as if he were not, but he was, raised in Yorkshire. 'Why did they sack you?'

'Who knows, John, why English people do anything? They said I made a mistake in an accounting column, but folk make mistakes all the time, and they do not get sacked. White folk like to punish Africans, I suppose. It is in White folk's natures, a superiority they cannot even see.' I heard his annoyance; he did not say that he was annoyed, but I heard it all the same. He sighed and relented. 'They sacked me. They would not have sacked an English lad for the same thing.'

I thought of what I could say: 'Well, you can still come and do some work for me.'

He gave me a very firm look. 'John . . .'

'Think about it,' I said.

'I don't think it's a good idea, John . . .'

His words saddened me, but I pushed it no further; I thought I might try again. We started to talk about other things and were soon passing through old Paternoster Row and were in the little black alley at the back of the Cathedral, nothing but a fluttering cape of shadow, entirely unlit. Only the sparest light of the moon got near us, no torches, nothing from open windows.

We could hardly see each other's forms. He was talking, turning towards me, saying something; I can't remember what. We were looking at each other, and whatever he said fell away. Suddenly it was time not for talk but for truths.

'Why did you run away that night?' I asked.

The unexpected directness of my question made him look downwards, his eyes running across the dark ground. 'You know why.'

'Because you asked me if I lived alone and I told you I had a wife.' He looked up at me again, but did not answer. 'Men have wives, Ned. Men like us feel they have to marry. They get married to save something, or protect themselves, or in hopes they can change, but then it is too late.'

'Too late for what?'

'To make another choice.'

'The world is full of bad choices,' he said.

'And most of them taken out of fear, and regretted for ever, Ned. Men like us, we are told if we just get married, if we just act normal, we will become normal. But look at us, we do not. We still feel our desires.'

I was talking in the plural, and thus about him as well as myself; he dropped his eyes to the ground once more. 'Well, I think I understand you better now, John. Those of us who are vulnerable in the world are presented only with bad choices sometimes, for that is all the world offers us. I understand how that can be true, but . . .'

'*But*, Ned?'

Some nocturnal cloud above moved, and moonlight fell upon us. Looking back up at me, his eyes were round and glittering with the moment. He pulled his lips in, almost pursed them, that mannerism of his that I had noticed the first day I had met him. 'But still I do not want to harm someone's unknowing wife.'

'And how would you do that, Ned?' He glanced away. I put my fingertips, gentle, to his jaw, to turn his face back to look at me. 'What do you think we would do that would harm my wife?' He was breathing very heavily, his chest vibrating with nerves. He knew I was talking of sex. 'You said you liked me, Ned. You said you liked me the night you ran away. Is that why you won't come and work for me now, Ned, because you are afraid of what might happen if you did?'

'Stop it, John . . .' My fingers were still on his face; the tips moved on his skin; he reacted to the sensation. I cupped my hand slightly; feline, he moved his jaw against my palm, but then he pulled his head away from my touch. 'Stop it, John,' he said more firmly. 'You are overwhelming me.'

I let my hand fall to my side. 'Overwhelming you, Ned?' He blinked. 'Or is what you truly want the thing that is overwhelming you?'

'John . . .'

'Do you think I don't understand the desire, and the fear of the desire?'

'John . . .'

I stepped forwards, and there, in such a dark spot in the heart of the city, I kissed him. As our lips touched, I felt his body tense with surprise. But then I heard his breath catch, desirous of my touch, this kiss. I moved further against him and he began to kiss me back. Our mouths opened wider.

It was more than I could have imagined. In the time since he had fled me, in the Temple gardens, since Mr Sellis, all of it, I had been dreaming of a moment like this, and now it was here, and it was as if some insurmountable wall had fallen away, to reveal on the other side, not shadows, mists and fogs, but a world bright in the most crystalline clarity. My hands moved over his body – long and lean, muscular and hard – then he moved his hands to catch mine. Our fingers entwined as we were kissing. I heard some footsteps, very distant at the other end of the alley. He looked around, spooked. 'No, John . . .'

Quickly I drew him into the gardens of the Cathedral; it was as black as tar among the bushes. Stumbling over grass, in total darkness, I put my hands down the front of his body, along his hip, into the lip of his breeches' waist. 'No,' he whispered, 'no, John, I can't,' as I started to push them down. My fingers touched the skin of his hips, a soft fuzz of hair on the dome of his buttocks. His erection – very hard – was caught in the top of his breeches, his tongue was in my mouth. He pushed me away.

'I'm sorry, John. We should not do this.' Looking up at me with shocked, confused eyes, he wiped the back of his hand over his mouth. 'We . . . we should not.' With his hand still held to his lips, he murmured: 'I am sorry . . . John . . . I am not . . . I am not . . .'

He kept looking at me unsteadily, unhappily. 'You don't want to?' I asked, confused.

That hand fell from his mouth. 'It is too fast, John. I am not ready.'

'Not ready, Ned?' The moment opened out before us, his refusal, but also the words he had said: not 'no,' but 'not ready'. I had been with many men, in many circumstances. I was not used to the refuting of a desire that we both knew he felt. His eyes ran all over mine, so fearful, a little ashamed, but not rejecting *of me*, and then I understood. 'You are a virgin.'

He nodded cautiously. 'Yes.'

'Have you not been with men, Ned, or not with anyone at all?'

He paused. 'Not with anyone at all.'

Just like the boy we had seen preaching about hellfire in the street . . . 'I see,' I said. I felt so protective of him in that moment. Powerfully, I only wanted him to trust me. 'It's all right, Ned.' I stepped towards him and extended my hand. He looked down at my fingers, my upturned palm. 'Take it,' I said.

Slowly, cautiously, he put his hand in mine. His skin was warm. I enclosed his hand gently, let his fingers turn, protected, in my palm. Lifting his hand to my mouth, I kissed it. 'There's no rush, Ned. I can wait.' He breathed out and gave something that was not quite a laugh and not quite a sigh of relief. Our hands slipped apart. 'Come on,' I said, 'I'll walk you home.'

'Walk me home?' he whispered. For a moment, I thought he might refuse, say the idea was silly. But then he smiled; deeply, happily smiled. 'All right,' he said.

I walked with him all the way to Mint Street, over the Bridge. We said goodbye not far from the corner of the Borough High Street, in the night shadows of the Marshalsea Prison. As we made our shy farewells, I called to him: 'So are you going to come and work for me?'

His face glittered with exasperated delight. 'You never let up, John Church.'

I shook my head. 'No, I don't, not when I know what I want.' His eyes went very round. 'We can get to know each other better. We can take our time.'

'All right,' he said again. *All right.* I waited at the end of Mint Street, as he walked along the cobbles back to his lodging-house. Halfway down the street, he turned and looked back at me. He lifted his hand quietly to bid me good night, those fingers of his separating in his softly feminine way. I raised my hand in return. He let himself into his lodging-house, and I heard the door's echoing bang as he closed it. I watched his empty street for a moment more, to commit it to my memory. Then I turned and walked back to my home.

Chapter Eight

or

Ladies Still Want To Be Ladies

Across a springtime . . .

I remember very clearly the first Sunday that I introduced Ned as my assistant. That morning at the Obelisk, he was nervous; I told him to relax. 'What will I say my job is?' he asked, as I swept up around the pulpit and he set down pamphlets in the pews. I looked over at him and smiled, to reassure him. 'My assistant. What else do you need to be?' He shrugged a little, without looking at me, still setting down pamphlets at steady intervals, like a gardener planting bulbs. 'Someone might ask my specific duties.' I laughed: 'Assisting me!'

Before the service, the congregation began to file in, and some people reacted to seeing Ned sitting in the front pew directly beneath the pulpit. He, for his part, kept his eyes on me. Lastly, Mr Linehan arrived, and standing at the very front of the chapel, stared at Ned so directly – with such an urgent air of moral enquiry – that I had to ask him to take a seat. Mrs Caesar and her group entered and, for the first time in however long, Lydia was with them. I did not know if Ned had told her that he would be there or if it was mere coincidence. They took their seats about halfway through the pews, forming a long line staring outwards, not speaking. With all their faces concentrated on the front, I realised that one or other had spotted him. Only then did they turn to murmur to each other, to turn further and whisper at length that Ned was sitting in the front pew. If Lydia had heard from somewhere about Ned's new job, had she come to embarrass him in some way? 'There are plenty of African chapels at which you could *assist*.' Except they weren't paying him, or offering him kisses, or laughing as they pressed him against a chapel wall, put their mouth on his neck and moved their hands down his body.

Afterwards, Mrs Caesar came up and congratulated Ned on his 'auspicious' new appointment. Lydia said nothing, neither to me nor to him. But she gazed at us both intently, and afterwards, Ned, instead of feeling relieved, as I'd hoped, appeared agitated.

★

Sunday was my busiest day, of course: secretly busy for me, having to go off to Vere Street in the evening. Sometimes he came other days. He had nothing better to do, he said; it was hard to find work. I nodded sympathetically and enjoyed the increasing amount of time we spent together. I paid him small amounts of money; he seemed bashful but relieved to receive it. Soon I would start to pay him more.

If we were alone at the Obelisk, I would lock the door from inside, just as Mrs Cook did upstairs at Vere Street, and we would sweep the space for loose change, lost hats, people hiding behind curtains waiting to find out more. Eventually our desires would overwhelm us, and we would, our mouths sewn together by kisses, we'd pull down pew cushions to the hard stone floor, to make ourselves a lovers' bed. But just at that moment where my breath was hard, and my blood was up, my fingers reaching for my breeches button to pull them down, he would stop me and say: 'No, John, that's enough.' We would say nothing of our obvious erections. I will not apologise for desiring him. But I respected his rules. I wanted *him* to want *me*, more than anything.

★

The molly house prospered across that springtime. Mrs Cook worried about the risk of her success, with how busy it was most Sunday nights. James Cook, on the rare occasion I saw him, would sneer: 'They're buying my grog, ain't they?' 'When the money rolls in, suddenly it's yours,' Philip Kett observed sharply, causing Cook to threaten to punch him. One Sunday evening, there was a wedding that was very well attended. Still I had not got right the words of the service.

The evening started to wear down. The clientele drifted off home and soon it was just me, Mrs Cook, Philip Kett and the Duchess of Gloucester, who hung around with an air of having a question in her. Mrs Cook and Kett cleared glasses, whilst the Duchess and I stacked up chairs so that the floor could be swept.

'Well, that was lovely,' Mrs Cook said, and we all agreed. 'They looked so happy.'

'There were a lot of people here tonight,' I said. 'Is this the busiest night yet?'

'Half of them didn't even know who the other half were,' Philip Kett said drily, over near the bar. 'They just came in hopes of a fuck and went home with a flower in their buttonhole.'

Mrs Cook laughed brightly. 'If Sweet Lips was here, she'd say that at least they had something in their hole!'

I couldn't help but laugh too, but I had a concern. 'When do you know that there are too many people, Mrs Cook? Is it a risk?'

She shrugged. 'There is risk in all sorts of thing, Reverend.' She went over to join Philip Kett at the bar. They put more and more dirty glasses into a large bowl of water. 'Philip, love,' she said, 'can you make a start on these?' She walked back towards me. 'Were you pleased with how it went, Reverend Church?'

'O, yes. I think I need to consider about the wedding service. "Doth this man take this woman?" and all that. We are men marrying, here at least.'

'Are you going to tell the girls that?' Mrs Cook joked.

The Duchess spoke most seriously: 'Ladies still want to be ladies, Reverend!' I looked at Mrs Cook, and she at me, pressing her lips shut lest we start to giggle. The Duchess set down one of the chairs she was stacking. With our attention on her, she asked the question that I had felt in her. 'Do you think there might be space for *another* kind of person at the house?'

Mrs Cook's brow furrowed. 'What kind of person, Duchess?'

'*August* persons, I mean.'

It was then I remembered when Sally had said that the Duchess of Gloucester was a gentleman's servant in one of the royal palaces. 'Good Lord, Duchess!' I cried. 'Do you mean who I think you mean?'

My words were bright and tumultuous; but Mrs Cook stared at me in confusion. 'Who?'

'O, tell me not the Prince of Wales!' I said. The Duchess's eyes widened with amazement.

'O, no, Reverend, the Prince's tastes are very much conventional!' The Duchess paused. 'It is another person. He would come incognito.'

Incognito: like a heroine in one of my wife's novels. 'Is it some prince?' Philip Kett asked flatly. The Duchess bowed her head as if to intimate but not quite say yes.

Mrs Cook still seemed confused. 'But will he still not be recognised?' she asked. 'Isn't his mug on some jubilee plate somewhere?'

The Duchess thought about this. 'He is not one of the *better-known* princes. The King has many, many children. Would you recognise them all, Mrs Cook?'

She blew through her lips. 'I'd be hard-pressed to recognise the King, lovey.

★

On days when we had no chapel business, Ned and I liked to go on long walks, rambling all over London. I enjoyed these walks immensely, both for the pleasure of proximity to his person and for the interest of his conversation. Always he was such sweet and intelligent company, with that delicacy of spirit that always intrigued me so, as it once had, long before, with William Webster. He had a quick mind, able to see parts of history all around us that were quite obscure to me. Once we went to the well-known meeting house on Old Jewry, to a political gathering. (I only went to please him.) Afterwards, he asked me if the name of that street made me wonder about London's history; I had walked that street a thousand times, and in truth, it had not. He asked me if I did not wonder that, in England, they could banish Jewish persons for four hundred years, and yet keep the name of this street – its very ancient name. 'What does that say about Englishmen?' he asked. I said that I did not know, and it made him laugh – almost flirtatiously. 'Englishmen,' he said, 'have managed the trick of doing absolutely the worst things but denying their evil afterwards, when evidence of it is all around. Eject the Jews but keep the name; enslave Africans and tell them it was to convert them to Christianity and save their souls; conquer India, close its factories and strip it of its wealth, and say it was to end *suttee*. Never to steal money and land. *Never* that.' He laughed again so brightly, as if enjoying a good joke he was making, yet clearly he was not. He was so thrilling to me in these moments; thrilling, but also mysterious, in the freedom of his intelligence.

*

Once we went for a walk after the end of a weekday prayer gathering. A pearly evening light fell over the city as we went over the Bridge and up past the Tower. Briefly standing on the brow below the Minories, we mused on all those who had lost their heads within, all those Anne Boleyns and Thomas Mores. Now that they no longer sliced heads off on Tower Hill, the building had crumbled to a ruin. Kings and queens like to live in comfortable palaces these days, not draughty forts. Recently there had been talk that the Tower might be opened to the General Public, as a kind of holy pilgrimage to England's past, or at least a day out from the Home Counties. From the brow of the hill, he pointed down south-eastwards, down the slope towards the docks that lined the river. The rigging of the massed ships there knotted like spiderwebs in mid-air, above the crooked factory buildings that ran down to Limehouse. Some of these ships would sail to Africa, India, all around the world, wherever Englishmen went now.

'The history of this country is as much in the contents of those boats as of that tower,' he said. 'Send English people down there to those ships to see their present, not up here to see their past, or rather the past of kings and queens who cared nothing for them. As long as horrors are performed five thousand miles away in Jamaica, the English will dream of the six wives of Henry VIII, and probably, in time, even Marie Antoinette, and think these the sad stories of history.' I wanted him to know that I was a freethinker, a radical, an innovator too. I began to think that I could trust him, to tell him about what radical action I had undertaken at the molly house. I wanted him to know that he could admire in me what I admired in him.

*

One idle midweek day, Ned suggested we go out to the country. We took the boat from Westminster Bridge to a place named Hammersmith, some way west of London. Hammersmith is a bucolic sort of place, all cosy little wooden buildings hugging the river's deep meanders there. Its streets are few and lined with trees and fields, and a mist rolls in from the river.

124

A hazy afternoon enveloped us as we walked, in conversation and silence. Eventually, we wound back to the river shore. Boys fished along the banks, sent there by their parents to work.

Walking side by side, Ned and I traced the deep curve of the Thames. He told me that westwards was a place named Chiswick, famous among radicals for a battle where Bad King Charles was repelled from London, saving it for the Republic. I had never heard that story before.

Here and there, fishermen's huts puffed white smoke from chimneys, ignoring the passage of time that London natively insists upon. We walked along a piece of low river – beach, as much sand as pebble. He said it was beautiful and I agreed. He asked me if I liked the country. Although it had not been my intention, I began to tell him about that summer of my boyhood, at Tunbridge Wells, about hedgerows and church bells, and the warm summer air moving over open fields, buzzing with bees.

'I thought you told me you were an orphan,' he said as I was talking about the woman who I took to be my mother. And so I had to tell him about the Foundling Hospital, about the horror of the wardens, the mystery of my origin, and how, briefly and happily, this woman who was not my mother had taken me out to the country to live. 'But why did you not stay with her after that?' he asked. I told him about her taking me back, the rejection, shock, the awful days after, waking up in the boys' dormitory and momentarily forgetting what had happened; just for a moment, thinking I was still with her. 'That's terrible,' he said. He looked at me with such emotion, because he had his own childhood, similarly unloved, abused. 'She should not – they should not have done that to you.'

We started walking back towards the boat-jetty at Hammersmith. Presently the boat to London would come, and we would be back in the world, among fellow travellers, and then in the city itself. I realised that this was the opportunity for me to tell him about Vere Street, whilst we were still alone but not at the Obelisk either. I told him it all: about the opening and location of the molly house; about Mrs Cook and the queens; about how proud I was about my moment of revelation, seeing that men like us had so little to mark our own lives; about the weddings I had performed, how sweet and good they had been; about how people had cried and said I was creating a wonderful world. I told him about White and Hepburn, how magical it had all been. But I was careful to talk about it in terms of radical action, of claiming our own stories, of reshaping words to fit our own narratives, to resist the hatred that forms us. Love could change lives radically, I said, but as part of a radical action. Men like us could be dignified – and dignify ourselves – in being allowed to show our love.

He was gazing at me unreadably. 'But how are they acknowledging it, John? They do not go to the Registrar. They do not tell their families. They write no letters to tell old friends the good news. They cannot.'

'But we are our own community,' I said. 'At the molly house. We acknowledge it before each other. In so doing, we acknowledge that we are worthy of love too. Do you not see the importance of that?' He said nothing. 'It is the most radical thing I have ever done. It is the most radical expression of my ideas yet.'

'I don't see it as radical,' he said.

I had expected that he should admire me. 'I don't think you understand what has been achieved, Ned. It is a kind of revolution, I believe, a first step, towards a new way of being for men like us. It has changed what can be known about love, if men like us are allowed to love, are allowed to marry—'

'John—' he began, but suddenly I felt under attack; I would not let him speak.

'I thought you who wanted to see the end of persecution

of Africans would also want to act against the persecution of men like us.'

At this he soured. 'They are not the same thing at all,' he spat, and I realised I had offended him. His eyes flicked quickly to one side. 'I was thinking I could try to get you a speech at one of the Free & Easy Clubs just outside London.' I remembered he had told me he had met Lydia Caesar at a political meeting at the Free & Easy Club in Whitechapel. 'What do you think of that?'

His words were crisp, threaded through with coldness. It was as if I had said nothing at all. I felt my anger rising – he was rejecting me. My throat swelled, my cheeks still tingled red; I knew my rage was possible, and I could hear the low drone in my head that accompanies it. He had felt shame, and so had transposed that shame on to me; he had shamed me to stop feeling ashamed himself; or at least, to share its burden. But then I remembered: I was not ashamed, not of Vere Street, and not of my desires and wants either. 'What I think,' I said eventually, 'is I want you to come to the molly house with me. I want my friends to see you. I want you to see them. I want us to sit in a world that would accept us—'

'John—'

'I want to hold your hand, and sit with you, and let people see how beautiful you are—'

'John, I don't want to go!'

I know I am capable of bad decisions, terrible rages, destroying things; I did not want to do that now; I wanted to be a good person, after all, most of all for him. I did not want to yell at him, or accuse him, or ask him why he had tried to make me ashamed. I wanted him to want to come to Vere Street. He turned and looked back downriver. In the distance, the boat from London was approaching; it would be there in five minutes. Maybe it was the approach of the boat, and its inhabitants, that stilled me. No one else was on the jetty; we were the only travellers. We were standing close together, out of sight of the world. I moved quickly to kiss his cheek. Briefly, he nestled into my touch, before pulling away, lest we be seen.

But I am always able to find hope. I *knew* he would change his mind.

A few days later . . .

I arrived at the White Swan Sunday evening. In the main room, I found Mrs Cook sitting with the Duchess of Gloucester, again dressed as a man. The mood was not so much sombre as clerk-ish; very 'any other business'. The Duchess spoke in her native, taciturn but respectful manner. She explained that she was indeed a gentleman – servant to one of the royal households. 'A prince' had confirmed he wanted to come to the molly house. The Duchess said it was important that no one guess who he was, and that we two – Mrs Cook and I – protect him.

'Will you not be here?' I asked.

'O, of course,' she said, 'but I would not be able to speak freely to His Highness. I need someone who can . . .' She paused. '. . . manage him.' She paused again. 'Princes come with their own peculiarities and peccadilloes.'

Mrs Cook and I gave each other knowing looks. My friend had had enough. 'Duchess! Will you tell us who it is?'

The Duchess of Gloucester paused with great portentous-ness. 'His Royal Highness,' she began at a stately pace, 'Prince Ernest Augustus.'

Mrs Cook kept gazing, absolutely blankly. 'Who's that?'

The Duchess looked surprised. 'Why! The Duke of Cumberland!'

Mrs Cook: 'I'm still none the bloody wiser, dearie.'

Now the Duchess seemed quite confused. 'The King's fifth son.'

'Fifth?' Mrs Cook cried. 'I am surprised even the King recognises him. He has all them daughters too.'

I had to stifle a smirk. 'That king has too many children,' I said.

'Fifteen . . .' the Duchess said, most gravely.

Mrs Cook rolled her eyes. 'No wonder the Queen wears such wide dresses . . .'

'When is he coming?' I asked.

The Duchess looked at me very penetratingly. 'Tonight, Reverend.'

At this time, Mrs Cook almost jumped out of her seat. *'Tonight?'*

It was a busy evening at the house, but those of us who knew who was coming could not help but feel antic. Around nine o'clock, Mrs Cook raced over to me and grabbed my arm: 'He's here!' Together we pushed through the crowd of bodies to wait by the upstairs door. I noticed it had been left unbolted. The Duchess, who had remained in male clothing, had already gone down to meet him, and now was ushering him up the stairs. Two other men were with them, one being the Italian, Mr Sellis, who had warned me of the need to be radical about love, to commit to it, and to pursue it when you think you are losing it.

When they got to the top, the Duchess looked at us. 'Mrs Cook, do not curtsey,' she whispered low. 'Show nothing. His Highness knows that you respect his station but the circumstance requires no etiquette.'

'Etiquette?' Mrs Cook repeated, in mystery.

The Duke was the most unremarkable man, tall, his hair very fair but quite thin and dishevelled, his body thick with good living, a hulking red face, florid and flabby from too much grog.

There was nothing regal in his bearing. If he had been pushing a cart filled with vegetables through Leadenhall Market, you would not have blinked. Mr Sellis barely nodded at me in recognition. With him was another man, an Irishman, introduced to us as Mr Neale. We were told quietly to call the Duke 'Mr Smythe' at all times. All of this was said in the Duke's presence yet he did not acknowledge the whispered conversation once.

'I am Reverend Church,' I said, before turning to my friend. 'This is Mrs Cook.'

'Do you run the place?' the Duke said to me, as if on a royal visit to a boot factory.

'Mrs Cook does . . . Mr Smythe.'

He raised his eyebrows: 'Extraordinary.' 'Mr Smythe' sat with Mr Sellis, Mr Neale and the Duchess, in a corner of the room, and did not hobnob with the hoi polloi at all. But after a short while, the Duchess came and asked me to join them. They were drinking brandy from a bottle, poured into four glasses; I was never offered a fifth. Once I'd sat down with them, the Duke gazed at me for a long time. The other men looked at me too, but I could tell that they were waiting for their master to speak. 'Tranter tells me that you perform marriages here.'

'Tranter?' I asked, then the Duchess coughed, and so I understood. 'O . . . Yes, sir, that is right.'

'Mr Smythe,' the Duchess corrected; how reflexively I had said 'sir'.

The Duke let his eyes run over those of his companions, with some cruel amusement. 'Well, why the hell would you want to do that, man? Marriage is between a man and a woman. Why would a man wish to marry at all if he did not have to?'

I glanced at Mr Sellis. 'Love, perhaps?' Sellis's eyes did not meet my gaze.

The Duke hooted with derision. 'Bally nonsense! A man has to marry for duty or money, or some such. You mollies are free

of all that. You are free men scrabbling to get inside a prison!'
He was all high-born contemptuous laughter. I felt only revulsion at him. We were here in a molly house, and he spoke of us as if it were nothing to do with him. I got up and asked to be excused. No matter what the Duchess had said about etiquette, there was astonishment. Princes are not used to being the ones found lacking.

I went to sit with Sally and Black-Eyed Leonora, greeting them: 'Ladies.'

Leonora had a feather fan with her, which she flicked open and moved slowly and elegantly. They were each drinking rum. Sweet Lips came over and joined us too.

'John Church, the light is shining out of you these days,' Sally said.

'Truly?'

'You look like you found the fountain of eternal youth.'

Sweet Lips gave a sharp laugh. 'O, give old Sal a sip!'

Sally did not even hear the jibe. Looking at me, she closed one eye. 'You have a young man, don't you?'

'Sally, you have the nose of a bloodhound.'

Sweet Lips: 'Wet and brown.'

'Who is it?' Sally asked. A pause. 'Will you not tell me?' She looked around. 'Is he here?' I started to shake my head. She glanced back at her friend. 'O, it's not Leonora, is it? O, you poor sod!'

Black-Eyed Leonora tapped her feather fan sharply so that it closed instantly. 'I would like a nice, tall man to walk me home at the end of the evening. I have to brave the dangerous streets all alone.'

Sally blew through her teeth. 'You *are* the danger!'

They were both laughing. I became aware of a man at our side. It was the Irishman, Mr Neale. He bowed to the ladies and turned to Black-Eyed Leonora. 'Mr Smythe' – was it intentional that he paused so, for dramatic effect? – 'yonder, wondered if you would like to repair to a bedroom with him?'

The three girls' heads turned like a weathervane in the wind – very much one direction. 'Which one is Smythe?' Sweet Lips asked. 'The handsome fellow?' She meant Mr Sellis. Mr Neale looked most sour.

'No, the other gentleman.'

The queens looked at the incognito fifth son of King George III. 'O, dear,' Sally said. 'No, thanks.'

Mr Neale stayed where he was, bowing to Leonora, staring at her directly. 'To be clear, the Duke is very fond of meeting African gentlemen. He prefers them more than any other type.'

Sally's eyes went wide and mouth went round, as if to say: *O, good luck, pal!* Black-Eyed Leonora's eyes were suddenly all ice. She leaned forwards, towards Mr Neale. 'Well, tell Mr Smythe that I do not like gentlemen who say that they prefer "African gentlemen".' She stretched out her hands, over which she wore ivory silk gloves, admiring her own exquisiteness. 'I prefer a gentleman who likes me for my own self, and I prefer them not to look like' – she raised her voice now – '*syphilitic barn owls!*'

Mr Neale went grey with shock. The three queens were laughing and laughing, and glancing mockingly over at the Duke, who shot to his feet and stormed out. Mr Sellis, Mr Neale and finally the Duchess scurried after him. It seemed such a sharp inversion of the world: the prince driven away ignominiously by the poor. Ned should see such an act! This was truly radical action! This was a revolutionary world! If only Ned would come to Vere Street, he would see how I – no, everyone in that secret place – had created that truly radical world of which we had been surely dreaming.

Chapter Nine
or
Hampstead

It came to pass that Ned told me he had spoken to someone who ran a Free & Easy Club far out in Hampstead. He said that perhaps one Sunday evening we might take a carriage up there, through the countryside, to give a talk. Somehow we no longer talked in terms of marriage, and Vere Street. Now it was the politics of my ideas of which he spoke, of tolerance as a tool, of how the mutual recognition of our shared humanity might help all mankind.

I could not complain, of course. How could I? Abolition was nearest to his heart, and I could not dispute that. But in this apparent denial that I had achieved much of value at Vere Street, I could only sense some trace of disrespect. I did not want that from anyone, but most of all, not from him. Yet despite the nature of how this proposal had come about, I was not entirely averse to doing it – to having my ideas acclaimed by a different audience. Still, I wanted to please Ned; that mattered to me too. I wanted to fit in around his beliefs, in hopes – eventually – he might fit in around mine.

I told Mrs Cook that I could not make that Sunday, and she told me not to worry, so we did the weddings on Friday. Through those few days before the trip, I felt nervous, not knowing what was ahead. We met to go to Hampstead at the carriage stop at the edge of old London, Chancery Lane, a few hours after we had locked up the Obelisk. When I saw him waiting for me next to the carriage – which was black and rough, nothing fancy – he seemed so still, his long, slim shape held perfectly as if in mid-air. But his beauty now had such an effect on me: it is trivial of me to say it, to connect outer perfection to some perfection within, but there it is; it was the truth.

Seeing me approach, he held out two paper stubs. 'I bought our tickets.'

'The last coach back to London is a quarter-hour to eleven,' I said. 'We shall have to catch that.'

There were three other travellers, in total making five, six with the driver up top. We sat in the carriage knocking knees, not quite looking at each other, as we rattled up the unpaved road of Grays Inn Lane. This was a very rough part, of open fields and thrown-up houses; vagabonds and street children lurked here, for whatever pickings they might find. We travelled on a muddy road up towards the big Hampstead Road north, riding in awkward silence before our companions got out at Kings Cross or Camden Town. When they were gone, we relaxed.

'About what are you going to speak, John?'

What did he think? 'The radical possibilities of tolerance, as we have discussed.' I wondered if he was checking that I was not going to sing the praises of Vere Street!

'Did you bring your notes?'

'Notes?'

He looked at me askew. 'You didn't write notes?' I hadn't. 'You are just going to talk off your head?'

I was smiling at him. 'It's what I do every Sunday, Ned. It's what I know how to do. They will lap it up, you watch.'

He shook his head, his lips pursed. 'You never lack confidence, John Church.'

We carried on to Hampstead, up a very steep hill, all the way to its top, where the village sits. Presently we were in wilder country, where the famous Heath begins. The village is famously a pretty place. Its little lanes wind and twist, and at the end of every one you can see the ancient green forest, a common land, on which the ordinary folk still graze their sheep and forage fruit. The air is very clean up there, away from the filthy coal smoke of London. Much of the village was built early in the last century, but its busy brick and sloping roofs already looked old-fashioned against the cool, repetitive elegance of modern tastes. Here and there, bluestocking types sloped around, turning books on second-hand stalls. Elsewhere hawkers cried for your attention, selling cakes, meat pies, hot sausages, even fried fish. There were many cosy taverns, where it would be nice to sit and drink an ale, but Ned was not one for inebriation.

Later, we went to the meeting hall, which was at the top of the airy Heath Street. To my considerable surprise, there were fifty people there, many more than I had expected. They were a rag-bag of types, from fashionable to farming folk. There was a sharp conviviality which suggested the crowd was familiar with itself, but no one greeted Ned; it was not clear to me whom he knew here to have suggested it. At the front, a large man with mutton-chops and bushy red hair was giving instructions to anyone who would take them. Ned went up and introduced himself. The man became gregariously interested in me, paying little attention to him. 'O, very good, Mr Church! We are most interested to hear your radical views!' He clapped his hands very loudly. 'Right, shall we get on?'

Even if I say it myself, I gave an excellent speech. Of course, the best speakers in such venues are those who are also preachers, or at least have the quality of the preacher. I spoke of how love and tolerance will create a great sea of egalitarianism, in which the last, truest revolution might take place and all human beings shall finally be free and equal. I quoted Galatians: 'There is neither Jew nor Greek, there is neither slave nor free, there is no male and female, for you are all one in Christ Jesus.' Then Romans: 'God shows no partiality.' Then good old Mark: 'You shall love your neighbour as yourself.' Lastly, I said the following: 'In time, this equality between men and women and between races shall extend outward and outward, and we English shall have to pursue that to its logical end. We shall have to give the Indian his freedom, and the Irishwoman hers, and the Welshman and the Scot. We shall set aside all prejudice in the name of tolerance and equality and a new, revolutionary freedom.'

Hands started going up as soon as I had finished, from folk with faces that were turning pink. A man asked the first question: 'When you say that equality and toleration should be extended endlessly, what do you mean? What about criminals? Murderers and rapists?' I replied that respect for others is a central tenet of tolerance, for tolerance is the very opposite of violence, and criminals break that tenet through violence.

A woman asked the second question: 'When you say set aside all prejudices, how is that possible? Men are born prejudiced. Do you mean that all manners of person, no matter their class, or nature, or race, might sit together and be as one?' Yes, I said, absolutely I meant that. I asked her for evidence that men are born with prejudice. Now I knew what to say, something that was true but also original: 'Men are taught every prejudice they possess,' I said. 'No infant has a prejudice except for apple sauce over pear.' I expected a laugh; there was frosty silence. I had expected acclaim; but here there seemed annoyance.

Another woman asked, did I not understand the Indian benefited from British rule? 'Think of those poor widows who got burned by *suttee*, and what about Anglican schools that have opened, and medicines, and Christianity?' I said to her that no one is freed by imprisoning others, and you cannot justify bad things by doing good things. You cannot free Africans whilst imprisoning Indians. Are you compelling a person in their beliefs just so that you have the comfort of them matching your own; or worse, because you use your beliefs to justify violence, as many Christians did during Slavery? 'That is purely vanity, delusion and self-comforting.' The woman folded her arms and looked quite cross when I said that.

Lastly, a thin, stooped man with his hand in the air got to his feet without me even asking him to speak. 'Sir,' he began in a cool, liquid voice. 'Is there no limit to the sort of person that you expect us to tolerate?' I said if there is no violence, then no. The man seemed quite pleased. 'Can you not think of *one type* of person that must never be accepted?' The room fell into an expectant hush. I glanced at Ned, who was staring back at me with a raw concern; I did not understand.

'I can think of no such person, if he is not violent to another, and acts consensually.'

The thin, stooped man grinned handsomely, to me and to the whole meeting, for he could smell the blood of his victory. 'What about the Sodomite, Reverend?' I felt my throat clamp shut, the sweat bead along my brow. 'In no part of morality is the Sodomite accepted,' he was saying. 'He can be executed before the law, he breaks many laws, he outrages all sensitivities, and he is despised in every religion. Yet perhaps what he does is with consent, but no one surely would say it is all right for a Sodomite to be accepted. Unless you mean to say we should accept Sodomites.'

Somewhere I heard a woman cry: 'For shame!'

I could feel Ned's eyes burning into me. At once I heard the hum in my head, loud and buzzing. Usually it starts quietly, so that I have some warning, but immediately the sound was roaring because the threat to me was so imminent. I heard the blood rushing in the veins behind my ears, my pulse thudding in

137

my brain. There was no way I could have said yes, not a single survivable way. No person of any substance had ever suggested in public that a Sodomite should not be punished. After all I had achieved at Vere Street, a true radicalism, a transformation of real meaning, here I was, Simon Peter, about to deny the Truth. I closed my eyes. I could hear the thin, stooped man's voice: 'Sir? What is your reply?' A second's pause; the roar in my head. '*Sir!* What is your reply?'

What happens to a man in a moment like this? Why does one man hold together and another break apart? But the question is not about what men do, but what *I* do. In that moment, so many things flashed through my head: Ned, and his smile when it was just the two of us alone, laughing; now, here, with that tense, concerned look on his face; his refusal to come to the molly house, to see what I had achieved; Sally Fox telling me about the pillory; always, always, the wardens of the Foundling Hospital calling me disgusting; my wife and her disappointments; always, always, the gilder and his wife locking me in the blackness of the cellar; the rustle of its rats, when first I used my rage to become powerful, to *achieve* power.

O, I know I started shouting. Sometimes the hum in my head, that awful sick-making drone, becomes overwhelming. I know sometimes I do stupid things, I know I lose control of myself. The beast of my rage returns, and I have to ride it – in order to save myself. That is what people do not understand, I think. The rage harms me but it also protects me from others' harm. I don't remember what I was yelling. I know I was calling them no sort of radicals if they believed that punishing people was the answer. I think I said that they had the morality of those who enslave – that they were nothing better than that – and immediately there was uproar and the risk of fists. I am not sure if they were mine. I suppose they were.

I don't remember how it happened – how he and I found

ourselves tumbling out into the black country night, there on the edge of Hampstead village, running, our heels echoing on the cobbled street, me in front of him. Were those radicals hurling insults or chasing after us? Were they hollering for our deaths whilst shaking their fists? No, I remember only two sets of feet clattering, echoing against the higgledy-piggledy houses of Hampstead, only two points of sound.

'John!' I heard Ned shouting, running behind me. 'John, stop!' What had I said to the stooped, thin man? I did not remember. I do not even remember now. All of it is blackened rubble to me afterwards, once the beast is gone. All of it is the shame of the rage that overwhelms me: there is the shame that causes the rage, and the shame that follows it; but also there is the knowledge that the rage saves me, that it is my most powerful weapon. This is a knot I have never untied; I would be afraid even to try.

I came to a dead stop, and hung breathless, there in the darkness. Now he caught up with me. He walked around me so that he was facing me. I looked up at him. 'John,' he murmured. 'John, what is going on? I don't understand.'

I looked down and felt that shame consuming me. I had made a fool of myself, worst of all, in front of him, when what I wanted was for him to like me. William Webster used to say that I could get too intense and frighten him, but I would never want that. 'You shouldn't have made me come here!' I cried. 'You shouldn't have tried to make me fit into this world, this world of . . . *hypocrites*!'

'I am sorry, John,' he said, confused but sincere, I could see.

'You have humiliated me!'

He took a step towards me, and I could see the conciliation that was in him. 'That was not my intention, John.'

'Those people . . .' I said, trying not to blame him any more. I could hear the emotion in my voice. 'Those people aren't radicals. They are shams of radicals. They are exactly the same as Inquisitors in Spain, breaking the skulls of those of whom they disapprove.'

Ned looked at me. 'I don't think they are, John.'

'Don't defend them!' I yelled, shouting straight into his face. Somewhere in the distance, a window opened. Someone wanted to see what the commotion was.

He did not rise to my anger; he spoke calmly, with care. 'I am not defending them. Just because you – we – don't like what they say, they are not the same as Inquisitors but—'

'They claim to be good Christians yet act like murderers, like torturers!' I cried.

He sighed. 'Then perhaps religion is not the route to tolerance. Maybe religion is the enemy of tolerance.' I was shocked that he said this. Could he truly believe it? He seemed to know he had to explain himself to me, without me even asking: 'Religious belief is fundamental, and radical religious belief is even more so, unpersuadable even. People hold these beliefs because of their religion, or what they perceive their religion requires of them. To ask them to change their religion is to ask them to change themselves, and people don't want to do that. Religion never makes people kinder or more merciful. It just confirms them in their prejudice.'

'Are you an atheist, John?' I asked. Atheists were whispered of in English society, not as Satanists of yore but as utterly alien. I had an image of him and Lydia Caesar, who herself never talked of God or faith, only of politics, in some little godless huddle; I did not know from where that image came.

'I told you I am on a journey, John. Part of a thinking person's journey is to give up things that you carry with you solely because your parents did, or your teachers did, or' – he took a small breath – 'whoever raised you did. But you can give up beliefs, and move forwards.'

'Is that a yes?' I asked.

He sighed. 'No. But it's not a no, either.' Somewhere in the distance, on the Heath, an owl was hooting, or maybe a fox was howling. Both of us turned at the sharp, sudden shriek; the sound made us shiver through the dark. 'Come on,' he said. 'Let's go and find the carriage.'

He turned and started to walk back towards the heart of the village. We walked in silence for a while, down its hill, towards the place where the coaches arrived from London. Waiting at the carriage stop for a long time, sitting close to each other but not so close to alert suspicion, the mood changed completely; the storm had passed, and always there is sunlight after. He told me funny stories about radicals he knew, stupid things they had said. I liked that he told me, that he did not take it all too seriously. I told him about the appalling Mr Linehan, whom he did not remember, who had come to the chapel for a bible meditation and talked to me at length on the issue of how faith can be expressed without acts of charity. As I watched him, a sausage roll was poking out of his coat pocket, half eaten; it was all I could do to keep looking at him as he talked and not the sausage roll. Ned laughed beautifully, sweeping his hand over his face. As I watched him, I was thinking: *I have shown myself to him, my true, turbulent self, and he has not rejected me.*

Now and then he checked his pocket watch, and kept saying times: halfway-past nine, a quarter-hour to ten, five minutes past ten, twenty minutes past, then twenty-five. After a good passage of time, the northbound carriage hove into view, its horses dragging the passengers slowly uphill. When finally they came to a stop, various local residents, come from town, alighted. We watched the driver tying up his carriage and unbuckling his horses; he was not going back to town. Ned said it was now more than halfway past ten. He called over to the driver: 'I say, do you know when the next southwards carriage will be? We have been waiting more than an hour without a sight.'

The driver looked at Ned and shrugged. 'Gone.'

'Gone?'

The man now grew irritable. 'Gone!'

Ned persevered: 'We were told the last one was a quarter-hour to eleven.'

'Not on Sundays, pal. On Sundays, it's nine o' clock.'

Ned turned to look at me; we must have just missed it. 'What shall we do? Walk back to Southwark?' I told him I did not mind, but that it was probably two hours from there. This was not a problem in itself, but the first hour was solid dark countryside until Euston. How would he feel, walking home through miles of woodland and rough pasture, in territory where gangs of armed child robbers and highwaymen roamed?

'Well, we could try to find a room for the night,' I said. 'There are inns with rooms in Hampstead, it is famous for it.' I saw something flash across his eyes, but he did not refuse. 'I can pay,' I said. 'I have money.'

We went to one inn, which the keeper said was full; he recommended we go to another, on a steep hill right on the edges of the Heath. Up there, the great blackness of the ancient forest loomed, night birds called, creatures scuttled in the darkness. It was near eleven o'clock by then. At the second place, the keeper said she had only one room. Carrying a candlestick, she showed us up steep stairs, down black corridors, over uneven, creaking floors. When she opened the door to show us the room, I turned to look at Ned; his eyes were round with terror. 'Is there only one bed?' he asked in a tight voice.

The woman looked at us like we were morons. 'O, good grief!' she cried. 'You are two big men, you will be fine. Stop being such women!' Her lick of shame made us pay up; of course, that had been her intention.

Neither of us had brought a change of clothes, or any kind

of nightgown. We each stood in the room, stooping slightly, staring at the bed. 'On which side do you want to sleep?' I asked.

'I don't mind,' he replied, softly. 'The left side?' He kept that haze of uncertainty about him. 'Let's get undressed – just down to our shirts – and get into bed.'

'We can order some drink up if you wish,' I said; he said no, quickly and quietly.

He walked around the bed and turned his back to me, and slowly he began to kick off his shoes, take off his jacket. In the candlelight, he hung there, slim-shaped. I could hardly breathe. My cock was already swelling. I took my clothes off and slipped under the sheets before he had a chance to see it starting to stand. I lifted my knees under the sheets, to conceal everything. Still keeping his back to me, he said: 'Don't watch me, John.' I started laughing, then so did he even as he cried: 'Turn around! *Don't look!*'

'I'm not looking! Why would I look?'

'*You know why*, John!' he cried with charming but nervous levity. I clamped my hands over my eyes, with closed fingers, hamming like a pantomime actor.

'I'm peeping through my fingers,' I said.

'Stop it, John!' He was giggling as he protested. 'You're making light of it!' Of course I was; by now my cock was fully hard. I heard the rustle of his clothes, then felt the bounce of his body hitting the bed. Still laughing a little, he slipped under the covers then turned to his side, away from me. I took my hands from over my eyes. There was a blanket and an undersheet on the bed, nothing more. Under them, our bodies were magnetically aware of each other, their warmth, the blood circulating around our forms, their physical pull.

'I think I should take the undersheet,' he said, 'and you can have the blanket. That way, we will not disturb each other sleeping.'

'No,' I said, 'it's all right, you can have the blanket. I don't feel the cold. I grew up in an orphanage. You never feel the cold after that.' The other advantage was that I did not have to reveal my erection; that might spook him. We each of us moved position to take our coverings. Unexpectedly our bodies touched. Warm, lean bodies, bare skin. Both of us jolted, then froze. Moments of silence stretched out across the bed. The two of us felt so separate and yet so entirely together, as if the rest of the world had vanished, and only we were left alive.

'You're going to try to touch me, aren't you, John?' His voice was shadowy and nervous and did not wait for my reply. 'I won't stop you, John. I want you to, I am ready.'

I turned to look at him; he was already turning to look at me. Tenderly, we began to kiss. We had kissed before, of course, but now it seemed like the first time. His lips were so soft, and as our mouths joined, I felt his breath, warm and sweet, inside mine. I moved closer to his body, until my bare leg was touching his. I pulled myself over him and put my hand against his cock; it was very hard, expectant. He drew back slightly; I was probably the first person ever to touch him there. I told him not to worry, I told him not to pull away from me. I put a kiss to his cheek and then, one, two, three more, on his throat. He tipped his head back, to reveal his neck to my lips. He let out a long, exquisite breath.

We fell into our lovemaking, and it was gentle and even – I did not want to scare him, this, his first time with man or woman. Face to face, I lifted his legs to loop up around my back – he did not know what to do – and all I could do was stare at him, his astonishing beauty, but also the beauty of his humanity, all the things I felt towards him then, his intelligence, his kindness, all of it. I spat into my hand and told him to trust me. 'I trust you,' he said. When I pushed myself inside him, very slow, he winced and put up his hands slightly against my body. I told him not to fight it, but to want it, to let me inside him, again, to trust me and, again, to want it. 'All right,' he whispered, and as he said it, I slipped completely inside him. His eyes grew wide and then he started to laugh a little, realising what had happened.

I could not believe it – I could hardly fathom it – we had made it – we had got this far. I felt so new, so unprepared for the moment. He was looking at me intently, and I was fucking him, all I had dreamed of for so very long. Let me tell you a secret. If it sounds silly, I don't care. (If it sounds silly, then that's on you.) I was not like this before that night; I felt transformed; he had said that he was not ready before, but perhaps it was me who had not been ready, and only now was I ready – to be transformed.

It was then he said to me, 'John, I cannot hold it in any longer,' and his semen sprayed up his body, a sign of his inexperience and excitement, I suppose. We both of us started to laugh, me still inside him, and him looking as if some astonishing secret had just been revealed to him.

*

I hardly slept that night, even as I heard him drift into his soft sleep-breathing. I lay there in the darkness listening to the Hampstead night: the gentle, woodwind hoots of owls, the distant screech of foxes on the heath. Once he woke up, and we made love again, but then afterwards he sank back into a very deep sleep. I must have slept for a while, for I woke in a strange violet light, which I guessed meant it was almost dawn. As I awakened, I felt a weight against my back. I realised what it was: his head resting against my shoulder and the curve of his hand over my hip, his fingers, unconsciously, slowly rubbing along the texture of my skin.

I lay there for a long time, and watched the light changing. Slowly I moved the position of my body, turning around, so that we were facing. He did not wake up. With his head now against my chest, I felt the ends of his hair brush my lips. Lightly, so as not to wake him, I leaned into his scalp and kissed the top of his head. I swept my arm up along his, and instinctively he nestled completely into my body, curling himself into me. And all I can tell you is this: I was so entirely happy.

In the morning . . .

The innkeeper's promise of a breakfast turned out to be little more than over-brewed tea and last night's bread with some honey. Ned did not eat much; me only a little more. Over the table, he gave me small smiles. Having bought new tickets on the midday coach in the morning, we decided to walk on the Heath for a while; I had never been there before and had heard of its ancient mystery and beauty. We walked away from the village, to the very, very top of the hill that rises out of London before sloping away to the far north. There was a famous tavern named Jack Straw's Castle. It was named after a great revolutionary from back in olden times.

There was hardly anyone around, save the odd man, walking on his own, down in the other direction to the right of the Castle. The sun came out, and was surprisingly hot. We walked into dense woodland, where knotted pale green trees as old as England, and fine sprays of bush and fern, conspired to block out the day. Now and then as we walked, suddenly, bright sunlight burst on our backs, almost shockingly warm.

We walked deeper and deeper into the tangle of the Heath, and as we did we were laughing and talking, and I heard our voices captured by the canopy of green above our heads. Rapidly we tumbled downhill, under enormous trees, beneath which vast seas of red earth opened up, some great, unnavigated plain. He lost his footing slightly, and I threw out my hand to

146

stop him falling. He caught it and I tugged him back towards me, making him call out as he swung round to face me. 'I feel very free out here,' he said – quite unexpectedly.

'Free?' I asked.

'Very unseen. Like no one is watching me.'

I felt so close to him in that moment, as if what had happened had changed and released us from some prison. We touched hands, as lovers might – real lovers – a man and a woman who do not know about the dangerousness of their love. 'There is no one to see us.' I pulled him towards me and kissed him, holding his body close to mine. Our lips touching, he was breathing in such anticipation; tiny little laughs escaped from his throat, one after another.

Walking onwards, downhill, in which direction I did not know (it's easy to lose your way on the Heath), we came to a stop where the ground was growing marshy. He started talking, as if picking up on a conversation we had had moments before, when we had not been talking of it at all.

'I don't remember my parents,' he said. 'I am not even sure what happened to them. It was never very clear whether I was purchased as an infant or born to a mother from whom I was later taken away. No one wanted to tell me, or thought that I should even have the right to know. I was kept as a pet, I suppose, by an old lady, whose husband was quite rich. I think they owned factories in Sheffield and Leeds.'

I realised what he was doing: he was telling me of his childhood enslaved. Once he had told me never to ask an African about it, but now he wanted to tell me. He felt able to reveal the truth of who he was to me, because in doing so, we would get to understand each other more. 'The lady pretended to love me and often told her friends how much she loved me, yet when no one was looking, she liked to pinch me, to say cruel things.' I wondered what things a woman would call a child she

147

pretended to love. 'She would slap my face if I made a mistake, or hold my hand over a candle until my skin burned.' He turned his hand over to show me his palm; he did it so quickly that I did not know if it was for me to see some mark, or for him to remember. 'Eventually, I learned never to cry, no matter what she did to me. One day, when I was sixteen or so, I found out that her husband intended to send me to Jamaica, where he was free to sell me, because I was no longer any use as a pet. I was too old at sixteen. I did not want to go to Jamaica, to be whipped to death in a field of sugar. I knew I had to do whatever I could to prevent that.'

'What did you do?'

'One night, I ran away. I left at night because they never locked the house. I had been there since I was a child. They did not expect me to run away. It didn't occur to them to lock the house, to lock me in, because it did not occur to them that I could make plans of my own, and perhaps until that moment, neither did I. But one night I waited until they went to bed, and I stole some money, enough to get me on a public coach to London, and I ran, and I ran, and I ran.'

'They never came after you?'

He shook his head. 'It was the last years before the Act abolishing the Trade. If they pursued me, they risked letting it be known they were shipping their household slaves back to Jamaica. They wouldn't risk that.'

'Is it illegal to do that?'

'Men do it all the time, but they do not want the world to know they do it. And remember, John, these people are all certain that they are good people. Not one of them thinks they are bad.' I did not like that he had said that, but I let him say it. 'They accepted their loss, I suppose.' He laughed bitterly to himself. 'Which was all I was to them, in the end. A thing. A property lost.'

His words were so bleak, I could not bear it, and I know it's because my own childhood was so defined by such lies, such loss, but I wanted to say something to comfort him. 'Perhaps she did care for you, the old lady, and she wanted you to escape.'

I knew at once from his intense stare that he did not want or need that comfort. 'At some point, John, you will have to accept that people are exactly what their actions imply, not what you want their actions to mean.' What people need, then, is not comfort but to be allowed to speak the truth.

Amid endless trees, so deep in the forest, the sunlight turned green. I was just gazing at him. It was so quiet there, not a soul around. And so, right then, I decided to speak the truth, too: 'I am in love with you, Ned.'

The words just slipped out of me, as easily as air exhaled.

'What?' he whispered in genuine surprise.

'I am in love with you, Ned. I have been falling in love with you since that first day at the Obelisk. You are the most wonderful person I have ever met. Last night, I was holding you in your sleep, and I felt so happy and so complete. I'm sorry. I'm sorry, if it's too much, but it's true, and I want you to know the truth, which is . . .' I gulped. 'Which is that I love you and I feel as if I am a better man for loving you.'

His eyes were so very wide, his lips had parted, I heard his breathing. There was such amazement on his face, almost shock, that I did not know how he would react. Then he stepped forwards, and took my face, cupped it in his hands, and kissed me.

Chapter Ten
or
Love

May blooms . . .

The first week of every month, my wife, Mrs Church, received a note from her father's bank, on Threadneedle Street, that she should receive a drawn-cheque which she had to go and cash. As her husband, I was required to go and sign for it; legally, a married Englishwoman may own nothing for herself, of course. In truth, her father resented very deeply that I might control her money. In anguished letters, he asked how his well-born daughter had found herself in such a state, with such a penurious beast of a man. ('What is a man? What is a woman? Answer me that, errant child!' he wrote to her several times, over several years.) The days where we lived on this drawn-cheque were long gone; I paid our rent now. I don't know if my wife told him that, though.

Although my wife did not come to the Obelisk to hear me preach, she liked to walk in the street with me, she liked the world to see me as her husband – the tall, handsome preacher at her side; what performances we had become. It was in the preparation of these walks that she and I maintained some semblance of intimacy, or at least, civility. My wife liked to dress with care when she went out. She liked to read about new fashions in journals from France, for with her education, she could quite effortlessly read French. (Autodidactic, self-created me, I cannot read a word.) She would ask me, quite sweetly: 'Husband, will you kindly help me with my dress?' She had grown up with servants – as any person of any financial substance does – but now all she had was me. 'I do not even have a maid,' she would say, hardly hiding her bitterness.

The day in May my wife and I were to go to cash the drawn-cheque, we stood in our rooms, able to hear the whispered gossip of our landlords and their customers through the floor-boards. I hooked up the back of the bodice of her cream after-noon dress, of which she was very fond, then helped her get the matching jacket over her shoulders. She put on her bonnet and tied its pale blue bow under her chin, twirled fashionable ring-lets down around her cheeks. Turning to look at me, already dressed in a coat with a white cravat tied tight, she put out her hands to show herself to me: 'Well?'

'Most elegant,' I said.

My wife pulled her face into a pout. 'John, a man must never say a woman is elegant. "Elegant" is *never* a manly word.' My wife said these things to shame me, to remind me of the sins we had once confessed to each other, which she suspected, cor-rectly, I had been unable to suppress.

Outside the weather was warm – a hot London spring sun-shine on people's backs. Hawthorn was blooming cream-white on trees here and there. We walked all the way from The Cut towards the High Street in the Borough. Even in the very worst parts of Southwark, my wife held her head high, on occasion nodding to ladies whom she thought 'appropriate'. Now and then she commented on the beauty of someone's dress, the fineness of the needlework. We talked of what we might do after we went to the bank.

'I thought perhaps we could go over to Mayfair later, to look at the new shops,' she said. That district had, in my own life-time, replaced the old City as the smartest place to go shop-ping. My wife liked to go there to daydream of the ladies of society – all those Augustas and Georgianas – who stepped out of coaches and exchanged greetings with old friends. 'Where shall we luncheon, husband?'

'Wherever we wish. If you wish to go over to Mayfair, we can eat at the Hindoostanee Coffee House there. They say it is the best.' My wife liked to eat a curry from India. This place had barely been open a year; it was a sensation.

'O, no, I would like to eat sooner, I think.'

We were near the Monument. I knew my wife liked a chop-house on the corner of Pudding Lane and Eastcheap. We went there and sat down in a bright bay window that faced out onto Pudding Lane itself, and ordered cuts of lamb in a thick stew of onions, which we ate with a glass of porter ale.

As we sat there, she chattered this way and that. My wife said she was going to buy herself a new coat, or else perhaps a fur stole, or a hat with a peacock feather. She had seen one on a lady in the street lately; the feather had been long and as white as fresh snow. How nice it would look, with a white jacket too. 'Or ivory or cream . . .' She said she also wanted to buy some novels; she had finished hers.

I was not listening. I fell into my thoughts, swirling, tumbling, of Ned. I wondered where he was sitting now. I wondered what he was doing. *Is he thinking about me? Perhaps he is not thinking of me at all. Why should he be?* my mind whispered. *Why should he not?* it whispered again. I had told him I loved him. Is that not narcotic to the unloved, to be told you are loved? *I love you*: to be told it, and to say it too. I dreamed of possible futures in other places, to which we could flee, me and him: Cambridge, Edinburgh, New York, the moon. How would we do it, how should we escape? I could leave a note for my wife, saying, 'You are free, go well, tell everyone I died, keep your money, I don't want a penny, marry again, have children, stop drinking, *live a happy life*.' Ned had said he was on a journey, but aren't we all, precisely to that point: to find a way to live our lives. 'Husband!' Still I was not listening.

I tried to picture my wife opening this note; an image of her smiling flickered through my head. Maybe she would run through the streets to some secret lover I did not know she had, bang on his door and whisper, 'He's gone. We are free.' I would not begrudge her her freedom. '*John!*' she cried, and finally my reverie broke. 'Are you not listening to me? I was telling you my sister's baby was born!'

I gathered myself back, sadly, into reality. 'Truly?'

'Isn't it marvellous news? A boy to replace poor little Edgar, their firstborn.'

'The Lord has blessed them,' I said. Their first baby had died, two weeks old.

'I received a letter.' Her eyes flicked up at me, with a certain meanness. 'I expect you were out all day, and I forgot or fell asleep before you got back.' Her eyes were on mine, and then they were not. 'I thought I might go to visit her in Surrey. I have not seen her for a few years. I should like to see my little nephew.' Her eyes moved up again, this time more searchingly. 'Should *you* like to come with me, husband?' She knew full well I should not. Her family would want me there even less; they despised me. I said I could not, and she did not resist. 'I shall go for perhaps a week and spend time with her and her children, and perhaps my other sister will come up from Hampshire, I am not sure—'

The most extraordinary thought rushed at me then, ecstatic, revelatory, crazily urgent. It was all I could do not to throw down my knife and fork, stand up and cry *hallelujah*. I was so transfixed by this little slice of genius that my wife must have picked up on my brilliant self-absorption. I heard her cry out: 'John! Aren't you *even now* listening to what your poor wife is telling you?'

No, I thought. *I am not listening to you at all.*

★

The next days passed in a blur of excitement. I told Ned nothing of my plan. On the day of her departure to her sister's, I walked my wife to the carriage stop at Marshalsea and waited with her whilst the coach south was loaded. She reminded me she would be gone a week. If only she knew: the day she was leaving, and the day she would return, were carved on my brain. As soon as the carriage wheels were out of sight, my excitement overwhelmed me. From there, I walked the few minutes to Mint Street, where I knocked at Ned's door. He seemed a little surprised to see me there, and said – in something of a panic – I could not come in. His room-mate was in their digs. I did not mind; I told him merely to bring a change of clothes with him to chapel the next day. 'A change of clothes?' I nodded and smiled. 'But why?' 'Just bring it,' I said. If he was shocked to see me there, I wrong-footed him by not staying, merely turning and calling: 'See you tomorrow, Ned.'

He duly arrived the next day just before noon with a hessian bag tied to a stick over his shoulder. He asked me why he had brought it, and I told him to wait and see. The afternoon passed with us looking at the chapel accounts and him asking me questions about where this money had gone, how that money was spent. I would struggle to remember at the best of times, but now it was almost impossible to think of it at all.

We worked for two hours, then I said it was time for us to leave. I pointed to his hessian bag, which he had set down on the ground. 'Where are we going, John?' he asked. 'You cannot afford to keep going and staying at country inns.' Saying nothing, I pointed at the bag again with a big theatrical gesture.

We walked the mile or so. He gave up asking where we were going, for each time, I pressed a finger to my lips. Finally, we arrived at our destination: The Cut, only moments from the cake shop. We walked through the clumps of filthy children playing in the road, past the body of a cat crushed under a carriage's wheels. A trio of cut-purses hanging around on a corner watched us passing with fixed eyes, until one, at the very last moment, straightened up and said: 'Good day, Reverend, sir.' We came to the cake shop, and stood outside.

'Cake?' he asked quizzically, an amused tone in his voice. 'You brought me to buy a cake?' For the last time, I put my finger to my lips and playfully shushed him. I walked to the shop's door and pushed it open, so that he could walk inside. His body passed mine, him glancing up at me and shaking his head at my silliness. Only entering the shop did he stop, seeing two white-haired dumplings staring back at him with some shock.

'Reverend Church!' Mr Gee exclaimed, but he was staring straight at Ned. It could not be the first time an African stood in that shop.

'This is my assistant at the chapel, Ned,' I said, and Mr Gee went 'O!' as if that explained everything. 'He has come to help me with the chapel accounts.' I gave a tight sort of laugh, aware of what risk I was taking; I was not so stupid not to imagine that there was a great deal of risk. Yet still, I knew, I would take it. 'They are . . . they are in quite a state, for I am no clerk. Ned is a very experienced account-keeper. He has been a great asset.'

'I see!' said Mr Gee. The four of us hung there in a weird, spacey silence. 'My wife has gone to visit her sister in Surrey for some days.' I smiled. 'We are going to take the opportunity to do some work.'

'I see!' Mr Gee offered again. The awkwardness did not lift.

'Welcome, Master Ned,' Mrs Gee said. 'Should you like a pie?'

I turned to look at Ned playfully, to ask, *Should you . . . ?* But he seemed so anxious and confused that I said nothing. We said good day to the Gees then walked up the stairs at the back of the shop to my rooms above. I could hardly breathe; my pulse was beating in my throat like a drum. 'John,' Ned hissed as we walked along the landing of the first floor, too low to be heard downstairs. 'John, what is this?'

Saying nothing, I put the key in the door. As the lock released, I turned towards him. Our faces were close; I leaned forwards and kissed him softly. Briefly he let his body fall against me, but then he pushed me away from him. As I moved out of the kiss, I raised my eyebrows teasingly and whispered: 'This is ours, Ned.'

When we were both through the door, I pressed it closed again. 'John, is this your home?' he asked, already knowing the answer. I said nothing, taking a step forwards and pushing him up to the wall next to the door. We started kissing deeply, but then he turned his face to one side, with a startled realisation. 'What are you doing, John? I can't be here.'

'Why not?'

'Because it is your home, it is her home! This is a madness!'

I shook my head. 'My wife is away for a week. It is ours for a whole week.'

He pushed my weight off him. 'That is not the point, John. This is her home, your home with her. I cannot be here. What about your landlords?'

'What about them?' I asked airily.

He turned, craning his head to look into the main sitting room, its table where we ate, the rows of books, a couple of chairs, the chaise where it was my custom to sleep. I could hear his heavy, nervous breathing.

'For the next week, this can be our home,' I said. It was almost as if he was holding his breath. 'It's ours. We will live here as any couple might.'

He walked fully into the room, then turned to look at interconnecting doors. There was the bedroom where my wife – and sometimes I – slept. His eyes widened to see the large bed:

'I – I should go, John.' But I knew he was not going to. I knew, in moments, he was going to let me fuck him on that same bed.

He turned to look at me, and his eyes were misty with hunger and trepidation. 'Two days,' he said, as if in a conversation we were not having.

'What?'

'Two days. I cannot stay all week. Your landlords will suspect.'

I knew he was right. Even I can see what's sensible *sometimes*. 'Two days but three nights,' I said, smiling at him, and he laughed.

'All right,' he said. *All right*: the same neutral way he always said it.

*

On the first morning I awoke, my body alerted by the proximity of his body in bed with me. I felt his weight against the mattress, a different tension in the sheets that stretched across us, then I remembered what had happened. The day before returned to me: coming back to my rooms above the cake shop, speaking with the Gees, Ned coming upstairs, and the two of us moving down onto the bed. In the evening, we walked along the southern shore of the Thames, west of the Bridge. Going down onto the sand of its little beaches, the river was low enough to show the shingle underneath. Afterwards, we had returned to this bed and stayed there ever since.

Instinctively, before I had even turned my head, my hands slid across the bed, and my knuckles touched his body, the leanness of his hip, its smooth, warm skin. Opening my eyes, there he was, asleep in my bed, the sheet pulled up over his body and half of his head; his slim, bony feet stuck out from the sheet's other end. I blinked a little and watched his shape rising and falling, the living breath in his body. I felt so completely, so perfectly, happy in that moment, as if nothing could intrude upon us.

I let out a long breath and felt my own emotion, in that way that you do not expect it. It was that which awakened him. He half turned, looking back towards me. He laughed a little, putting his hands over his face. 'O, was I snoring?'

I smiled. 'No, no, not at all.'

'My room-mate says I snore sometimes, but I think it's only because I say he does. He comes home drunk and snores like an ironworker's hammer.'

'No snoring,' I said. 'And no farting in the night, you were the perfect houseguest.' His hands fell away from his face; he laughed again, but now riotously, scandalised.

'Are you hungry?' I asked.

He nodded, crinkling up his nose. 'We ate no supper last night.' I had forgotten that; perhaps I had not even noticed that we had not eaten. I was not thinking of anything else by that stage. He pulled himself into an upright position, the sheet falling away from his body to reveal the concave slimness of his stomach and chest. He ran his hand over the top of his head. 'O, my hair,' he said.

'What about it?'

'It's a mess.' One side of his hair had flattened against the pillow overnight. His fingers started softly teasing its ends so that they would release their shape. 'I should cut it.'

'Don't cut it,' I said. 'I like it like that.' He was pulling its ends with light, quick fingers, absent-mindedly before me, in this small intimate way. And that was what I liked: that absent-minded intimacy that now existed between us.

★

That first day we did not leave my rooms before evening. The afternoon passed in idle conversation and then lovemaking again. We waited until the Gees had shut up their shop before venturing out to find some dinner, eating at a tavern past the

158

Blackfriars Road, on Stamford Street. We sat near a window where you could see the open fields on which they had not yet built (but were going to soon), so that sunset shimmered over the rippling marshland, its sparse clumps of brush. We left and picked our way over that marshland, a very circuitous way home, and we told each other funny stories, and tried not to slip from the sodden clods of ground, but when we did, we laughed, and his laughter was so joyous and carefree, it patterned the very air with happiness.

*

On the second morning, we made love yet again. Afterwards, with my body naked over his, my chest and stomach over his back and buttocks, he sighed happily. 'I like to feel your weight on me, John. I like to feel your weight *on top* of mine. I wish I could feel it like this all the time.' His words struck me like a thunderbolt. Lifting my head from him, I looked into his eyes and I could see him react to my intensity. Without blinking, I said, 'We should take a room somewhere, you and I. We shouldn't give this up. We shouldn't let it go. Some small room, where we can meet, and spend time together like this. You could stay there the rest of the time.'

He laughed nervously. 'And who is going to pay for this room?'

'I will! I will start a Saturday morning service and send the collection plate round twice, to raise the rent.'

'You are going to cheat your worshippers, John?'

'No, not *cheat*!' He was acting like it was all so ridiculous, but momentarily I wondered at its possibility. I saw the possibility of a life, a moment filled with sublime moments, all the sublime acts I could perform to show him how much I loved him, so that he could love me back. 'Don't you want to?' I asked, sensing his uncertainty.

'It's not that, John. Is it even possible?'

'Everything is possible, Ned!' I cried, lifting my body up until I was on my knees, naked before him, between his legs. *'Everything!'*

*

The second day started to pass, and so our time together was starting to slip away. My mind was doing its tricks, thinking constantly of this future in which we might actually live together somewhere, some secret world the two of us could build. Even as he talked to me about this or that, all I was thinking, in truth, was of this other life we could have. Of course, it would not be as husband and wife, but in some performance in which we would never be suspected. Could I afford a room somewhere, and how would it work if I went there? It would take a while to raise enough money, I knew, but after a few months, it would be possible. Or even inevitable.

He moved around the room, picking up the books that were strewn about. For a while, he sat in a chair picking through Miss Edgeworth's *Castle Rackrent*, flicking through the pages, his leg hanging over one arm of the chair, his bare foot dangling in mid-air, arched slightly, an absorbed tension. Now and then he read passages aloud; how beautiful his voice was to me now, its lulling depths, its husked-flat northern vowels, its light femininities, soft sibilances.

Picking backwards through the book, until he was almost at the beginning, he read: ' "We cannot judge either of the feelings or of the characters of men with perfect accuracy from their actions or their appearance in public; it is from their careless conversations, their half-finished sentences, that we may hope with the greatest probability of success to discover their real characters,' " and laughed to himself afterwards. 'Did you enjoy this novel?' he asked. 'It seems very radical in its views on Ireland.'

I had never read it; it belonged to my wife. 'I enjoyed it very much,' I said, and yes, it was a lie – I know – but I wanted him to believe that I was the person who might read such a book. He picked up another book and began to look at that. I continued to watch him, his face absorbed in his little game of flicking pages and reading just shards of a story.

'Are you enjoying being here, Ned?'

He looked up at me and smiled broadly. 'Of course. Are you enjoying it?'

'It's wonderful.' His head fell back against the back of the chair and he was gazing at me happily. 'It makes me think again about Vere Street, about the molly house. About how we should enjoy being together in places, spaces, where we are . . .' His eyes had changed; my voice faltered.

'What?' he asked, with his head still tilted backwards but his eyes harder now.

I gulped the word: 'Safe.'

'Safe?' he said back to me. He kept gazing at me for a few seconds, then crinkled up his nose and shook his head. 'I don't think I want to go there.'

'We could spend time together, in a place, as lovers. People could see us in love.'

It was this that made him straighten up a little, lifting into a more upright pose. 'Is that *necessary*, John, that people see us, that people *know* about us?'

I heard it then: his shame. O, it made me sad, for I know how corrosive such shame is, a poison that is spread on the Sodomite's skin from childhood, that seeps slowly through into his flesh, so poisonous.

*

I did not sleep much that night. I thought over and over again about how the two of us might have the flickering possibility of a life together. But how, in a rented room paid for by me doing an extra service at the chapel, the vagaries of a Southwark collection plate? My mind raced, with solutions and problems and fantasies. I wanted this with him. I wanted *someone somewhere* to know that this was what we felt for each other. Why should we not? Because the world disapproved? In my impulsiveness, my impetuosity, I can care nothing for what the world thinks. At least, that is what I'll tell myself.

★

In the morning, the last of him being there, I got up early and left Ned sleeping, to work at my writing desk. When he awoke, he got up and walked across the room towards me. He was naked before me. His long, light form slid onto my lap. I remembered how shy he had been physically that night at Hampstead. Now he appeared before me, like Apollo stepped down from a painting, sent by the gods; a messenger of love dressed in nothing but his own beauty. He kissed my cheek gently. 'I am going back to Mint Street today,' he said. 'You've remembered that, John?'

I turned my face fully to his, so our mouths were only two inches apart. 'Stay another day,' I murmured.

He laughed, as if it were a joke, then kissed my lips. 'I told you I would stay three nights, two days. Don't try to pretend you have forgotten. I know you well enough, John. Don't try to shift the terms now.'

'Try to shift the terms?'

His forehead fell against mine. 'I have loved being here, John, but we said three nights and two days, so we go back to normal now. It is important to me that I am not compelled to do things I do not wish to do. I want to keep to terms I agree, and not to be compelled to do things that are not part of my own . . .' He paused. '. . . autonomy.' His spirit changed, into something

162

lighter. 'Besides, my landlady might clear my things if she thinks I've moved on.'

'She won't. Don't be foolish.'

'O, she will, she brooks no nonsense.'

I wanted to ask him, if I found one, would he take that room. But I did not ask. He slipped from my lap and padded back to the bed, folding himself down onto the mattress, but with his head and shoulders propped up against the pillows. He opened his arms to me. He meant that I should lie against him, let him embrace me. For a moment, I felt afraid. That was not our role: I was the man. I was the embracer. 'Come on, John,' he said. 'Come to me.' I knew I would go. I got up and, fully dressed, lay down against his naked body. He parted his legs so that I crumpled into his form. He placed a kiss through my hair. I felt his ribs and the muscles of his chest and his sinewy, slim arms folding around me. Gradually, I let my weight go so that it sank into his, and he drew me tighter into that embrace. And then I realised the saddest thing: I didn't think anyone had ever held me like that, in thirty years of life. I tried to think back through my life – my native mother, my fake mother, William Webster, the gilder, the endless parade of lovers and johns I had had, my poor wife – I don't think *anyone* had ever held me like that.

*

Understand this: I wanted only for us to be happy, him and me.

Chapter Eleven

or

I Am Not A Woman!

A Sunday evening, in the same May . . .

A glorious evening light fell over London the next Sunday, burnishing the city's west-facing windows. After an afternoon working at the chapel, I said to Ned that perhaps we could go for a walk. 'Down by the river?' he asked, but carefully I said, 'Let's walk into town.' As we drifted towards the river, every part of the sky west of us was a riot of red, purple and gold, and our skin was bathed in the gilding light. Sabbath day, the day of rest, yet the Southwark streets were busy with fashionable types' carriages heading back from Brighton for the week. We did not cross on the old London Bridge but the 'new' West-minster one – already sixty years old, but that did not stop Londoners calling it that. As we crossed, ordinary folk were walking in great number to the south side against the tide of seaside returners, dressed up for Sunday and pink-eyed with grog. They were going to the Pleasure Gardens at Vauxhall, that louche place, once quite grand. Now the Gardens were famous for raucous public singing and dancing, wandering fingers in private places. Back in the last century, as I told you, it was a very smart thing to go and dance with mollies in full women's clothing there, but now of course, to do so would only invite violence.

We walked up Whitehall and the Strand. He did not know

where we were going; I had not told him. His mood seemed very light; light as air, as people say. I knew he was happy just to be with me, in that moment; those few days at The Cut had been a good time for us, had deepened our mutual understanding. We turned off Drury Lane, to cross Princes Street and pass through the maze of alleys that were Clare Market. The light was fading into golden shadows, causing him to ask why we were in that part of town at that time of day, just when its reputation grew darker. I did not answer. In moments, we were on the end of Vere Street, standing outside the White Swan. And so my trick was revealed, to you at least; not quite yet to him.

Through the great tavern windows, I could see James Cook, tall and brooding, standing at the bar, in animated conversation with other men. Presently he became aware of someone watching them and turned and looked straight at me. He did not acknowledge me in any way, his eyes just held mine for a moment, close, conspiratorial, disdainful. He returned to his fellows; someone must have made a joke, for they were now all laughing that hard, mean laughter shared among Normal men.

'Why on earth are we in Clare Market at night, John?' Ned asked me, returning my attention to him. He was always alert to the possibility of violence, it seemed, but I just smiled at him.

'This is it,' I said.

He did not get my meaning. 'This is what?'

'This is the molly house.'

Confusion swept his face. He glanced into the windows of the White Swan, filled with ordinary drinkers, then back at me, flat with shock. I thought he would be happy I had done it, but instead he spoke with naked anger: 'You have tricked me, John!'

'What? No! Ned, no . . . I just want you to see it—'

'But I told you I didn't want to come. Why didn't you listen?'

At this, I became harder. 'I *did* listen, Ned. I absolutely did listen, and in fact, you told me you would think about coming.'

I could see the confusion on his face. 'Did I?' In fact, he had not said he would. The confusion cleared. 'No, I told you I didn't want to come.'

His eyes searched mine angrily. I saw the tension around his mouth. 'You don't have to go in if you don't want to,' I said, but if I am honest, I did not mean it; I wanted him to come inside and see the world we had created there.

Finally, he spoke: 'If I go inside with you this time, will you stop trying to force me to come?'

'Ned, I am not forcing you.'

His jaw seemed so set. 'That is precisely what you have done, John.' He still buzzed with some anger but then something in him relented, but only resentfully. 'I will go in with you this time, and if I do not want to come again, you will respect my wishes.' He was not asking questions. 'Promise this, John. Promise me this, or we should stop this.'

'Stop what?'

'Stop all of this, John. All of what goes on between us.'

I felt such horror that he could even say it. 'All right,' I said. *All right.*

We walked around to the side entrance, and from there up the stairs to the door into the molly house. I put my face up to the spyhole and rapped three times. 'Who is it?' came the voice from within; it was Philip Kett. An eye appeared in the glass; the eye and nothing else.

'John Church.'

The door unbolted. Philip Kett let us in. 'That's not the code, Reverend, and you know it.' He looked at Ned, not with surprise but weariness. 'Is he trade?'

'No,' I spat. 'Are you?' I did not even know if Ned knew what the word meant, but he looked at Kett with some trepidation.

We walked through to the main room, where Mrs Cook was standing drying glasses with a cloth. 'Who's this, then?' she cooed, her eyes filled with interest.

'This is Ned,' I said. Mrs Cook almost licked her lips with intrigue. 'It is Ned's first time at a molly house, so be gentle with him, Mrs Cook.'

She gave him a warm smile and let her hand brush his arm kindly. 'Well, it's very nice to meet you, Ned. I hope you will enjoy it here, and if there is anything you want, just ask me. Don't be nervous, either. The queens are as good as gold. Their bark is worse than their bite.' Ned glanced at me as she said this, whilst politely thanking her for her welcome. Mrs Cook turned to Kett. 'Philip, go and get Jimmy and tell him that Reverend Church is here. He wants to speak to the Reverend.' I wondered then if James Cook's looking at me earlier had suggested more than I'd imagined. Kett went off whilst Mrs Cook asked Ned if he wanted to see the rest of the molly house, implying that he should leave us alone for a few minutes. When he was gone, she pulled a chair towards me as if to make a conspirator's whisper.

'Have you heard the rumours from the palace?'

'Palace . . . ? What rumours should I hear from a palace?'

Her husband appeared and swaggered across the room towards me. He did not offer to shake my hand, merely dragged a chair towards himself. 'Does he know?' he growled.

I was beginning to tire of this mystery. 'Know what?'

And so Mrs Cook told me of a story heard around town, but which had not been published in the newspapers yet; it was being suppressed, apparently. The official story was that the Duke of Cumberland had awoken in his palace apartments in the night hearing someone screaming. Quickly, in the official story's version, he realised that a person – a man – was in the room with him, meaning to attack him with a knife. Rising, under blows, the Duke realised the attacker was none other than Mr Sellis. Most dramatically of all, Mr Sellis had slit his own throat. As even this story unfolded, I thought it all incredible . . . until Mrs Cook told me what was being whispered around town.

The palace servants, alerted by the screaming, had arrived to find the Duke covered in wounds and Mr Sellis bleeding to death – naked in the Duke's arms. The coroner reported Sellis's throat was cut by a right hand; but Mr Sellis was left-handed, and a person is unlikely to be strong enough to slit their own throat with their weaker hand. Other whispers were blooming now: Mr Sellis's clothes were found hanging in the Duke's closet; the Duke could not explain why, refused to; the Irishman Mr Neale had vanished from London, allegedly at the Duke's order, fleeing to his native land.

So the *real* story, the *deep* story, was this: the Duke had drawn Mr Sellis and Mr Neale to enter into a *ménage à trois* but Mr Sellis had rebelled. He had made ultimatums to his lover, the Duke, who had refused them. And now he was dead. I remembered that night he had told me about the commitment to love. Love requires radical action, he'd said. What had Sellis done, or what had been done to him, if he had issued foolish threats?

There was no chance to say anything else. The moment the tale was done, Ned walked back into the room. We all turned, in a sudden bolt, to look at him. He gazed at us nervously by return, confused by our alarmed eyes. Mrs Cook got up and said to him in a bright, sweet voice: 'Can I get you something to drink, lovey?'

He looked at me then back at her. 'May I have a cordial?'

Mrs Cook glanced at me, with the edge of one who is not sure if a person is joking. Had anyone asked for a cordial at a molly house before? She looked back at Ned: 'Of course, you can, lovey. Of course you can.'

She walked towards the bar, and Ned stood beside her, to

receive his glass, leaving me with James Cook. 'What does all of this mean?'

He looked at me as if I was the stupidest person in the world. 'Don't you see? It means we have some *leverage*.'

'Leverage?'

'Against Cumberland, should we need it.'

I did not understand at all. 'Why do *we* need leverage against Cumberland?'

He shrugged. 'Who knows?' Then he grinned maliciously. 'But there is always a way to profit from things, or perhaps if you need to defend yourselves.' I felt very strongly that I did not want to know what he meant, not at all.

The queens began to arrive at half past seven. There were no 'real' weddings that night, but I knew that there might be weddings of the other sort. In the way of the house, when people entered, they had a quick look around the space to see who was there. Although there were new folk coming all the time by then, Ned earned long, lustful looks from some. He hardly seemed to understand why men were looking at him. I, who had rented on the streets, who spent half my life in places like this, knew all too well. He had no awareness of his beauty; none at all. Or maybe, even, he was afraid of it, of what his beauty might bring him.

Eventually, Mrs Cook stood on the lower rung of a stool and clapped her hands. 'Will the ladies *please* prepare!' There was much laughter and a stampede of feet off to the dressing room. I noted the Duchess of Gloucester had not come that night. I hoped she had not been caught up in the events at the palace. In a few seconds, the number of people in the main room had halved. I could see Ned's uncertainty; he had no clue as to what was about to happen.

The first queen to appear – first because she wore no wig and little make-up – was Black-Eyed Leonora, in a long blue dress the colour of lapis lazuli, a white turban which glowed like silk, holding a large yellow sunflower. From where had Leonora got a sunflower in London in May? Then came Miss Sweet Lips, tall and loose and lovely – all her native knowing, ambiguous charms on display. Other queens appeared, young and old, beautiful and comical, about eight in total, until at last came Sally, dressed quite prettily in a pink-striped gown but also an ancient, white-powdered wig that looked like the mice had been at it. Miss Sweet Lips spun around and pointed at her: 'Who even wants the key to *her* door?'

Sally grinned happily: 'Gentlemen, it's only a farthing per entry!'

Sweet Lips: 'Still too fucking much!'

Ned was gazing in mute bewilderment. Sally Fox and Miss Sweet Lips took one look at him and were hooked. They sashayed towards us, like two actresses across a stage, perfectly in step.

'Is this your new fellow, then, Johnny boy, the one you've been keeping from us?' Sally cried.

I looked again at him – and he, nervously, at me. I smiled. 'This is Ned.'

'Pleased to meet you,' Ned said to her.

Miss Sweet Lips pouted and preened. 'And what about me, Master Ned? It must be *awfully* nice to meet me.' She let out a purr of a laugh and put her finger in her mouth, letting it hang there, all suggestion.

'Pleased to meet you,' he murmured.

Sally sat herself down beside him, her hip right up to his. She folded her arms to conceal her damaged one. 'How long have *you two* been courting?' She said the word 'courting' like a country grandmother. Black-Eyed Leonora joined us and the mood seemed good; Ned began to relax a little and his soft, gentle presence charmed Sally. But I could sense Sweet Lips growing restive; she liked all eyes to be on her, no one else.

'Are you going to get married tonight, Sweet Lips?' I asked, to give her some attention. She had a glass of rum at her lips and, without removing it, flashed her eyes left and right around the room to see who was in; it was slim pickings.

'I am not making any promises, eh, Reverend?' I laughed a little. Sweet Lips's gaze fell away from me to Ned, who was still chatting to Sally and Leonora. And as she listened to him speak, her voice grew loud and hard, mocking in the queens' way: 'You've got the best of the bunch, *dearie!*' Ned looked up at her, aware that she was speaking to him. 'It's an early night and an end of cucumber for all us other girls.'

'Other girls?' Ned asked. (But thankfully, not 'cucumber'.)

Sweet Lips was marvellous and terrible in equal measure, of course. 'There are those who like to *be* the pipe, and some who like to *take* it, if you get my meaning—'

Sally turned forwards in sharp reprimand. 'A plank of wood could understand it, darling.'

Sweet Lips was not to be dissuaded. 'And we all know that the Reverend here doesn't take no pipe, so why everyone is being mean to me for saying who's got a sore backside and who hasn't, I don't know!'

'Sweet Lips!' I cried. Ned was wide-eyed and mute. Sweet Lips stood above us, like Zeus, dressed like a woman but still chucking thunderbolts.

'*She* was the one who asked who was a girl and who was not, and *she* should learn that *she* is the girl!'

Ned was all confusion. 'Why are you calling me "she"?'

Sally chimed in: 'Shut your hole, Sweet Lips!'

'Ha!' Sweet Lips cried. 'I only wish I still could, dearie! But the truth is men have dicks, and girls take dicks. That's the law of nature!'

'What about Sapphists?' Leonora asked (not unreasonably).

Sweet Lips was never one to let things cool: 'I am *just* telling *her* who's a woman and who's a man, aren't I?'

Ned's face grew tense. 'I am *not* a woman! Stop calling me "her"!'

Sally decided to come to the rescue. 'O, ignore *her*, Ned, love.' This only made him more confused. Sometimes pronouns are not as helpful as people think. 'She's just jealous 'cos you've got the best one.' Sally patted Ned's arm. 'So is he treating you nice?'

'He is very . . . nice.'

Sweet Lips was having none of it: '*Nice, nice, nice.* Why is everyone so nice? Why can't a man just fuck your brains out any more, who cares about being nice? And you two should know' – she meant Sally and Ned – 'what it's like to get your brains fucked out by his big one!' Ned's eyes were shimmering confusion; he had absolutely no preparation for how the queens talked. Sensing blood in the water, Sweet Lips pointed straight at my crotch. 'We've all heard how big it is but only you and Sally here have had the pleasure of riding it! You must have a hole like the Fleet River sewer by now, dearie!'

I leapt to my feet. 'Sweet Lips, shut up!'

'Ha!' she continued. 'I would love the opportunity to have a canter around on it, but no luck for me!'

Sally: 'Shut it, Sweet Lips!'

Ned was looking at me sharply: 'I think I'd like to leave, John.'

'Forget her!' I cried.

Sweet Lips: 'O, charming, I'm sure!'

'She is just playing with you,' I tried to reason, but Ned's face was suddenly cold fury.

'I – I just want to leave,' he murmured. And at that very moment, as if things were not going badly enough, James Mann, the slippery friend of Tommy White, appeared at our table, to deliver the absolute fucking *coup de grâce*. 'Philip Kett has drunk too much and is getting his cock out!'

Sweet Lips positively whooped. 'Unfurl the monster!' The crowd was parting to reveal the scene, as surely as the curtains on a Drury Lane theatre stage. There, Philip Kett, also known as Lady Godiva, of the famously large member, looking like he had been drinking steadily all through the evening, was pulling off his clothes, whilst all around him, the denizens of Vere Street clapped as if at a country jig.

'I am leaving,' Ned spat. He did not say another word. Getting to his feet, he quickly pushed his way through the room, past the ridiculous scene at hand. I called his name but he did not stop, did not look back, the door was open. He disappeared down the stairs, and I chased after him.

He ran down Vere Street, onto Portugal Street. I followed after him calling his name, pushing through milling bodies, trying to get him to stop, until we were almost up to Lincoln's Inn Field. On Newman's Row, in the blackness along the high stone wall that bounds off Lincoln's Inn, we were suddenly completely alone. Only then, released from the eyes of others, did he slow down and let me catch up with him. We came to a stop, an exhausted heap. There were no lights around there, no shops, few houses, the street was empty and dark. The night was perfectly quiet, almost the only such spot in London. He was blinking slowly. I could see his anger.

'Don't mind Miss Sweet Lips or Sally or any of them,' I said. 'They don't mean any harm. I know it's all very cheeky and rude, but honestly, it's just how they talk.'

He took a long breath in. 'You tricked me into coming here. I did not want to. I knew I would not like it, but you would not leave it be. Those people, they were worse than even I could have imagined—'

'Don't say that.'

A single tear running down his cheek glinted in the moonlight; he wiped it away. 'I never want to be forced to do things, go places I don't want to, ever again. My whole life was once being told what to do, being treated like I could not make decisions for myself, not being permitted to, showing nothing, living in fear of someone else's reaction or intention. It's the worst thing now, forcing me to do things I don't want.'

'I'm sorry, Ned. I just wanted you to see it. I thought you might like it.'

'But instead I hate it!' he hissed, and it shocked me, that he said it so hard. He was gazing into the centre of the street, at nothing. His words, when they came, were mean and bitter, words I would never have associated with him before: 'Did you truly do it with that . . . that creature?'

'Who?'

'Sally, whatever he named himself.'

At this, I felt my anger flare. 'Yes! Yes, I fucked her. So what?'

'Him! Don't say "her", say "he", he's a man!'

'Not there she isn't. Not if she doesn't want to be. There she can be a she! It's not up to you to tell her she's not! And yes, I fucked her, and now we are friends, and what of it? Why shouldn't that be? Do you want me to pretend that I was a virgin like you, feel shame like you do! "I am not a woman!" For fuck's sake. Then what are you?'

'A man!'

'Who takes it in the arse!'

I only said it to be cruel, to shut him up, to stop all this, to silence him with shame, I suppose; a very unflattering admission on my part. His eyes flared. 'Then maybe I shouldn't,' he said quietly. He seemed so brittle then; so vulnerable, yet so angry with me too.

'I'm sorry, Ned. Truly, I am sorry. For all of it.'

When he spoke next, it was quite calmly. 'You knew about the coach in Hampstead, didn't you?'

The unexpectedness of his question caught me unawares: 'What . . . ?'

'You knew. You knew on Sundays that there was no late

coach. And you knew about the risk of robbery if we walked home in the dark. You knew that we would have to stay overnight in Hampstead and that I would give myself up to you.'

'No, I swear.'

'I don't believe you, John. I think you have been fooling me all along into thinking these things are innocent, but I am not sure they are. I feel like I am a puppet and you are holding the strings.'

'Don't be ridiculous!' I protested. 'I love you. I wish you trusted me! I wish you could just once show me that you trust me!'

'I don't like lying, John!'

'I did not lie,' I said.

'Yes, this *is* lying. You deceived me into coming here. You ignored what I said about not wanting to come.' We stood there in silence, a clear minute, him just thinking, me just waiting for him to continue. Finally, he did:

'When I was young, John, I was very effeminate. I know I am still sometimes effeminate now, but then, I was almost half a girl, half a boy. To be an effeminate African boy is to be watched every moment of your life. Your whole life, you are aware of people watching you. Sometimes now I think to be like us, and to look like me, you don't have a childhood in this country. Normal people take it from you – they steal it from you, with their violence, their hate, their watching. When you are twelve, thirteen years old and you swing your arms when you are walking on your own, or you sing a song to yourself as you work, or you talk like a girl, they just watch and watch you. O, they will punch you, or call you "faggot", or call you "girl", like that is the lowest thing, but what they do mostly is just watch you. And the watching is the worst thing, precisely because somehow it is quite benign, when in fact, both sides know it is a slow, smirking poison.

'They watch you to remind you of your worthlessness. They watch you to remind themselves of their higher worth. For as long as you are like that – African and effeminate – they are higher than you. If they are African, they are higher than you because they are not effeminate. If they are White and effeminate, they are higher than you because they are not African. If they are White and Normal, then they are the king of kings. So, as a boy, I wondered to myself: how can I change, how can I stop them watching me? I could do nothing about being African, so I realised I would have to stop myself being effeminate. And it became my life's task, and I gave my whole life to it, for many months. I practised, every free moment I had to myself – for I was enslaved and had so few – how to walk differently, how to speak differently, how to stop my hands moving when I talked, how never to sing a song I liked, or never to comment on a pretty colour or piece of fabric.'

There were tears in his eyes now as his eyes ran along the ground, trying to avoid my gaze. 'I killed that girlish boy I was, John. You say I feel shame, and you are right. Firstly, I am ashamed that I killed that girlish boy, but secondly I am still ashamed that I was ever him. All my life, John, I have been ashamed of who I am, and what I feel. And to be among those people, who are so proud, and so fearless, I felt only my double shame. And I was angry because you made me come here and feel this shame, even if that was not what you intended.' All I wanted to do was to hold him. The tears cleared. 'After my childhood, after everything I have had to fight for, I want to feel safe, John. I don't want to feel at risk, from others, or even from myself. I was so happy those few days we spent together in your rooms. I felt that I could trust you to make me safe, to protect me and love me . . .'

'I will always protect you, Ned.'

He looked up at me suddenly. 'I want to believe that, John.'

There seemed nothing left to say, at least that would not make things worse. I moved against his body and he sank against the barrier of the high stone wall, receiving my kisses, there in that empty, dark spot. Our faces close, I could hear him breathing slowly, cautiously. 'I want love, John,' he said softly. 'I want love, and I want someone to respect my wishes, and my limits.'

'And your autonomy,' I said, and he smiled a little, so sweetly. I had said the right thing. I reached out to take his hand in mine, there in the silent, lonely darkness of that part of town. We began to walk, hand in hand, unseen because there was no one around to see. To men like us, the dark offers safety from the eyes of others. His fingers began gripping my palm more tightly. But after not as much as a hundred yards, I saw a figure in the distance, in the night. There was just enough moonlight to reveal him staring at us. Ned pulled his hand from mine. Only then did I realise who it was: Mr Linehan.

I had forgotten he lived up this way. That was why I had seen him when the molly was murdered just down the road at Bell Yard. Had he seen us, two men holding hands, in the dark?

'Reverend Church!' he cried as we came into each other's view. His face bothered, seeing Ned. 'This is your *African assistant*!' He said the words with a scandalised urgency.

'Mr Linehan,' I said, shocked, feeling like we were exposed. The man shook his head, as if it were all too confusing.

'Why are ye here, like this, in this place, with this . . . person, whose name I forget . . .'

'Ned,' I said – stupidly. (Why did I say his name?)

'That's right,' Mr Linehan said. 'Ned.' (It was so stupid that I said his name.)

'We have been to a church meeting, Mr Linehan.'

The man's brow furrowed, all malice and suspicion. I heard the drone start low in my head. 'Which church around here is open at this time of night? I know them all.'

The drone is caused by panic, but then hearing it only makes me panic even more. 'St Clement Danes,' I gabbled, not thinking. It was a ruin of a place near the White Swan, empty for years. At once, Mr Linehan looked even more brutishly confused.

'What kind of service goes on at Clement Danes any more? I thought it was a haven for derelicts of all sorts these days. Does it even have a vicar appointed?' Mr Linehan looked at Ned again; his eyes were all horror. The drone suddenly grew so loud, as if my head was about to split open. 'I don't know what this is *at all*, Reverend Church! I don't understand any of this at all! I shall speak to ye Sunday about this, Reverend.' He nodded to himself, in some confirmation of his own morality. 'I shall speak to ye Sunday!'

It was too much, this threat. I felt my rage overwhelm me, blind me, turn me mad. I lunged forwards and pushed the man so hard in the shoulder, he started to stumble backwards. 'You know what, Linehan! Don't come back! Never fucking come back to the Obelisk! You are a snivelling, conniving hypocrite, and I despise you, and I never want to lay eyes on you again, all right? That's what you can take for next Sunday, me telling you if I ever see you again, I will rip your fucking head off!' I pulled my hand back as if to throw a punch. Linehan squealed like a piglet before the blade. 'Now fuck off before me and my *African* assistant kick your arse down Fleet Street!'

Mr Linehan was gazing at me with open shock. His lips started to mewl but made no sound; he turned and scampered away, whining at the night. I turned to look at Ned, who was looking at me in the most ghostly way.

'You shouldn't have done that, John,' was all he said.

I was afraid that he might be right. 'Come on,' I said to him instead, hiding my fears. 'Come on, let's go.' This time, I did not offer to hold his hand.

I walked Ned home all the way to Mint Street. He said that his room-mate was away, out of town for a night or two. He said he wanted me to come inside. I had not expected him to. I had thought he might reject me, but instead he took me inside. In his tiny, empty garret room, the two of us for the first time lay on his bed, and I fucked him, until dawn was blinking in the windows. And staring into the miracle of his eyes, almost ready to ejaculate inside him, I said to him: 'I will always protect you, Ned. I will always keep you safe.' He just smiled, as if he did not know why I said it, but to me, it felt like an oath.

*

O, and there is one more thing that I need to tell you. I *did* know about the last coach on Sundays in Hampstead.

I'm sorry, but I did . . .

Chapter Twelve

or

Disaster Strikes

May turns itself into June, then June becomes July . . .

The weeks that followed were itchy and strange. I had the sense
that the wider world around us had rearranged itself. Mr Linehan had made threats about what he was going to say that
Sunday and I had told him never to come back, but in the cold
wasteland of the morning after anger, I knew that he needn't
stay away just because I'd said so. I knew he could come hammering at my chapel door, like Martin Luther with his endless
constipations, or much worse, the Patrol. The rearrangement,
then, was of threat.

All week, I felt the trepidation of what I would say or do, if
he came, stood up in the pews and yelled: 'This *so-called* reverend has many questions to answer about his *assistant!*' Ned was
shivery with fright the whole time, and talked about not coming
on Sunday. I had to be quite firm with him – I may even have
shouted – to tell him it was essential he came. Not coming was
the most dangerous thing of all. When I said that, he became
annoyed; it was my actions that had endangered us, he cried. I
was amazed at such an accusation.

Yet Mr Linehan never returned to the Obelisk after that
night at Lincoln's Inn. Week after week, he did not come. In
those unfurling weeks in which the questions railed through
my head – *Has he left? Is he not coming back?* – I began to have

unsettling, intense dreams of Mr Linehan, night after night, as I had once about my abandoning mothers. Sometimes he came to me at the Obelisk, in the dream, and he made accusations, and sometimes he asked me to kiss him. If I refused, he went to the Patrol. If I relented, I ended up fucking him, revolted but still plentifully hard, which only compounded my sense of disgust. *You're hard now, Reverend, so you might as well stick it in me,* he might grin at me, with all his teeth knocked out. *You're hard now, Reverend, so show me what kind of man you are.*

Other times, he merely appeared in my dream as if to make hissing accusations but never said what he knew about me. It became like a puzzle-game to get him make an accusation but he would never quite say it, so that the dream got sweatier, more infuriating, never resolved. Still more times, he came and then, as I tried to placate his accusations, a crowd of listeners would be revealed, behind a curtain, and I would be exposed and arrested. Then again, at the very last moment, with slobbering lips, he would whisper to me: *Kiss me, Reverend, Sally Fox told me all about you, kiss me, Reverend, she told me what you have between your legs, make me a woman with it, Reverend, just like you made your African assistant a half-girl again.*

Mr Linehan haunted me; *haunts me.*

★

A London summer arrived, all hot, sunlit days and warm, soupy nights. Life at Vere Street, in the White Swan, continued. Although some faces started to change, others stayed the same (Sally, Leonora, Sweet Lips, and I suppose me). Ned came back close to me, remained working at the chapel, and we continued to give ourselves to our passions. He always said he did not want to return to the molly house, and said to me that he was sorry, it was not his world. I hid my disappointment. He never once asked me not to go, though.

One Sunday, after a well-attended service, Ned and I cleared up in the chapel. We worked a long time in silence. 'I was thinking about that room,' I said to him, although in fact, I had not been particularly.

He seemed not to understand. 'What room?'

'I said I should rent a room for you where we could meet.'

He furrowed his brow. 'When, John?'

I could not believe he had forgotten. 'When you were with me on The Cut. I said I should rent a room for us to be together.'

Something hazy, airy, crept into him. I walked up to him and drew him towards me, against my chest, my mouth a couple of inches above his, and I kissed him twice on his lips. 'Everything is going to be all right,' I said to him.

His head moved slightly in its position. 'What do you mean, "all right"?'

'Nothing,' I said. Stupidly, I pulled away from him. He was staring up at me, more concerned than annoyed.

'John, what is going on?'

I felt my chest so tight, airless. 'Let's go away,' I said.

'Overnight somewhere?'

'No, not overnight,' I replied. The thought I had had about he and I running away somewhere, the day I was out walking with Mrs Church, returned to me then. 'Let's go to – I don't know – Cambridge or Edinburgh—'

'For how long—' he began to ask, but I just kept talking:

'Or New York—'

'*New York?*' He gave a laugh that was not a laugh at all but a splash of cold shock. 'What do you mean, go to New York? Do you mean, go away, *to live?*' His face was all cracked confusion. I was aware of how panicked I was making him, what a fool I was being, how I had to appear saner, because this is what had driven people away before.

'Forget it,' I said. 'I'm only joking. It's going to be all right.' His eyes were nothing but disquiet.

The second Sunday in July . . .

I was supposed to perform joke weddings at the molly house on the Friday evening, but I knew I would not go. Somehow a new intensity was gripping me. I could not seem to concentrate, to line up my thoughts in a straight row. I sent a note saying that I was unwell, that the 'weddings' would have to be cancelled. The Sunday, I did not go to the molly house either. I half expected Mrs Cook to send a messenger boy, asking what was going on, but she did not.

Leaving my Sunday service at the Obelisk, I dawdled home, thinking this way and that. I found my wife in our rooms above the cake shop, staring into the mirror on her dressing table, slowly brushing her long hair. She barely turned as I closed the door behind me. Staring at her reflection, she gathered most of her hair back to pull it into a chignon. A few strands were left loose around her face to curl with the hot iron.

'Would you like to go for a walk this afternoon?' I asked. She turned, looking at me; I saw the surprise in her eyes.

'What kindness is this, John?' So rarely she called me John, and when she did, it was because she was happy.

We decided to head towards Vauxhall. From The Cut, you have to walk across open fields first. There are still farm cows at Lambeth, to supply the city with milk. The sun was good that day and my wife, carrying her fashionable parasol, seemed so happy. I helped her step over stones where the ground was still marshy, though they were going to drain it soon, apparently. I took her gloved hand, and at every turn, she said very sweetly, 'Thank you, John, thank you,' and said I was 'a gentleman'.

Six o'clock: my wife said she was tired and wanted to go home but she had had 'a wonderful day'. I asked her what she would like to eat for supper, told her that I could go out and find some pasties or a pie, but she said it was not necessary. She had some bread from the day before and a thick pork broth to soak it in. That would make us a meal. She asked if I would just go out and buy some ale. We ate our supper and she drank her first bottle of ale; I hardly touched mine. Sitting in apparent contentment at our dining table, we played cards with only odd scraps of conversation. I sat and marvelled at how I had had Ned in these rooms, not all that long before. Now it just seemed like a dream, something that had never truly happened. My wife won the hand; she laughed so merrily and asked me if I would play another game.

Nine o'clock: the cake shop was shut but I could hear the Gees still there, talking. Suddenly the door downstairs slammed open, and I heard Mr Gee shout, *'Oi!'* Footsteps clattered up the stairs. My wife and I looked at each other in alarm, as if robbers were about to burst in. There was a banging at the door and a woman's voice, its accent Irish: *'Reverend Church!'* Of course I knew who it was at once. *'Reverend Church!'* Every muscle, every fibre in my body, tightened. Why had Mrs Cook come to my home?

My wife's voice was instant suspicion: 'Who's that?'

'I don't know,' I lied.

Through the door it came again: *'Reverend Church!'* The banging resumed. Through the floorboards I could hear the Gees shouting: *'What's all this? What's all this?'*

My head rushed with thoughts, panic, fear, terror. *Why did she come here? What did it mean? How could she come here? How stupid of her.* I raced to pull the door open, and there she was, her eyes red, her face as grey as death.

'Mrs Cook,' I hissed. 'What's going on?'

'I went to your chapel, Reverend, and a person there told me where to find you. I have a carriage outside.'

'A carriage?' I cried.

My wife was on her feet. 'Who is this, husband? Who is this woman who comes to our home?'

Mrs Cook just stared at me and then at my wife in open-mouthed, trembling horror. Here I was, in my real life (or was it my fake life?). Her eyes drew back to mine, as she gulped twice in terror. 'Reverend Church, the house has been raided. They've arrested everyone.'

'*What . . . ?*'

'Everyone, including my Jimmy.' The first death knell of disaster boomed in my chest. 'Sally, Leonora, Sweet Lips, everyone! Even Philip Kett! Everyone! Everyone has been arrested!' I felt my chest compress, my throat close as if around a knife. It was like that moment just before you faint: lights around the eyes; shifting colours; unable to breathe; the sense that you might be falling. 'Reverend Church!' she cried. 'You have to come with me into town!'

My wife was all alarm. 'John, what is going on? What house? Who are these people? I've never heard any of these names!' And in that moment, I again felt like I was falling – but not just falling – sinking – drowning.

Mrs Cook was shouting, almost screaming: 'Reverend Church, we have to go!'

And my wife was shouting too: 'John, what is going on? Who is this person? Who are all these persons of whom I have never heard?'

I found some words: 'They are just some worshippers of mine, that's all. Just some worshippers of mine, who are in trouble with the Patrol.' (Later, my wife would accept this explanation of these events. Just as the gilder's wife accepted her husband's lies: sometimes it's the easiest way.)

Only at the very last moment did Mrs Cook steal another look at my wife, and my wife at her. They were each ghosts staring at the living.

*

I don't remember all that happened in the next hours. Some of it has been wiped from my mind, scrubbed away by panic and fear. I remember leaving my rooms with Mrs Cook, with my wife calling after me, asking me when I would be back from helping my worshippers. I remember the Gees following Mrs Cook and me out into the street, shouting about things being 'most irregular'. I remember Mrs Cook had a covered trap waiting. She had hired it to bring her here and take me back. The expense of that alone spooked me.

She and I must have talked, I suppose, because folk in the first flush of disaster will talk and talk and talk, make deals with each other, with the devil, with their destroyers, with any fucker, frankly. I don't remember of what we spoke. I can recall an image of her staring out of the carriage window, deathly still, her eyes round with fear, her lips parted and white. I also remember her crying bitterly and me comforting her, telling her not to cry. When was she still and when was she crying? I cannot seem to put it back together, even now. I must have asked her to tell me what she knew, and she must have told me she was not there when the house was raided, because I knew somehow that she had not been. I knew that the Patrol had broken in through the bolted door, or that someone within the house had let them in, unbolting the door. I knew that there had been Patrol officers at the house, secretly, for weeks; but I don't remember her telling me. She must have, I suppose.

*

Did it not occur to us what scene we would see when we got to Vere Street? I cannot remember if we discussed it or not. It was late – it must have been, because it was July and yet it was already fully dark – but the whole street was still writhing with bodies, a nest of human rats come to eat a corpse; our corpse. The tavern downstairs had been closed up by the Patrol, but someone had already smashed the windows, jagged shards of glass too perilous for anyone to climb inside. Other people were carrying things out from upstairs, artefacts of the molly house: pictures, furniture, bottles of drink, even the curtains. Bodies stood around a bonfire onto which they threw bedding and clothes, the male clothes of the queens who had been arrested in their female ones. An image flashed through me, as I stared into the flames, of the queens in a crowded gaol, dressed as women, just meat for the men who would stare at them, grabbing their crotches and grinning darkly.

I peered out of the carriage a little; it was safer for me than for Mrs Cook, who might be recognised as the tavern-keep's wife. The people swarming in and out of the upstairs were laughing and having a good time, carrying away whatever they could. I asked a man nearby if he knew what had happened. He said twenty-three men – *twenty-three!* – had been taken down to the gaol at Bow Street, and that the crowd there was much bigger. They were burning effigies hung from ropes; effigies of us. I thanked the man, smiling but cold to the bone, then sat back in the carriage. Instinctively, without a word, I caught my friend's hand. Did I think her fingers would be like ice? They were as hot as hell.

*

It was all I could do to dissuade Mrs Cook from going to Bow Street; I'll admit I just did not want to risk it. So we went to her other tavern, over at Long Acre, in Covent Garden. There was no gathered crowd outside; she told me she had locked up hours before. Afraid of being spotted, we rushed upstairs to the rooms above the tavern where she and her husband lived. I had never been there before. We stood a long time in absolute silence.

I watched her gazing, staring, down at the floor. 'I am so very glad that they did not catch you, Reverend,' she said softly.

'What?' I whispered. She said the words kindly, sincerely. I felt sick. I did not feel glad, about any of it.

There was banging on the tavern door downstairs. Mrs Cook went rigid with terror. The mob could easily have connected the two taverns if they knew James Cook had been arrested. Seeing how terrified she seemed, I said I would go down to check who was there. How afraid I was as I crept down the stairs to the tavern door, not knowing what mob of murderers awaited. I would pose as merely a friend, a priest come to comfort a parishioner. Some innate respect would be afforded me.

Outside, through the great tavern windows, I saw no blaze of torches, heard no yelling from a mob. Visible through the glass of the main door were two Patrol officers, I guessed from Bow Street, standing perfectly still. I opened the door. When I explained who I was, they almost winked at me, as if we were on the same side, me the man of God and they the keepers of his morality. They asked Mrs Cook a few questions. She denied ever having been to the rooms upstairs at Vere Street, said she did not believe her husband kept a molly house, insisted it was all a mistake. One of the Patrol officers told Mrs Cook to think of somewhere she could stay for a few days, or a week or so, 'just to keep out of trouble'.

'Trouble?' she asked.

'People are not kind to the wives of Sodomites,' the other officer said.

Once they were gone, I felt a compulsion to leave too. I did not want to stay there any longer, amid all that horror. I wanted to get away from London, back to Southwark, as if crossing the river offered me some form of protection. I asked Mrs Cook if she wanted me to stay; when she said no, I felt relieved. She would go to stay with her sister at the far side of Soho. 'I'll be safe there a few days, I should think,' she said. She looked around at the walls: 'I hope they don't burn me out.' She gazed at me a moment, in that way she had when she was studying you, preparing for something to say. 'What will you say to your wife, Reverend Church?'

I flushed with fury, raising my voice: 'What has this to do with my wife?' I am not sure I had shown that side of me to her before; she seemed quite amazed at my anger.

★

What time was it by then? I don't remember. I cannot work it out. The city was dark and quiet, though. From the top of Covent Garden, I picked my way back towards the Bridge, of course avoiding Clare Market. I wondered if the White Swan was a ghost now, a hollow husk, razed to the ground, dismantled brick by brick. I sniffed the air; I could not smell burning. As I sloped down along Fleet Street and off towards the Bridge, the huddled bodies of the city's homeless hardly stirred under blankets as the last of their fires sputtered out. Here and there, I saw bargemen picking their way down towards the river's wharves to start their early shifts. And around and about, drunkards staggered or lay gin-prone in the street.

As I reached the river, I did not know what to do. Dawn was not quite upon the world. The quality of the night-time was changing, away from dense midnight-blue into something purplish, glowing, miasmic. The stars seemed to be shrinking back into space. I decided not to walk to the Bridge; I did not want to see people, who would be crossing even at that hour. I would pay a bargeman at the river's edge just to carry me over. I found a young lad, no more than seventeen, who said it would cost tuppence. I sat in the back of the barge as he pursued me with questions. 'Been out drinking, is it, sir? – A good night, is it, sir? – What is sir looking for now? – Is sir looking to spend some money, 'cos you know, I got some time, if sir is looking to spend some money—' I knew this drill. This drill used to be mine. I did not answer his questions, just listened to the sound of his oars breaking the surface of the river. I reached over the side and put my fingers into the water, feeling it on my skin, ice-cold and silted with dirt.

By the time we alighted on the Southwark wharves, I already knew where I was headed. When I got to Mint Street, I stood outside the workhouse with my back to its wall. By then, the sky was streaked pink and peach with the arrival of the morning; the city soon would wake. I looked up at the patterns in the clouds of unformed colours.

I watched Ned's building, ran my eyes up its wall, to work out which window was his, from that one night I had slept there. I found some small stones and gently lobbed them up, to hit the glass. One, two, three. The first one missed. The second hit but not hard enough. The third was harder; I flinched, thinking I might crack the pane. His face, just awoken from sleep, appeared at the window. Seeing me, he furrowed his brow. 'Let me in,' I mouthed to him. He shook his head, pointing downwards, meaning to meet at the front door.

When he opened the door, his feet bare on the step, he was still pulling a jacket over and around his thin white nightshirt; the gauzy line of his naked body was visible underneath. His hair was pressed sharply triangular in one direction, flattened by his pillow, as it had been that first morning he had woken in my bed at The Cut, when he had laughed and covered his face with his hands. 'What is going on, John?'

'Can we go inside?'

He shook his head. 'My room-mate is here.'

'Let me in . . .'

He furrowed his brow. 'You know I cannot. My room-mate is here.' His eyes searched mine. 'What is wrong?'

Somewhere in the distance, a wagon was rumbling through the dawn-lit streets. We both turned, alerted by the sound, then looked back at each other. 'The house on Vere Street has been raided,' I said.

'*What?*'

'Most everyone has been arrested.'

He lifted his hand to his mouth. '*Jesus*, John.'

'I want to protect you—'

He stepped back slightly, afraid. 'Why do I need protecting?' His eyes grew darker, more panicked. 'I should go in,' he whispered, turning to look at the empty black corridor behind him. 'It's not safe. I should—'

I put my hand out to stop him shutting the door. Only as I did it did I see his surprise; he had not intended to shut it at all. 'All I want is to protect you,' I said.

'John—'

'Keep you safe, keep us safe.'

His lips parted and he let out a long, echoing breath. 'John, you're frightening me.'

'Let me come inside with you.'

'No, John.'

No? I whispered. I think I whispered it; the hum, the drone, was suddenly so loud. *Or did I yell it?* It's hard to – *it's hard to remember.* 'Be quiet, John,' he hissed. 'I need to go inside. You'll wake folk up with your shouting.' I wasn't shouting – *or was I?* I don't remember. I remember his face, alarmed, so I must have been shouting – at him. I had never shouted *at* him before, only to get him to recognise my emotions. But isn't that all shouting is? Isn't that the only reason we shout at all? Rage wipes my memory clean: I have already said that it is the beast I ride, recklessly, in hopes that I may be understood. And I thought he was the one who understood me. *Was I wrong?* 'Look,' he began hesitantly, 'let's not see each other for a few days. Let things settle down.'

About what was he speaking now? I reached to grab his hand. Then – I could not believe it – he pulled it away from mine: His eyelids were flickering very fast. 'It's just a few days, John,' he was saying – *as if to a stranger.* (Was I that stranger now?) 'I will come to the Obelisk in a few days.' He touched my arm but only very briefly. 'Keep calm, John. Don't do anything silly. It's just a few days.' His eyes were glowing like the moon. 'You haven't done anything foolish, John, have you?'

'Foolish?' I asked, a lump in my throat. 'What do you mean?'

He smiled, and perhaps it was the last time I saw him do it. 'All right,' he said, finally closing the door. *All right*: I had always thought it was neutral and cool, but now I wondered, was it actually manipulative? I stood there, and all I wanted to do was kick that fucking door in. All I wanted to do was scream at the top of my lungs and burn his house down to the fucking ground.

But I didn't, *did I*?

Chapter Thirteen
or
Ghosting

July and then August . . .

FROM *THE MORNING CHRONICLE*
(I cut out this clipping and hid it among my things)

In consequence of its having been represented to the Magistrates of the above office, that a number of persons of a most detestable description, met at the house of James Cooke, the White Swan, in Vere-street, Clare-market, particularly on a Sunday night, a privy search-warrant was issued, and was put in execution on Sunday night last, when 23 persons, including the landlord of the house, were taken into custody, and lodged in St. Clement's watch-house, till yesterday, at eleven o-clock, when they were brought before Mr. Read for examination; but the circumstance having transpired, a great concourse of people had collected in Bow-street, and which was much increased by the mob that followed the prisoners when they were brought from the watch-house. It was with the greatest difficulty the officers could bring them to and from the Brown Bear to the Office; the mob, particularly the women, expressing their detestation of the offence of which the prisoners were charged.

*

About half the men arrested at the White Swan were released within a few hours, ostensibly for lack of evidence. 'Lack of evidence' is a ruse for Patrol officers, lawyers and hacks, who together made sure the city knew before the men were released. A baying crowd assembled. The men could be seen, named, to be beaten and damned by their neighbours; they say they only just escaped with their lives. If they could not be charged with anything that would stick in court, the Patrol released them to the fury of the crowd. If justice cannot supply punishment, the mob will.

FROM *THE TIMES*, ON THE SAME DAY
(And my wife asked: 'Why have you bought all these newspapers, John?')

The prisoners underwent a long examination. Several were discharged, the proofs against them not being sufficiently strong to warrant their detention for trial; but their liberation was instantaneously productive of the most dangerous consequences. The multitude, male and female, fell upon them as they came out. They were knocked down, kicked, and covered with mud through every street in their endeavours to escape. The women, particularly those of Russell-street and Covent-garden market, were most ferocious in the application of this discipline; but the lower order of the male spectators were by no means lax in their exertions to mark their detestations of these wretches.

Out of the whole number, eight were ordered to find bail for the misdemeanour, and in default were committed to prison. They were housed for a time at the Brown Bear, in Bow-street, until the crowd should disperse. The crowd, however, continued to block up the Street and its avenues. A coach was drawn up before the door of the Brown Bear, for the conveyance of a part of the Delinquents to prison. This afforded a fresh signal to whet the eagerness of the mob, who pressed close round the carriage, and could not be kept off by the constables. It was, therefore, seen that any attempt to convey the Prisoners that way, must have exposed them to extremely rough handling, if not to order.

★

Reports in newspapers of the numbers and the names of those remaining in prison kept changing: sometimes seven, sometimes eight. Once I read eleven. Among the names were my friends, and James Cook, but not White and Hepburn. No one came to arrest or question me. In the days after the house was revealed, I saw no familiar faces from the world of the mollies. No eyes connected with mine – either silently ashamed or shamelessly bawdy – on the rammed, narrow streets. Whatever community we had been, it was hiding itself away.

Time started to pass, but still I did not hear from Ned. I waited for him to come back to the Obelisk but he did not come. He had said a few days, but a few days passed and then a week. As time opened up, merciless and empty, my own rage was coursing through me, so that sometimes I would find myself standing in the pews, thinking, rocking back and forth, my fingernails slicing into the flesh of my palms. But none of this changed one hard fact: *still he did not come.*

My mind began to race again, to twist and to betray me. I awoke thinking about him and went to bed the same. My thoughts were neither good nor kind, not towards him and not towards myself. I ranted and raved in the depths of my brain, accusing him, or bargaining with him. And what was the bargain? *Come back; I'll do anything. I have done everything I could; so come back, please, just come back.* Now and then my wife would say to me, 'Are you talking to yourself, John?' and I would realise that I was muttering under my breath. That was my mind, you see, chattering and bargaining and betraying.

I felt so afraid that he had left me, that I had gone too far on his doorstep that night. Or perhaps it was the night we went to Vere Street, or the visit to Hampstead. I told you that sometimes I go too far; perhaps this was one of those times. Sometimes I sat all day in the Obelisk, waiting for him to come, as he had said he would, but he did not; *had he intended to lie to me from the start?*

A week after the arrests, the Sunday evening next, when in a different time I would have gone to Vere Street, I knew I had to go to Mint Street. Still I had heard not a damned word from him. It was one of those glorious London summer evenings when the heat of the day peaks late then melts into the night. I stood on his street, staring up at his building, willing him to come out, but he did not. Had he turned away from me, abandoned me? Did he go to another chapel now? Did he walk on other streets, talk to other men, let them inside him? I called him traitor, I called him whore, then felt only shame. *My God, how did I get like this?*

I kept my eyes on his window. I thought about knocking his door, as I had the night that the house on Vere Street was revealed, but again, I did not. This was not control or sanity on my part; it was paralysis. I was afraid if I knocked the door of what I would find out; but at the same time, I knew this paralysis would not last for ever.

I stood there for a long time. It began to rain. It absolutely pelted down for ten minutes, and even though I stepped back against the wall of the infamous workhouse to gain some shelter, I became soaked to the skin. A sound slowly penetrated my thoughts: a human sound, of such joy. Women's voices, above my head. I looked up, and there at a barred window two young women stood, their bodies pressed against the bars, with their hands waving outside. They were trying to catch the raindrops. As they did so, their laughter seemed so happy and free – the pretty, joyous laughter of girls. I watched their arms stretching out, swaying like reeds in a river, into a world that no longer belonged to them, back and forth, back and forth. And all the while they kept laughing.

I heard a loud clanging, a truncheon whacked against metal, the doors of what must have been their cell, and a man's voice – a workhouse warden – shouting: 'Get down, you filthy fucking *sluts!*' Suddenly the women's laughter was gone, their hands had vanished. There was silence save for the thudding of rain. It was as if they had never been there at all. Had they? *Had they?* I pulled up my collar and left.

★

I was frightened, frightened for my sanity, frightened for my friends, frightened for him. Most days, I bought a newspaper, hunting for news of our extermination. Eventually two stories emerged. The first story I read whilst having tea in the morning with my wife. She had grown quite light of spirit in those days – I was at home much more, no longer disappearing in the evenings. As we sipped the tea, I read that a royal footman had mysteriously shot himself dead in St James's Palace. At first, it did not occur to me what it meant, but then I read the name: 'Tranter'. Remember when the Duke of Cumberland used that name for the Duchess of Cumberland? I was certain he had called her Tranter.

'O, Duchess . . .' I murmured to myself.

'What duchess?' my wife asked. I had forgotten she was even there. I looked up and smiled at her, cracking open inside.

'Nothing . . . Just a story about one of the Prince of Wales's horses. Had to be put down.'

'What do you care about the Prince of Wales? Or horses, for that matter?'

I shrugged. 'It's nothing. Forget it.'

★

One day, a few weeks on, sitting at my breakfast, I read a second story in *The Morning Chronicle*:

> *Yesterday at Bow-street, the Ensign brought up by Revett, the officer, from the Isle of Wight, in consequence of a charge against him*

of an inhuman offence, at the Swan public house in Vere-street,
underwent an examination before Mr. Justice Birnie. The prison-
er's name is Hepburn—

I tore the page from the newspaper in one quick rip. My wife
was in our bedroom, singing to herself, laying her small things
out on the bed. I vomited almost noiselessly, straight into the
remainder of the newspaper. I stared down at the sick, caught
entirely into the well of the paper. My wife had not heard me
puke, above her singing, in her preoccupation with her task. I
scooped it all up and took it downstairs and threw the papers
on the street's rubbish heap; wiping my mouth with the back
of my hand, I stood on the street for several minutes, staring
and staring at the air, staring at its invisibility, staring at its
nothingness; and so mine.

It was several days before I found out that White had been
arrested too and taken to Bow Street; *still I had not heard from
Ned.* (Was he afraid, reading these same stories, and staying away, hiding from me out of plain fear?) Inevitably, the
story of the arrest emerged in the press. Do you remember
Tommy White's friend at the molly house? He was named
James Mann; he had a slippery quality to him I had never
liked. It was he who had accused them, said that they had
importuned him, and he was so shocked at the sexual suggestion, he had fled.

This was a lie. You remember that he and Tommy White
were good friends. I had seen them together at Vere Street,
month after month after month. So I smelled the rat. Either
a journalist had got to him or he had sold the story, out of
malice or succumbing to this same, extending-outwards, ever-
rippling fear that owned London's Sodomites now.

★

I decided to write to Ned. One letter was sweet, saying that we were 'good friends', and we should meet to discuss things. He did not reply. Another reminded him of what we owed each other, of how he had asked for protection, how I had always been willing to give it. I asked him, hand-delivering it to Mint Street, to write to me. I always signed the letters 'your friend, John Church', nothing that could be suspected if someone intercepted them. Still he did not reply. I did not understand how cruel and heartless he was now.

Eventually, I sent a letter that was angrier, I confess, in which I garbled words about who owed whom what, about how harsh he was being, demanding to know when he would keep *his* promises. I asked him to meet at such a place and such a time, and I went that day, and waited an hour and a half. He did not come.

*

Time seemed to bend and blur. The moment of the story of the raid passed but there remained much discussion in the papers. All sides agreed that the Vere Street mollies must be punished: liberal and radical, Tory and Whig. People were named; attacks on and arrests of mollies became greater and greater in number. I lost track of myself, of who I was before. I receded into my thoughts, and increasingly they turned on me. I began to dwell on what I had done wrong – so many things – and what I could have done otherwise. And all along, I thought about him – and what he had or hadn't done. I was trying to understand how the world could so betray what was right, what was good, what was true. I knew all the answers; there are few surprises in a world trained to hate. And yet, I looked at what I had achieved, and still could not quite bring myself to believe I had been wrong about so much.

*

There was only one person to whom I could talk, the only person I had left. I walked from The Cut to Covent Garden. When I got to Long Acre, Mrs Cook's tavern was open. She saw me enter and a grey panic descended on her face. Saying nothing, she nodded towards a doorway, covered with a pinned-up blanket, showing that I should go there. I went through and let the hanging blanket flap behind me. It was another minute before it flapped again.

I smiled at her, but she remained tense. 'Can I get you a drink, Reverend?' she asked, pointing to the bar from which we had just walked. I shook my head.

'How long did you stay shut, Mrs Cook?'

'I only just reopened, Reverend. It wasn't safe before. I had to stay closed. I stayed with my sister at Soho for a while, but then her neighbours rumbled it, so I took a room at Camden Town for a few weeks.'

'Camden Town?'

'No one knows me in the country, do they?'

I nodded. 'Is it safe now?'

'Folk are no longer threatening to burn me down, but they ain't coming to buy my beer either.'

'You are struggling?' I asked, but she snapped back at me:

'What do you think? My husband is in gaol, we owe a lot of money on the tavern in Vere Street, and my business here is shot. What do you think about whether I'm struggling, Reverend?' She let out a long, tearful breath. 'I'm sorry, Reverend, I shouldn't take it out on you. You've done nothing wrong.' She was silent for a moment. 'You've had no trouble, Reverend?'

'Me? No.' I thought of what I should say next. 'Not yet.'

'They've no reason to arrest you. You weren't at the White Swan that night. Them's still in custody won't betray you. Sally and Leonora, they think the absolute world of you. Miss Sweet

Lips, she won't talk. She is as tough as old boots. She'll give the judge a mouthful.'

She tried to laugh but failed; her laughter shrivelled in her throat; we knew that the queens' smart, funny put-downs were worth nothing in the meat grinder of English justice. 'What about your husband?' I asked.

'I went to see him.'

'They let you in?'

She rubbed her fingers together to mean a bribe. 'Jimmy thinks someone grassed on us.' She cast her eyes around bleakly. 'What do you think, Reverend? Do you think it could be true?'

'But who?' I asked. It was clear she had no idea.

'Jimmy is obsessed with it. It's driving him mad. He says if he ever gets out, he'll have his revenge.'

I looked at her and smiled as best I could, feeling utterly sick. And then I asked her if she needed money; she said yes. I gave her what I could, which wasn't much at all. I saw her look at the coins in her hand and then up at me. What strange emotion was in her eyes, I cannot tell you.

*

My mind felt like it was collapsing. I couldn't get things to make sense. Fleeing back across the Bridge, I remember rushing down onto the top of the Borough High Street, my body slamming into strangers, and people turning and going, *Oi!* I did not care. I could not have it in me to care any more. But it was not until I was virtually at the white and red Church of St George the Martyr, across the road from the Marshalsea, that I realised where I was going – where perhaps I must have been going all along: Mint Street.

And so I found myself back at his door – I don't remember the last part of my journey at all – even now – and the first I remember was that I was loudly banging on it, and no one answered, so I ended up kicking it. Finally, his landlady appeared – her face green with outrage – and she was screaming at me: 'Fucking hell! What is going on?'

'I want to see Ned,' I said, the words splattering out of me and onto her. The woman was looking at me as if I was a madman.

'Well, he's gone! Moved out!'

I let out a long, hard breath. 'Moved out?' The words popped on my lips.

'Yes,' the landlady growled, 'and you should fuck off too, sling your hook!'

'Where has he gone?'

The landlady's anger at being so disturbed had not abated. '*I* don't know! He paid up and left, said someone was bothering him.'

She slammed the door shut. I let my head fall forwards against it. Who was bothering him? *O, Ned*: was someone threatening him? Did he not want my protection any more? Had he fled in terror of what was overwhelming us? He should have come to me for help. I would have saved him. I would *never* have abandoned him.

FROM *JACKSON'S JOURNAL*

Seven of the detestable club of Vere-street, viz. Wm. Amos, alias Fox, James Cooke, Philip Kett, Wm. Thompson, Richard Francis, James Done, and Robert Aspinal, were tried for conspiring together at the White Swan, in Vere-street, Clare-market, for the purpose or exciting each others to commit a detestable offence. Mr. Pooley stated the case for the prosecution. The witnesses against the prisoner were Nichols, and another of the Bow-street patrol, who were sent to the house by the Magistrates, to watch the proceedings of persons assembled there. They gained admittance into the back parlour, which was the principal rendezvous of these miscreants, and were considered as persons of the same propensity, and treated without reserve.

For three nights they witnessed such disgusting conduct and language, as to place beyond all doubt the intentions of the company. They gave information of all they had seen, and the prisoners, with a number of others, were brought before the Magistrates. The evidence being closed, Mr. Gurney, who had cross-examined the witnesses while giving their testimony, said that he was placed in the awkward situation of Counsel for the defendants, and had undertaken that task because he felt himself bound to do so by his oath, and duty as an advocate.

In the course of the evidence he had done that duty to the best of his judgment, by giving the defendants every benefit of cross-examination. He found the testimony so clear and uncontradicted, as to leave no ground of palliation upon which to make any appeal to the Jury, upon circumstances, which, if true, would go to excite an idea that the horrors of Sodom and Gomorrah were reviled in London. He must therefore decline trespassing on the time of the Jury, and leave them to form their own conclusions.

If the prisoners had any thing to offer in their defence, he had no doubt they would meet with every indulgence. The prisoners being then called on, each told his story, but it could have made no impression on the minds of any discerning Jury, and all the prisoners were found Guilty.

Amos, having been trice before convicted of similar offences, was sentenced to three years' imprisonment, and to stand once in the pillory in the Hay-market.

Cooke, the keeper of the house, Kett, Thompson, Francis, and Done, were sentenced to two years' imprisonment, and the pillory in the same place; and Aspinal, to one year's imprisonment only.

On sentence being pronounced they were all handcuffed, and tied to one chain in Court, and ordered to Cold Bath-fields prison.

On leaving the Court, a numerous crowd of people, which had collected at the door, assailed them with fists, sticks, and stones, which the constables could not completely prevent, although they were about 40 in number. The prisoners perceiving their perilous situation, immediately ran in a body to the prison, which they reached in a few minutes, and the constables, by blockading the streets, prevented the most fleet of their assailants from molesting them during their inglorious retreat.

Chapter Fourteen

or

Killing

The September . . .

The pillory was to be held at the old Hay-Market, at Panton Street. It was just below Leicester Square, so that after the violence, one could go and enjoy the diversions there. It was only a street away from where I had once told Katherine, Mary and Arabel that the Lord loved them, and William Webster that I loved him. We had all been so happy and transformed then. Now, the smiling faces of my past seemed to stare back at me in a mirror, grim inquisitors. Mrs Cook asked me to go with her to witness the punishments. She did not say that it was for me to perform the duty; she did not have to. But now I felt such a horrible, collapsing fear within me; I did not want to go.

The prisoners were being held in Newgate and the procession to the pillory would begin there. I met her on Ludgate Hill at about half past eleven. It was so near the spot where we had first spoken, the day they hanged Richard Oakden. It was only then I saw it, that we Sodomites are bound to repeat these moments over and over again, for as long as we perform the duty, for as long as we are to be killed.

Mrs Cook's eyes were red and puffy, and her body was wrapped up in layers and layers of coats and scarves, though it was not cold. I felt anxious to see her that way: to perform the duty it is important to be as invisible as possible. We walked in silence up the hill towards St Paul and then on to Newgate. The shops were all closed, their windows shuttered up. 'They are expecting trouble,' I said, more to myself than her. She let out a fearful breath and stumbled, as if to faint. I caught her and she said she was all right, pulling her arm from my hand. She refused my touch.

We pushed through the crowd, our eyes down, to deflect identification. We found a few steps, not empty but with space, leading up to a nailed-shut doorway with a heavy stone canopy above it. The canopy would hide us away a little. The steps would give us height to see straight to the gates from which prisoners were brought. It was not so that we had a good view; it was so that they could see us. The rule of the duty is that you should be seen by those about to be destroyed, so they know they do not face their task alone.

At midday, the bells of the churches began sounding around the City; London was being called to see justice done. The crowd in front of the Old Bailey started swirling like a tide, a huge number of people alerted by the infamy of 'the Vere Street Coterie'. There was something indefinable in the air, like a congregation of birds all whistling as one, a long, ugly, vast gull screech. The great doors of the old gaol began to pull back. At once, the sound of the crowd became a deafening wall of shrieks. My eyes hovered over that swirling sea of heads. Different flavours of radical presented themselves: Abolitionists and Republicans, religious men and political ones. None of them came to protest what was happening that day. They came to celebrate it. A woman with a child in one arm, wearing the red Phrygian cap they had worn during the Revolution in France, was waving a bread knife in her hand with the other. She was shrieking like a lunatic, just yelling over and over: *Kill them! Kill them! Kill them!* whilst her baby screamed and screamed. Only at the last moment did I see stitched into her shawl the old radical phrase: *Liberty! Equality! Fraternity!*

Through the gates, the first cart appeared: on it were Sally Fox, Black-Eyed Leonora, Miss Sweet Lips – all dressed as men, in prisoners' rags – and James Cook. They were standing in the open cart, tied to a pole so as to stop them either jumping or being pulled over the side. It was two months since the house on Vere Street had been revealed, two terrifying, fear-filled months; for them and for all of us. A second cart followed, with the remainder of those to be pilloried that day, men whom I did not know so well. Among them was Philip Kett.

The Patrol officers, about sixty in number, filed out around them, and held up a mixture of lances and rifles to contain the crowd as it surged forward. The officers formed into a chevron to pierce the throng, to slice a way through, but as they moved on, men tried to attack the carts, to topple them over, to leap onto them, to punch and gouge at the tethered sinners. I watched Leonora's face – immaculate, exquisite Black-Eyed Leonora – saw the sheer, cold fear in her eyes. The crowd began to throw things at the prisoners: stones that could strike out an eye, coins that could rip open a cheek. Fearless, fast-mouthed Sweet Lips started yelling insults back. How I wished she would not; it would only make things worse. Normal people prefer it when those they attack just shut up and take it. James Cook was tied to his pole, sobbing like a child, protesting his virtue. 'I am innocent, innocent,' he screamed. 'I am like you! I am not one of these *perverts*!' People were laughing at him, every snivelling bit of his self-humiliation.

The caravan of justice began to make its way out onto Ludgate Hill, parting the crowd like Moses and the Red Sea. Ripping hands pursued the Israelites. Further away, people just stood around chatting and laughing with neighbours and friends, talking about what they were doing for the rest of their day off, how well their sons were doing in the church school. As the carts rumbled past, the Pelting, an old custom, began. People had come with handcarts filled with mud and shit, and you could pay a little money to get yourself a great clod.

The first cart rattled slowly past Mrs Cook and me, and for a moment, already splattered with muck, its occupants turned and looked at us: Leonora looked first, seeing me, and she whispered something – no, of course, I could not hear them – and then Sally looked too – I watched their lips moving – almost a kind of prayer. They looked and looked at me like they could not understand which of us was alive and which of us was dead. *Is that you, Reverend, back from the grave, or is it us?*

A rock flew through the air and broke the skin on Sally's forehead. She screamed, and blood immediately covered her eyes and mouth. The cheering grew louder and the Pelting intensified, the crowd thrilled with its first bull's-eye.

FROM *THE ANNUAL REGISTER*
(Why do I keep these things? Why? To hurt myself?)

Such was the degree of popular indignation excited against these wretches, and such the general eagerness to witness their punishment, that, by ten in the morning, the chief avenues from Clerkenwell Prison and Newgate to the place of punishment were crowded with people; and the multitude assembled in the Haymarket, and all its immediate vicinity, was so great as to render the streets impassable. All the windows and even the very roofs of the houses were crowded with persons of both sexes; and every coach, wagon, hay-cart, dray, and other vehicles which blocked up great part of the street, were crowded with spectators.

The Sheriffs, attended by two City Marshals, with an immense number of constables, accompanied the procession of the Prisoners from Newgate, whence they set out in the transport caravan, and proceeded through Fleet-street and the Strand; and the Prisoners were hooted and pelted the whole way by the populace. At one o-clock four of the culprits were fixed in the pillory, erected for and accommodated to the occasion, with two additional wings, one being allotted for each criminal; and immediately a new torrent of popular vengeance poured upon them from all sides. The day being fine, the streets were dry and free from mud, but the defect was speedily and amply supplied by the butchers of St. James's-market. Numerous escorts of whom constantly supplied the party of attack, chiefly consisting of women, with tubs of blood, garbage, and ordure from their slaughter-houses, and with this ammunition, plentifully diversified with dead cats, turnips, potatoes, addled eggs, and other missiles, the criminals were incessantly pelted to the last moment.

*

Of course, this was only the start of the day; the easy part, you might say. We made our way to the pillory site on the corner of Panton Street and the Hay-Market. In grim, near-total silence, we hid in a wooden scaffold around a new building, waiting for them to arrive. When they did, they were splattered with so much shit and blood, you could hardly recognise them. Their faces were shredded by what had been thrown at them, cheeks swollen inches out, the whites of their eyes red with blood.

Sweet Lips – beautiful, imperious Sweet Lips, bringer of trouble, dazzler of men – her mouth torn open now, belching out blood. Leonora – do you remember her in her golden turban and red lips and her knowing, withering glances, her soft sensitivities? Now she was lacerated and crumpled over with pain and exhaustion. (*Do you want to turn from the descriptions? Then shove your face against it, for it is the truth of what was done.*) Cook had long since collapsed, and hung like a wet, ragged corn-dolly from his pole. Last of all, I saw Sally: only she stared outwards, impassive and brutal, with her face smashed beyond recognition, and her clothes almost torn off her. She turned her face up to the sunlight and I watched her sigh most deeply. Sally knew the truth more than any other. She had been to the pillory before. She knew that the worst was yet to come.

Mrs Cook started to weep. She could hold in her grief no longer. I told her it was time for us to go and she kept saying no, she had to stay, but I knew there was too much risk. We could not show our grief to anyone. The two of us drifted in shocked silence across Leicester Square, back to the Charing Cross Road, onto the western end of Long Acre. We stood in that spot, clinging to our silence, there in the great press of bodies between St Giles and Covent Garden, for an unknown number of minutes. Around us, people in good cheer gnawed at pork pies and dripping puddings and swigged ale from jars. I felt sickened; I felt repulsed. Was that our friends' blood splattered on their clothes, was it the little pink spots on the happy faces of their children at their feet?

'Thank you, Reverend, for coming with me . . .' Mrs Cook started saying, but her voice cracked halfway through. Her face was grey with horror and her eyes so empty. That was it; she said nothing else to me. She turned and walked up Long Acre. I watched her go for a moment, not moving myself. She did not look back once, and in the end, I turned right and walked down towards Charing Cross.

(I do not remember from where I tore this page but it remains an artefact . . .)

On Wednesday Ensign John Newbolt Hepburn, of the 4th West India Regiment (whose apprehension at the Barracks at Newport was stated in a former paper) and T. White, a drum boy, were tried at the Old Bailey, for a detestable crime. The prisoner Hepburn accosted Mann, the boy, whose evidence supported the prosecution, while on parade in the Park, promising to introduce him to White. The witness and White afterwards received an invitation to dine with him. They met at the

house in Vere-street, where the detestable gang was discovered some
time since, and dragged to punishment. In consequence of information
communicated by Mann to the Sergeant-Major of his Regiment, the
prisoners were apprehended . . . The Jury found both prisoners – Guilty.

★

Hepburn and White admitted that they went through a form of
marriage performed by a priest, 'a person unknown'. A terror
ran through me, even as I was still not exposed. But nonetheless, the idea of me revived in the press. There had been talk of
weddings at Vere Street, but now here were two men who had
committed that foul crime. And I was the man who had enabled
it. The two men (*do you still remember that happy night, when Mrs
Cook cried and Leonora said I had created a wonderful world?*) were
not sentenced to the pillory. No, they were sentenced to hang:
the gravity of the crime, their lack of remorse, their mockery of
Christian values demanded harsher punishment. And so, with
everyone else in prison, I knew it was down to me to perform
the duty. Suddenly I thought that this was the last time. After
that day, I would not do it again.

Newgate was filled with a pretty pale light the day of their
killing. It was months since the raiding of Vere Street, and
Hepburn and White – John and Tommy – had been in gaol a
long time by then. The scaffold was set up, two nooses hanging
expectantly. The crowd was not nearly as large or voluble as on
the day that Sally and the others were pilloried.

London had moved on from the Vere Street scandal, or so
it seemed. History had intervened. The old King, to whom
Mrs Caesar had once wished death, had gone blind, deaf and
mad; a kind of death, after all. His useless, detested son, the
Prince of Wales, had formed a Regency. In the war, things were
going badly for Napoleon in Spain, yet there were rumours he
intended to invade Russia next.

At the back of the crowd were a number of very good-quality coaches lined up, and from within, aristocratic noses peered out at the sight. Only later would it be claimed in the press that Tommy White had prostituted himself among the city's great and good; a kind of Sodomite conspiracy. It was of course a vicious, deluded lie.

Tommy was led out first, seeming almost aerial in mood. His hands were bound, but he seemed so fresh-faced, not at all like one who had been in gaol for months and was about to be killed. They say sometimes those condemned to die are almost relieved when finally the day comes. He wore a white, frilled shirt; from where had he got such a good shirt after months in prison? Slowly he raised his face to the thin light, as if to bask in summer heat, although there was none.

After several minutes, John Hepburn was led out, hands also bound, followed by a vicar, the hangman and some Patrol officers. As he appeared, Tommy White turned around expectantly. They would not have seen each other since their trial, though they were held in the same place of correction. Hepburn looked grey with worry, much older than before, so that their effect as a pair was even stranger: one shattered old man and one dewy and lovely Adonis. They stood next to each other on the scaffold. To my great surprise, White gave Hepburn the most wonderful, joyful smile. It was like glorious sunshine in the bleakest midwinter. Hepburn slowly smiled in return. I understood then why Tommy wore that shirt: it was to appear beautiful for his loved one, no other reason than that, to be seen beautiful once more by the one you adore. Hepburn began to look happier and happier, as if all his cares had fallen away.

A strange disapproval entered the front of the crowd. People had come for punishment, not to see some perverts' love, far greater than anything they had experienced themselves. Sinners can never be victors! People began to jeer, but White did not take his eyes from Hepburn's once, a small smile on his lips radiating that if this was what their love demanded, then so be it. The mean little vicar, horrified by such sincerity and happiness, spat that it was time. The executioner pushed Hepburn's head through the noose, and without ceremony – no time for a prayer – kicked him forwards off the scaffold. He fell hard; the sound of his neck breaking was as loud as fingers snapping next to your ear. He was still and dead immediately. Only then did Tommy White's calmness shatter; he started to jabber and panic and cry out, 'John! John!' (*My name . . . He was shouting my name . . .*) The executioner punched him, told him to be quiet, then roughly shoved a black mask over his head and kicked his body from the scaffold too. It all seemed so horrific, so fast and yet so slow, as beautiful, sweet Tommy thrashed in the noose fully two minutes, screaming and screaming, before, finally, he died.

I had had enough. I turned away; this was the last of it, the end of what had happened at Vere Street. Head half down, I pushed my way backwards through the crowd, even as I could feel my body weakening, the release of exhaustion that had been pent up for so long. I passed near where the grand coaches lined up. I let my gaze scan the occupants' hawkish faces. To my surprise, I recognised one of them: the Duke of Cumberland. Briefly, his eyes connected with mine; he gazed straight at me. His stare narrowed as one who just momentarily, thinks he has seen a face before. But his eyes did not linger; he found no meaning in me. He merely looked away, sat back in his carriage, and spoke to an unseen companion, who then, in turn, looked out at me. It was the Irishman, Mr Neale, the third part of the Duke's *ménage*, and now love's victor. It was his love which had triumphed in the end, not Mr Sellis's. He smiled at me thinly then sat back, in the dark. I stared and stared at their elegant carriage, I could not look away, until finally, I heard a voice inside tell the driver to go, and the fellow on top cracked his whip at the horses, and they started to pull away.

★

In the days that followed, I found I was drawing further and further into myself, in that dangerous manner that I know takes me in perilous directions. I found myself madly running over things in my head, again and again, things that could have been done differently, things done that were mistakes, things I could not change, things I did with or without remorse, things others had done to betray me, things I had done to betray others. Each day, I roamed around London, to no actual effect. I told my wife that I was most busy with things to do with the chapel, but I came home every night, so she was happy. It was not her fault, but that happiness felt like a knife stuck in between my ribs. Each night, I went to sleep in our rooms, thinking that my wife knew nothing of what had gone on in my life: how we obscure ourselves, almost entirely, from those who imagine they know us intimately.

★

One day, I walked far from home, thinking and thinking and thinking. I kept trying to put it all back together, everything that had happened in those last awful months. I was trying to see what had gone so wrong, what could have been done differently. There were so many things; it would humiliate and condemn me to recount them here. I tried not to think of Sally and Leonora, of Sweet Lips and the Duchess, of Hepburn and White; it was too painful now. *I have to think of my own sanity*, I kept saying to myself, but instead, always I ended up thinking about Ned, sometimes as that pure, wonderful person with whom I had fallen in love. I thought of that miraculous 'understanding', that unique connection we had surely had. And then

214

again, I thought of the mystery of how he had just vanished from my life, how cruelly he had treated me. How I hated him then! But I chastised myself. People were frightened. He had cause to be frightened; we all did. I needed to feel compassion, to remember that we had loved each other.

I had been rambling three hours perhaps – the City, Moorfields, Clerkenwell, out to Islington and Kings Cross, through villages like Euston and back into Bloomsbury. My legs ached, and my mouth had grown dry. I think I must have been almost in St Giles when I caught someone looking at me in the crush of bodies on the street. Momentarily I did not recognise the young woman, although she was gazing at me very directly, yet without attempting to catch my attention. Only gradually did I see it was Lydia Caesar. I had not seen her for a very long time by then, though she looked precisely the same, with her pale bonnet and her defiant eyes.

As soon as she realised I had seen her, she dropped her gaze from mine, and turned to walk away. I don't know why but I felt the need to pursue her. I felt so wronged in those days that perhaps I wanted some explanation of her and her mother's disappearance from the Obelisk – O, I don't know. But *some* morality was rising in me: I had deserved better treatment than this! I called her name in the street – 'Miss *Lydia*! Miss *Lydia*!' – and she turned around with such determination.

'Reverend Church,' she said flatly.

'Miss Lydia, have I done something to offend you? Whenever we speak, you seem almost unable to hide your contempt for me.'

'I don't know what you mean, Reverend. I haven't seen you in months, so how can you come to such a summation?'

'I know. I wanted to ask why you no longer come to the Obelisk. I wondered perhaps if you had some other religious belief now.' I thought of how once I had imagined her – and Ned's – atheism. 'Or none?'

She fixed me very firmly with her stare. 'A person is free to go wherever they please, Reverend.'

I gasped aloud to hear her brutality. 'Truly, Miss Lydia, I do not understand your contempt for me.'

She looked at me piercingly, more than she ever had before. 'I am a free woman, Reverend Church, and I do not have to explain my likes and dislikes.'

Still she assaulted me! 'I have always welcomed your mother and your group at the Obelisk.' This seemed only to irritate her.

'You used us, Reverend Church!'

'Used you?'

'At your chapel. For some kind of . . . *authenticity*. My mother was too polite to tell you to get lost, but I am not, Reverend Church, *I am not!* I am not afraid to tell you what I think of the predatory nature of English priests!'

She was glaring at me with such despicable disdain. I did not need this; I did not care about this woman; let her go, off to her faithless life, and I would go off to mine. I was about to bid her good day and turn away, and then, in her gleeful sense of superiority over me, she said the most remarkable, the most wonderful thing: 'And if, Reverend Church, you are hanging around here to pester Master Ned, you should make your way, sir, because he is not interested in knowing you any further.'

My entire body went perfectly still, my flesh like ice. 'Ned?' I whispered, so innocently.

Her high dudgeon – her enjoyment of her own vilification of me – prevented her from stopping to think what she was saying. 'I assume that's why you are hanging around here, Reverend, because you know he moved to Drury Lane after he left the Mint. Well, let me tell you, he has no interest in seeing you or listening to your silly theology or your excuses for your terrible behaviour. He is a different man now to when he knew you. He stays with his own kind—'

Instantaneously, all my ill-feeling was gone. I felt like I was floating on air. She had revealed the truth to me. She had revealed to me where he was. She was still talking as I turned and walked away from her. On the air, I could hear her bright outrage: 'Reverend Church! I warn you, Reverend Church!' But I did not care one jot. She could talk as much as she liked. *I had found him again.*

*

The next two days, I waited for him, on every part of Drury Lane, my eyes searching, searching for him. I stood, in a haze, in a new dream, one in which perhaps fresh starts are suggested – or terrible reckonings. It was a dream/a madness. I was hungry to see him, but what would I say or do if I did? Just a simple, spare greeting. Just a thump in the face. Just sudden, rushing kisses, as we stumbled backwards, tearing at each other's clothes. I waited, perched against walls, squatting on doorsteps. Hours seemed like seconds, yet each day dragged on like whole seasons: winter, spring, summer, autumn, turning on a slow rhythm.

On the third day, the weather was fine. That morning, I had hardly eaten anything; an oversight or an act of faith. By the afternoon, I was hungry and my feet and back hurt from standing around. I remembered from when they starved me at the gilder's shop that when your stomach is empty, you should drink water. I knew there was a water-seller at the top of Drury Lane, selling at a ha'penny a gulp. I found her, a Welshwoman, and bought two cups, drinking them one after the other as she stood talking to another customer. Her voice was pretty and light, that melodic Welsh accent that I love. Now and then she dipped into her own language, strange and elastic. The other customer replied in English throughout, but – mysteriously – understood the Welsh. Their sentences ran Welsh/English/Welsh/English.

Then there was laughter at something said in one language or the other; or both; all this understanding, all this mutual comprehension, when I had none.

The water made me perk up a little; I bent my ear to see if I could pick out any words in the Welsh, but I could not. I actually started to turn my head, so intently was I listening to that which I could not understand. I turned so far, eventually, I was almost fully staring south down Drury Lane. It was then that I saw him.

He was just standing there, that long, angular line of his body, looking at something on a market stall. He exchanged a few words with the stall owner, and I saw that soft shyness as he smiled at something they said. I blinked slowly, watching him, and I could not bring myself to believe that this was truly him. He seemed as tangible as a cloud; untouchable, unreachable; no more and no less real than that. It felt as if he was a dream, or we were both a dream, just going about our business, in a way that makes no sense observed rationally but entire sense within the dream.

With that sudden shiver on the neck of one who knows he is being watched, he straightened his back. He turned and looked at me. Thoughts tore through me, of what he might say of our reunion: *you came back, you found me, I waited and waited, I love you, how could I do anything but love you, John?* All my anger was floating out of my body, and his goodness, his beauty, everything I had admired in him and wanted from him, and for him, was filling me up.

His eyes widened, his lips parted. I smiled a little, uncertainly, but, astonishing and inexplicable to me, his face grew stern, rejecting. He turned and began to walk briskly away, southwards into Covent Garden. I realised that he was fleeing me! Seconds ticked out with my poor, frazzled mind trying to make sense of what was happening. During those ticking seconds, his back began to vanish out of view. I began to run after him, dropping the water-seller's cup to the ground. I heard it clatter, then the girl shouting after me. In a moment, I was running down Drury Lane. I started shouting his name: *'Ned! Ned! Ned!'* He did not turn around. He started to run too; running from me! *'Ned! Ned! Ned!'* I kept yelling, as if his running away were some kind of mistake. What else would make any sense?

We got to the top of Long Acre, not so very far from the tavern on Vere Street. At the crossroads of the two streets, he swung round to face me. I crashed to a sudden stop. His eyes were red with upset – or alarm.

'What do you want, John?'

His hostility was everywhere around me in the air. *I could not understand; I would not understand.* 'You run away from me now?'

'Why do you think it's all right just to turn up at places where I am?'

'What?'

'The Corporation Hall, you just turned up there. Mint Street, you used to turn up there. Now here. How long have you been watching me, John?'

Watching him? 'I am in love with you,' I said quietly. 'Have you forgotten that I love you?'

He did not even acknowledge what I had said. 'Lydia told me she'd seen you lurking around.' He was shaking his head. 'I cannot see you, John.'

He said it so emphatically, it shocked me. 'Why not?'

'You know why. People are dead, John. People are in prison.'

Suddenly, not knowing what else or how else to speak, I began to speak as a preacher. I began to sermonise my truth. 'I have come to tell you that I have come to see that the only goodness in the world is love, Ned. It's not revolution, it's not radicalism, it's not even religion. It's love. Only love. Whatever else the world might do, if there is love, there is goodness, and those who love—'

'Stop it, John!' He was glaring at me angrily – why?

'No, Ned, those who love – who love each other – maintain that goodness, keep it alive, and if you and I still love each other—'

'Stop it, John, you sound like a madman!' *A madman?* I understood none of this rejection. We had had such understanding. We were the same, he and I, and now? What were we now? I felt like I was drowning. Like he was drowning me.

'Ned . . .' I begged.

'Get away from me, John. I never want to see you again. I am not the person you thought, and you are not the person I thought.'

What? 'Don't say that.' I reached out to touch him, but he just pulled himself away.

'Get away from me, John!' Now he was beginning to shout. People were starting to turn. It was so dangerous to us. How could he, of all people, take such a risk? 'Get the fuck away from me, John!' I did not, could not, move. *'Get the fuck away from me!'*

His eyes were so wild with anger, but at the last moment he seemed to falter. Did I think he was changing his mind, relenting, admitting what he truly felt? He turned and strode off, and on broken steps, I started to follow him. Then, at last, he swung round, on Drury Lane, and screamed at the top of his lungs: *'Get the fuck away from me, John! Don't follow me any more! Leave me alone!'*

His eyes were hot with fury, and so finally, I understood love had turned to hatred. That there was no love from him; only hatred. Finally he had turned to hate too, just like those people who had watched my friends pilloried and hanged. He stormed away and I knew that it was time to surrender. I had given him everything, but he would give me nothing by return.

★

I staggered away, through the streets that ran downhill to the river. Soon I found myself standing on the northern end of the Bridge, looking out eastwards. My mind was floating and destroyed. And here at the river's edge, I come to confess the truth. I haven't told you something about myself. I kept it from you, not to deceive you, but to protect myself from your judgement.

When William Webster left, I tried to kill myself. When I told you I had lain on the floor of our rooms and I had realised how to forge a future for myself, forgive me, but that was a lie. I deceived you. I wanted to make myself seem more impressive – more whole – than truly I am. Because the real me is just fragments of a person; that child I never actually sewed back together, after all. I told you I was Something, or Someone. But my deep fear is this. I am still Nothing. Never more have I vanished down into my nothingness, that fear I have that I matter to no one, am loved by no one, and can hold on to no one, than in the sharp moments of rejection in my life, of which that day on Drury Lane was one.

Here is my last confession. The day after William left for Essex, I came here, like all those who drown themselves in the river do, and stood in this exact spot, above the fast rapids of the east side of the Bridge. From here, people throw themselves in because the pressure of the torrent of the rubbish-filled arches beneath is so high, your death is fast. Your neck breaks as soon as you hit the water.

That day, all those years before, I had climbed up to jump, I had had every intention of dying. I actually made the leap, but some fellow rushed forwards and caught me right at the last moment, his grasp holding the weight of the coat I was wearing, thinking its heaviness would help my fall. But just for half a second, I flew into the safety of the air – and my death.

Now with Ned, as with William, I stood there at the Bridge's precipice, facing the possibility of self-extinction. How good it felt, and how wonderful and safe, that I would not be here any more, not to feel all this horror of being alive. I was blinking, staring at the rush of the water, the crash of dirty white waterfalls one side to the other, and I remember thinking:

I am a love that cannot be expressed.

I am a love that inspires fear in those that receive it.

I am a love that destroys itself and everyone around it.

I am a love that must, that will, in the end, be abandoned.

How can anyone continue living, knowing these things about themselves?

O, I did not intend to kill myself that day; I just went to remember that perhaps back when William left, I should have ended it all. If I had, I would not be doomed to repeat my failures. So, instead of jumping from the Bridge, I merely blinked away whatever tears were in my eyes, turned south, and began to walk slowly home.

PART THREE

Eighteen Months Later,
The Year Finally Becoming
Eighteen Hundred And Twelve

Chapter Fifteen
or
Monsters!

I was enveloped in a fog of my griefs. I felt as if my body was smashed out of shape, into different – new and frightening – forms. I felt like I had been broken down into pieces – not for the first time in my life, no, but more profoundly than any time since, well, William. I felt like I was not a man, I was just human pieces, dismembered and eviscerated but still alive. I wanted him to understand what he had done to me, but then how could he? I did not exist for him any more.

★

Slowly, that fog lifted, and I felt such anger for him: feelings of ire, hatred, destruction, revenge. Yet even that passed, this desert of recriminations, and what was left then? Nothing was left. It had all become nothing. And that was worse: nothing in a world of nothing. My old life was gone; all my friends were dead or in prison. I had fallen, expecting eventually to be caught in a net. But the net was gone. I had fallen and fallen and fallen, and when my body finally hit the ground, it just smacked into it, *bang*, without anyone to catch it.

★

Ned and I could have been friends – in another world. Perhaps, like Sally and me, we could have laughed about our old connection. But when the other side remains so icily cruel, what is left? Regret. Misunderstanding. That peculiar grief about the remaining of regret and misunderstanding. *What if, what if, what if?* And then: *fuck you.* Is hatred easier than love? Was that what I was learning in those desperate days? If so, then I had lost my faith that the world could get better – would inevitably get better. It can get worse, or at best, refuse to change.

★

O, another thing I must tell you; something you'll find sad, only naturally. My poor wife suddenly sickened and died in this break of time. The coroner said she had drunk herself to death, and her liver was as black and shrivelled as a prune, but I would not believe that. She just gave up. Life was too hard for her. How I wish she had just left me, as I had told her, gone back to Hampshire, said I was dead, and married again. If England was a nicer, fairer country, it would have allowed us to divorce. Then again, if that were the case, England would allow a lot of things.

★

No sooner was she in the grave than the Gees kicked me out of our rooms. They said they had had enough of me and all my 'curiosities'. I asked them if they could not respect a widower, to which Mrs Gee quite unfathomably said that they had not respected me as a husband, so why should they start now? I had brought 'all sorts' to their door, they said, and now I could 'push off!' I wrote a long letter to my wife's father, returning the last drawn-cheque he had sent his daughter. I expected him to write back gratefully, knowing I had acted honourably in not cashing his money, perhaps finally to set old enmities aside. A week later, I received a letter from Hampshire, which I opened and inside found a sheet of paper, written on which was only a single word:

MONSTER!

One afternoon in the autumn of 1812 . . .

The war had turned in England's favour, everyone agreed, and after twenty years of fighting, since before they killed King Louis and Queen Marie Antoinette, it seemed like the end was in sight. *Might England win?* people whispered in wary hope. Napoleon was on the run, losing in Spain, in Russia, fleeing madly across Germany, back to his rat-hole, Paris. *Might England be the greatest country in the world again?* they wondered. Who knows when hopes are in vain?

And yet, because history is cruel, and likes to take with one hand and then take with the other too, those years were also very hard. It was a time of terrible weather, dark, cold summers, and so failed harvests and hungry winters. Prices soared even further, ever and ever upwards. *How long can it go on?* people asked, but they had asked that question twenty years before. Let history whisper the answer: *It can go on for fucking ever, you morons!* Despite talk of victory, around England there was clamour, unrest, unhappiness. Ordinary folk smashed up the factories of owners who paid them less and less, and organised huge marches that made certain classes of Englishmen nervous. But still it went on, the sense that things in our once-great country were getting worse and worse . . .

Soldiers, dismissed from a war growing quieter in Europe, sat cadaverous with hunger on street corners. Employers were unable to pay their staff, and so landlords received no rent, and tenants were thrown out, children, elders and all. The choice to starve or to whore yourself or your children is not a good one. The itinerant swelled the streets, and as the weather was so bad, their clothes turned to blackened, mouldy rags; eventually, so did their skin.

That summer, the newspapers spoke of none of this.

Journalists wrote breathlessly of shiny things. One was a *new* war – as if there had not been enough war! – this time with America. The Yankees had invaded Canada, and the British, the papers said, were trying to protect the native Indians, whose interest we had always been protecting, it appeared. They also wrote feverishly of the famously infamous Lord Byron, who had that spring published his poem *Childe Harold*. Never before, people pronounced, had someone become so instantly famous as he. He was a new sort of Briton, everyone declared, a man who rejected reason in favour of emotion, sensibleness in favour of sensuality. There was talk that Lord Byron was a Sodomite, or rather, in truth, a Pederast, his reputation as a ladies' man serving solely to obscure the fact. Last of all, a madman shot the Prime Minister, Mr Spencer Perceval, dead. The press reeled with the news. On London's streets, you often heard muttered: *'They should shoot the fucking lot of 'em!'* But if you think I come to speak kindly of the lot of the blameless poor, mistake me not. The number of mollies being arrested and prosecuted kept increasing, more and more taken with every bad turn of events, their pillorying and executions never better attended, never more applauded by radicals and reactionaries alike, men who said it was to protect women and children, the same men who raped their maids and sold their slaves.

Now, in the radical world, I saw only charlatans, liars, self-seekers, self-deluders, those who proclaimed morality only to do ill; and in the streets, a rabble who presented with unrest, hunger and uncertainty decided to bay for the blood of those more vulnerable than they. The days when I had believed in the goodness of human beings seemed far away. My faith felt so destroyed. Yet I continued to trudge into the Obelisk, numb with grief and shock – I still needed to make a living – and delivered sermons – using the same old words, like glass in my mouth.

Do you need a paradox? (Or is it an irony? Don't ask me – I am not educated enough to know the difference!) Well, know that the chapel prospered greatly in those days, doubling, tripling its numbers. Yet every Sunday, I stared out at those rows and rows of faces, thinking only: *What are we all doing here? What performance is this now?* The fame of the Obelisk continued to grow among the city's radical Christians. I had invites on occasion to speak at other chapels who wished to hear my views, now that the politics of the city were growing more radical too. Preachers are always looking for new markets to explore. Sometimes they paid me; sometimes it was worth more to have my name bandied about, north of the river. And so – it felt – my performance of a new and empty life, successful but meaningless, continued.

*

One bright, golden afternoon, I had been to speak at the very well-heeled and ornately liberal Grosvenor Chapel in Mayfair. It had felt like a success. I walked away in the sunshine with a spring in my step. Sometimes other denominations could be shocked by the simple purity of my own radicalism – love, acceptance, tolerance, nothing else, without conditions – but that day, the attendees had admired it, and thought themselves very good people indeed for doing so. Afterwards, as I was walking home down Piccadilly, I heard a voice behind me say my name: 'Reverend Church . . .' I thought perhaps someone from the chapel had followed me to ask me more questions, but turning, I saw who it was.

'Leonora!' I said.

Even dressed simply and soberly as a man, I knew her at once: short, neat, impassive, yet sweetly smiling. She opened her arms to show her small body in its modest, well-cut black suit. 'You recognise me even now?'

'My goodness, I would recognise you anywhere, Leonora,'

I said, almost laughing, and she smiled, and I knew that she was real; alive and real. It was then that I realised we might be speaking too loudly. Her eyes moved around us, to see the risk of detection, yet I could sense that she wanted to talk.

We walked a few minutes to find a place to sit discreetly in the Green Park, which they said was to be landscaped out again once the war was over. In the past, the Park had been the rural fringe of London. Young soldiers had gone there to duel over matters of honour that had probably never mattered. Nowadays, young scientists experimented with flying balloons or weather devices on its grassy undulations; that seemed like a good thing, science before gunfire.

We found a mound of soft grass, secluded under some trees, from where we could see all the way down to the sharply vaulted rooftops of Westminster Abbey. Sitting down, we were far enough away from any path not to be heard by any person strolling by. 'It's good to see you, Leonora.'

'You too, Reverend Church.'

'How long have you been out of gaol?'

'O, a short while now, they let me out early.' She shrugged as if she did not particularly know why.

I studied her face momentarily. There were small scars on her jaw and around her mouth, healed now but reminders of what she went through on that awful day two years before.

'Where are you living now?'

'I live on Saint George Street, just over there.' She pointed up towards Mayfair; Saint George Street was a *very* fashionable place to live.

'How can you afford that, Leonora?'

She gave me a soft, small smile, one of her loveliest. 'I have a gentleman of some means.'

I laughed. 'You bagged a rich man!'

'He is actually a very intelligent fellow, a scholar. I like that about him. He writes poems and such. But he inherited money and a house there from an aunt.'

'You are a lady of means now, Leonora.'

She lifted her face to the light and delicately placed one hand over the centre of her chest, like a Bourbon princess. 'Indeed, Reverend, indeed.'

I smiled at her performance. 'Do you live openly together?'

'O, no,' she went. She leaned forwards. 'But I am going to live the life of a lady of property! So no matter what anyone tells you, remember this: Black-Eyed Leonora *does not rent*.'

I laughed very merrily and so did she. 'Do you hear from Sally?' I asked, when we'd settled.

'She is still in prison.' I had forgotten: she had received a longer sentence than the others. 'Mr Cook is out, I believe, and Sweet Lips.'

'Have you seen Sweet Lips?' She nodded quite brightly and rolled her eyes, as if to say: *you know Sweet Lips*. 'Is she still beautiful?' I asked quietly.

Leonora grinned. 'Sweet Lips doesn't need anyone else to tell her she is beautiful.' I nodded at the truth of that statement. It wasn't an answer; perhaps that was for the best.

'Did you hear about the Duchess?'

Leonora's eyes fixed rather. 'I heard a rumour but I haven't seen any facts.'

'What do you mean?'

'I mean you should show me a grave, Reverend, and I'll mourn. Until then, I'll be optimistic. I'll have hope. That's my nature, Reverend, though it might surprise. I'll always have hope, if there's any hope to be had.' I remembered when I could have said the same thing of myself. It affected me very deeply, that after everything, Black-Eyed Leonora could say such a positive thing.

We hung in the awkwardness of not knowing what else to say. 'What will Sally do when she gets out?' I asked.

'She always had a wealthy lover who kept her to her liking.' I laughed; I had no idea. 'She says that we will be like two dowager duchesses in our old age, terrorising all the shops in Mayfair.'

'That seems a nice old age to have.'

She nodded so merrily. 'I'll see how it goes with my fellow on George Street. Sally and I might end up running our own molly house, Reverend. Eighty years old, with Philip Kett still behind the bar, even older.' She gave me her detached, amused smile, the one I now understood was also a performance. 'Do you go to any houses now, Reverend?'

'No,' I said. 'I don't even know where they are.'

'There are plenty of them.'

'Even now, with all the arrests?'

Leonora looked at me as if I were mad. 'Of course now. Do you think desires disappear just because they are under threat? Are the parks still busy at night?'

'I wouldn't know.'

'Of course they are, Reverend. The parks will be full at night on the Day of Judgement. Our natures do not cease because our enemies seek to destroy us. That is what our enemies never understand. You cannot kill a person's nature, you can only kill the person.' She sighed long and slow, her eyes moving across the grass. 'What happened to your young man?'

'O, it ended.'

'After the house was raided?' I nodded. 'People get scared,' she said kindly. 'Don't hate him for being scared. He loved you.'

'Do you think so?' I asked, surprised that she should say it.

'O, it shone out of him, Reverend, that he loved you.' Was this more of her hopefulness? I was not sure what to make of it, if so. 'You know, Reverend, I will never be able to thank you enough,' she said, suddenly changing tack.

'For what, Leonora?'

'For what you did for us at Vere Street. You told us we were worthy of love, Reverend, as worthy as any other person. You did wonderful things for us, no matter what happened in the end . . .' She took a small, tearful breath – then, just as quickly, cleared her throat. 'You showed us there was goodness in a world that allowed us no goodness, that allowed us only hate. You showed us—' Her emotion stopped her but I knew what she was going to say.

'That you could be loved.'

She nodded, then apologised if she was being silly, which she absolutely was not. In that moment, I felt in my soul a spark leaping from flame to straw, and I wondered: could I believe in the possibilities of love again?

Pulling a pocket watch from inside her jacket, she got to her feet and said she had to go. She raised her hand and turned and was gone. I sat there a long time alone in the Green Park. The sunlight intensified and was so beautiful, painting the grass and the trees the brightest, most summery green. I was smiling.

Some short time after . . .

In the days that followed my meeting Leonora, a new sense of hope entered me, and I felt happy again, for the first time in so long. Folk at the Obelisk said that I was 'like a new man altogether', although they had said nothing of my mood in the two years before. But I knew there was a fresh spirit in my preaching, and very strongly, I felt a renewal of my beliefs in the goodness of human beings, and the capacity of societies to come together in ways mediated not by hate or resentment but by mutual and reciprocal love. This also brought a reinvigoration in my interest in being at the chapel, so much that I would go every day now, to witness its community and its mission. I started to leave the chapel open for the destitute to gather, during the day, as price rises and worklessness had soared through the year. These were hard times, and it became part of my mission to help provide respite and feed those who could not feed themselves. After Leonora, I had my faith again; I felt restored.

One evening, in the middle of the week, I decided to check on the Obelisk to make sure all was in order. To my surprise, I found it all but empty. Usually, by now, the hungry would have started to gather. If it had been raining, the sodden would have sought shelter. But the days had lately been sunlit, so perhaps people did not need to come all the way to Kennington to find relief. As I arrived, an old woman with a mangy dog at her heel was going in before me, like a worshipper entering on Sunday morning, looking up into the cavernous ceiling, awaiting God. Alerted by my presence, she turned to ask if there would be soup that evening. 'If the ladies of the congregation bring it,' I said, 'but I'll come back later with some bread.'

'O,' she grimaced. 'I was hoping there'd be soup or else I wouldn't have bothered!'

'You can wait awhile if you wish, mum,' I said, but the woman just groaned. Grumbling to her dog, she shuffled off to the other side of the chapel to find a seat.

I walked forwards to the pulpit, hardly noticing the solitary other figure present, seated very still in the front pew. What little I perceived of him was a blackened, hunched male figure, staring out at nothing in particular. This was often the manner of the destitutes who gathered at the Obelisk. He did not greet me, but as I walked past him, I heard a familiar – a distantly familiar – voice behind me: 'Evening, Reverend Church.' I turned to look at him, and in the middle of saying good evening back, I shuddered. It was James Cook.

He looked at least fifteen years older. His prowling handsomeness was entirely wiped from his face. He had become a racked, crooked line of a man, old before his time, swollen and colourless. 'Surprised to see me, Reverend?' he asked, all sarcasm.

'How long have you been waiting, Mr Cook?'

'A long time.' Finally he looked at me more directly, and there was such a viciousness in his eyes. 'Such a long time, Reverend . . .'

I felt the hairs on the nape of my neck prickle. 'If I had known—'

He interrupted me: 'I came yesterday, and again today, and waited hours and hours. What do you think that means, Reverend?'

'I don't know.'

'It must mean that I am awful keen to see you, mustn't it?' His eyes grew even harder than they had been before, but now there was a mockery in his stare; its object was me. I wondered at how I should bear myself, how I should protect myself.

'How – how is Mrs Cook?' I faltered.

'Like you care.' His tone was bitterer now.

'Care? I care for Mrs Cook very much. She is my friend.'

'Yet you dumped her once you were in the clear.'

'*In the clear?*'

He kept talking: 'She lost the tavern on Long Acre. Creditors came for her in the end. Out on her arse she was, poor cow.'

I paused, trying to assess what this was. 'When last I saw her, I knew she was struggling,' I said.

'And you did nothing to help her?'

'What could I do?' He did not say what; it was stupid of me to ask.

'We live in a room above the Old Cheshire Cheese now,' he said.

'That tavern on Fleet Street?'

It is a famously ancient place; all Londoners know it. 'They

235

give her shifts now and then, down in the tavern, and a room for free.'

'Can she not get another tavern?'

'Can you fly up to heaven, Reverend, to have a visit with Jesus?' he spat.

I blinked. He still had not revealed why he was there. 'How long have you been out of prison, Mr Cook?'

'Not long.' He sniffed. 'Did you say something about soup coming?' I told him perhaps later, and he nodded, looking at me all the while. 'Do you have some money?' I did not reply; he gave me a thin, hateful smile. 'Do you have *money*, Reverend Church?' he said again, with a much darker force.

I looked across the chapel. The old woman was talking to her dog about some wrong someone had done her, who knew how long ago. I heard voices outside the chapel – either those come for shelter or come with soup. Now I just wanted him to go; I could not risk him making a scene. 'I have a few pennies on me, I think, but it should be enough for you to buy some supper.'

He laughed nastily. 'That's not what I mean, Reverend, and you fucking well know it.'

So blackmail was his game. 'This is a chapel in Southwark, Mr Cook. You must know I am not rich.'

He looked up at the ceiling. 'You own this place, don't you? It must be worth a lot.'

I repeated what I had said before. 'I don't have any money, Mr Cook. I am sure you want money quickly, not the two or three years it would take me to sell a chapel building like this.'

'My lawyer is writing a pamphlet to defend my good name. Because I ain't no faggot.'

My back straightened. 'You only took faggots' money.'

His eyes were swollen and white, just like the rest of him, but this was not decline; it was hatred. 'How about you, Reverend?'

'Me?'

'Yes, Reverend, you.' He sighed. 'I think you must have friends in high places, given that you never got accused of nothing two years ago. But you *are* a faggot. A faggot through and through.'

I gave him no satisfaction: 'What do you want, Cook?'

He smirked now, realising that I saw his true intentions. 'The thing is, Reverend, what does that matter, how many dukes or duchesses or princes or prime ministers or Patrol sergeants you have in your pocket, if some ne'er-do-well driven mad by bitterness just floods the streets of London with pamphlets naming you not just as a faggot, but as the man who married mollies on Vere Street? How would you like to be revealed finally as the parson who married them disgusting perverts Hepburn and White?'

I felt a cold wave of fear hit me, but I did not show it. 'Whose money *you* took?'

Cook smirked thinly, to make clear that he did not care one jot about my disgust. I could feel myself shaking, no matter how ridiculous it was; after all, ridiculousness has never stopped any rumour or any court. 'Does Mrs Cook know you are here?'

He laughed at a joke I did not understand. 'Do you know why I married my wife, *Reverend*?' He kept emphasising the word, knowing it would grind on me, and it did. 'I married her because the street I want to live on is Easy Street, *Reverend*,' he growled. 'What do I have now? An old wife with no tavern, and no money, and look at me now, *Reverend*. Do you see what the pillory and prison done to me? Do you think I don't know how I lost my fucking masculine charms?' His eyes had an evil glow. 'Think of what prison will do to yours. If they don't hang you, of course, for your sick inversion of the' – he spoke in this mocking, pathetic way – 'of the Lord's *Holy* Word.' I was still shaking; could he tell? 'So, tell me this, *Reverend*, where do I find Easy Street?' He tilted his head back and looked up at the chapel's vaulted ceiling. 'I think I must have found it here.'

'What – do – you – want – Cook?'

'Twenty pounds,' he said smartly. I burst into laughter – entirely genuine. Most Londoners don't earn that in a year. 'Ten, then,' he bargained. The sudden drop in money might have seemed welcome, but people who suddenly cut their price are desperate; and desperate people are dangerous people. But I could not open the door to blackmail. Blackmail is the dog you pet to calm that just bites you anyway.

'I'm not giving you any money,' I said. 'I don't have any money to give you.'

'My wife said you were married to a most fancy lady.'

I blinked, thinking of what I might say. 'My wife is dead.'

'Lucky you,' he said, his eyes still horribly aglow. 'Or lucky her.'

It was then I began to pull him out of his seat. I started slapping and punching him around the head and the shoulders. 'Get out!' I yelled. 'Get out!'

He screamed and bowed beneath my fists. 'I'll get you, Church!' he was half shouting, half laughing as I pushed him out down the chapel aisle, between the pews. 'I'll get you!' Finally, I pushed him out into the evening, and watched him running away. I couldn't help but remember that night when I had yelled at Mr Linehan in the street, and Ned had warned me, 'You shouldn't have done that, John.'

The next day . . .

I knew what I had to do; go and see his wife, my erstwhile friend, at the Old Cheshire Cheese. I marched north through Southwark and on to the Bridge. I tumbled off its northern side and into the City, and from there picked my way to the tavern itself. You enter it down a long wooden alleyway. There inside,

I asked the fellow behind the bar if Mrs Cook worked here still, and he said yes, she was in her room. 'Upstairs, two flights, third door on the left.'

'Is her husband with her?' I asked.

Pfft, he went. 'Not likely, pal! He comes and goes only when she gets her wages, and today ain't pay day!'

At the end of a black, uneven corridor on the second floor, I found the third door and tapped on it gently. There was no answer. I pressed my ear to the wood; there was no sound at all beyond. 'Mrs Cook?' I called. Again, nothing. I tapped again and put my ear against the surface to listen. A few seconds' silence, then I heard footsteps moving; I jumped back from the door just as it started to open. There she was, looking exactly the same as when we were friends. Her husband was transformed, and yet she looked as if it were only the day before that we were laughing together at Vere Street. 'Reverend Church,' she said without surprise.

There was no fire in the room when she bid me enter, only a single candle. There was a chair and a mattress on the floor, and almost nothing else. The single window was so tiny and so grubby that almost no light would pass through it. I imagined her here alone, over endless hours, with her husband 'likely not' with her.

'Will you sit, Reverend?'

I looked at the lone chair. 'No, Mrs Cook.' She was quite impassive in my presence; there was nothing soft or kind about her. 'I know you lost the tavern on Long Acre,' I began, 'but—'

'But you did not expect to see me as reduced as this.'

'No, I did not,' I said, frankly. 'Do you know your husband came to see me?'

She looked at me a moment. 'Yes.'

'I see . . . Do you know that he asked me for money?'

'Yes.'

239

I am not sure if this surprised me or not. 'Was it you who sent him to blackmail me?'

She was hot with outrage. 'No, Reverend, I did not! I would never do that! It was Jimmy's blooming stupid idea. He thinks you can pay up. He ain't happy you were so free with your fists, you know.'

'Not so happy he got his arse whipped by a faggot?' I said, and she looked down at the floor. 'Why did he come and see me?'

She looked back at me, lifting her hands into mid-air. 'Look for yourself. We are desperate, Reverend.'

'Why not someone with actual money, like the Duke of Cumberland? I thought he was supposed to be our leverage!'

Ha, she went – bitterly. 'He's already knocked on that door.'

'Jesus Christ! What happened?'

'They told him to sling his hook. Told him they would get him arrested again for something else if he didn't keep his trap shut. Someone came and warned him he would get Australia, or a bullet.'

'Did you take the threat seriously?'

She looked at me as if I were mad. 'Didn't Mr Sellis end up dead?'

'Jesus Christ,' I said again, but now barely a mutter.

'Jimmy is obsessed with revenge for what happened to him.' She was suddenly talking quickly, on the edge of tears. 'I worked hard all my life, Reverend, and only tried to do good things, and look, we have had everything taken away from us. Jimmy was in gaol and they called him molly and madge and he had to use his fists every day he was in there! Almost every day, someone tried to kill or rape him! A molly in gaol is just a free hole for anyone to abuse, he said.'

I felt my fury – and my fear. 'Do you think that is any different for Sally? Or Leonora? Or Sweet Lips? Is your husband's hole any more sacred than theirs?'

'They were *my* sisters! They were my friends too.' We were silent a moment, an ill and unhappy silence, a landscape of lost loyalties. 'Do you remember when I said that Jimmy thought someone grassed us up to the Patrol?' I nodded. 'He thinks he's worked out who it was.'

'Who?' I asked.

She looked at me fully ten seconds. 'You, Reverend . . .'

I heard the hum in my head. I wanted to scream at her to take it back. 'That's ridiculous!' I cried, outraged.

My anger unsettled her. 'You got off scot-free!'

'*Scot-free?*' I yelled, so loudly she blinked in fright. 'Is this what you consider scot-free, Mrs Cook? Tommy and Hepburn are dead, my friends are in prison, I live in terror every day, Ned left me! Do you think that *scot-free?*'

'I showed only kindness to my girls!' she protested, as if I had accused her of what was actually an accusation in her own head. 'They called me their sister, their mother! I only showed them goodness!'

'Is your showing goodness sending me to the pillory, or the scaffold too, Mrs Cook?'

A shiver passed through her. 'I only wanted to be a good woman, a kind person,' she whispered, terribly quiet, 'and do what's right.' She looked at me starkly. 'Jimmy has a lawyer who is trouble,' she said. 'His name is Holloway.'

It felt like accusation had switched to warning. 'Trouble in what way?'

'They are going to publish a pamphlet about Vere Street to try and clear Jimmy's name. They are going to talk about Tommy White and Mr Hepburn getting married, and even the Duke. And I think they might try to name you, Reverend, or if not name you, they shall speak to a hack, drop them your name.'

I felt sick, panicked. 'I shall sue them for libel!'

'On what cause?' she asked.

'That they are lying.'

When she spoke, her words had a deadly effect. 'But they won't be lying, Reverend, will they?'

FROM 'THE PHOENIX OF SODOM'
Written by James Cook's lawyer, Mr Holloway
(Published all over London around this time)

... *the statement of Cook cannot be subject to any such misrepresentation, for it is matter of record: – thirty of the parties he describes to be the constant frequenters of the house were apprehended by the Police officers, and that on a Sunday evening; they were all examined by the Magistrates, and their guilt established, though in different degrees: and the dreadful shocking consequences of their conviction ended in the execution of a sentence so disgraceful to humanity, so contrary to the punishment awarded by the laws of England, that the foulest page in the history of savage ferocity must blush at the relation of that ruffianly scene of human degradation; a scene that never could have disgraced the streets of London but in the Sheriffalty of Mr. Matthew Wood; and never can happen again, until Sheriffs and Pillories are made of the same materials.*

Cook, under an idea that it would procure him a remission of the pillory, was desirous of disclosing the names of a great number of persons involved in the transactions: and a meeting took place, at the Secretary of State's Office, upon the subject; but which produced no other effect, than an order to put Cook in the Pillory the next day, which was accordingly done; and, upon his return to Newgate, Suter, the head turnkey, said to him, 'Cook, it was not intended you should have come back alive!'

Chapter Sixteen
or
Remember When I Wrote Some Letters?

Some months later, with the year transforming itself into 1813 . . .

So let me start by wrong-footing you in the conduct of this narrative. The pamphlet 'The Phoenix of Sodom' was published but my name was not in it. How frightened I was, first reading it, that I would be exposed. I read it a second time and a third time, to check and to check again I was not implicated, but I was not. I do not know why at the end they omitted my particulars; was it on Mrs Cook's account? The text was mainly an attempt to clear Cook's name, which did not particularly succeed. Winter came and went, and I heard nothing more of the Cooks, or blackmail; nothing else about plots against me; nothing.

During that time, or slightly before, I am not sure which, I was invited to lodge with a lady from my congregation, by the name of Mrs Hunter. Truth be told, the chapel was profitable enough for me to take my own rooms, even a servant perhaps, but Mrs Hunter was agreeable company and her home comfortable. She invited me to use her parlour to expound my ideas on love and its possibilities to her own well-to-do friends. Some of these ladies said I could be as great a preacher as Mr Wesley, and I waved my hand and said no, self-deprecating in the English manner. But even as they said it, secretly I thought: *why not as great as Mr Wesley?* Indeed: *why not greater!*

At Mrs Hunter's house, I met a young man named Adam Foreman. He was ten years younger than me, a lad of athletic beauty and hungry eyes. After weeks of apparently inane conversations – in which he never mentioned girls, in which stares were held meaningfully, in which the smalls of backs were touched a moment too long, and details were told of when he might be found bathing in the outhouse, or how Mrs Hunter snored so loud she'd never hear a sound – finally, I asked him, 'Do you bolt your chamber door at night, Master Foreman?' A grin as sensuous as the devil's flashed across his face, and he said *no, sir*: 'You'll find me *open* all night, Reverend.'

When the house was asleep, I crept barefoot on floorboards and pushed that unbolted door, to find him waiting, naked on his bed. As we made love, Adam let out his sharp, intense groans of being fucked. True enough, Mrs Hunter, in the room downstairs, snored like Methuselah. Adam let me inside him several times more over the following weeks, before I began to regret doing it. I knew I was making a mistake. Men are such fools, always placing our own desires before sense or safety. I finished it with him, and so earned sharp looks from him whenever I saw him after that. But I'll admit this to you, as it is the truth: it was a short and sweet affair, nothing more; and it should have stayed that way.

THEN!

One Sunday morning, I went down to breakfast and Mrs Hunter was sitting there, atypically in a very grey countenance, as if she had not slept a wink. But I had heard her snoring all night long, even from my more distant room. She hovered around me bringing plates of bacon and black pudding, and bread she had already buttered. There was a newspaper on the table, folded and placed directly in my usual seating place.

'Did you sleep well, Mrs Hunter?' I asked.

'Sleep, Reverend, is a very rare commodity these days!' Her tone was mysterious but very sharp. I stared at her but she did not look at me, instead busying herself with the breakfast.

'Have you been out yet? Is the day warm or cold?'

'*I* don't know, Reverend!' even sharper.

Standing, she turned her back to me. I could not work out what infraction I had committed, and she was not a person much given to moods or sulks. 'This all looks very nice,' I said, surveying the food. 'Shall I make some tea, Mrs Hunter?'

'If you wish, Reverend!' so very icily.

I paused. 'Is something wrong, Mrs Hunter?'

At this, my landlady swung around. For a moment, I thought she might strike me. 'Have you looked at the newspaper yet, Reverend?' She knew I had had no opportunity to do so. 'I left it folded precisely so you should read it, Reverend!' She gave a strange, whistling *harrumph*. '*I* propose you should read the paper quick-sharp, Reverend.' She paused and narrowed her eyes at me. 'You are on the front page!' What hot, sick panic overwhelmed me! I unfolded the newspaper, the *Weekly Dispatch*, famous for its hatred of Sodomites.

THE following statements will fully explain the motives which induced the Editor to expose the crimes of the individual who is the subject of them. The demand for those numbers of the WEEKLY DISPATCH in which they appeared, was so great, that many hundreds of persons were unable to procure the papers, as no more could be printed than those which were called for on the days of publication. The Editor, therefore, wishing to extend his efforts in defence of religion and morality as widely as possible, by holding up to all mankind a true picture of a blasphemous hypocrite who is a contemner of the one and a violator of the other, has thought it advisable to publish the whole of his narratives and remarks in

a separate pamphlet; to which are subjoined many additional facts
that could not appear in a Sunday Paper. The reason this publi-
cation has been so long delayed was, in expectation that JOHN
CHURCH would have been brought to trial—

There it was, my name, for all of London to see:

JOHN CHURCH . . .

I looked up at Mrs Hunter. Had Cook gone to the press and had his revenge after all? A bloom of sweat, cold and cloying, formed, rainbow-shaped across my hairline. 'Jesus Christ,' I whispered. I thought I was going to puke.

'It's you, isn't it, Reverend?' Mrs Hunter cried. 'How can it *not* be you, Reverend?' I did not answer. I tried to read on but the words fell in fragments, cut up and hateful. Testimony from the Gees, quoted from their cake shop on The Cut: deriding my dead wife, her drunkenness, naming mysterious people who came in and out of our rooms. A young man in Ipswich, who does not even feature in this narrative, had accused me of indecency. The paper complained this young man's mind was 'completely destroyed, so fatally has the event preyed upon him', when I remember him riding my cock like a jockey rides a pony on Derby Day. So many lies about me, about the Obelisk, my wife. I had not yet reached the worst part. No, this was nothing like the worst!

. . . I can only say I wish you was as much captivated with sincere
friendship as I am but we all know our own feelings best . . .
. . . having already proved what human nature is I must conceal
even those emotions of love which I feel, I wish I had the honour of
being loved by you as much and in as great a degree as I do you . . .
. . . Sometimes the painful thought of a separation overpowers
me . . .

. . . I find, dear Ned, many are using all their power to part us but I hope it will prove in vain on your side . . .

. . . I am confident if you love me now or at any other time my heart will ever be upon you nor can I ever forget you till death . . .

. . . Your leaving of me will break my heart . . .

These were the letters I had sent Ned, after he had left me. I know it: I misled you before, as to their number. Perhaps, with the passage of time, I have misled myself as well. Here they were, though, published in their multiplicity, letter after letter after letter. Only slowly did I realise what this worst part was. It must have been Ned who had betrayed me to the *Weekly Dispatch*. He had sold them my letters.

Then I read the most evil lie. It claimed that the recipient of these letters – named only as Ned B., to save his honour, no doubt – had been 'harassed' by me for many months after ending our association, his period of employment at the Obelisk Chapel. *Harassed*: I did not understand. How could he say such cruel, deceitful things, tell such lies? *Harassed?*

. . . why not speak to me last night in the street when you heard me call, Stop! Stop! Ned! . . .

. . . Cruel Ned, deaf to all entreaties . . .

. . . Why was I permitted to tramp up and down the New Cut after you . . .

. . . I never, never thought you would deceive me . . .

. . . I cannot sleep, 'tis near three o'clock . . .

. . . Why did my dear friend Edward deceive me . . .

. . . How can I bear the piercing thought, parted; a dreadful word, worst of sensations . . .

. . . O that I had never, never known you, then I should never feel what I do . . .

Reader, it is to you I should apologise. I know that you now realise that I did not tell you about all of these letters, the intensity with which I behaved. I know that you are now thinking I have manipulated you, misdirected you, have led you to think I behaved in ways that perhaps I did not. Don't think those things of me. That good man you knew before: I am still the same man; I am not changed; I just believed in love. I harassed no one: I believed in love. All I have done is love him. And all he has done is harm me.

Here are my final, final confessions: I wrote him all those letters, letter after letter after letter, to show him just that, how much I loved him, in hopes that he might admit he loved me, by return. I want you to remember how he drove me to the edge of madness, and then beyond. The manipulation was his not mine. Never once did he tell me he loved me (did you notice that?). It was never my intention to do wrong. Like I said, he drove me to the edge of madness . . . and then beyond. He drove *me* mad. He broke *me*. Yet he says I harassed *him*.

Fists started thumping at the kitchen's back door. Mrs Hunter cried in surprise then went to answer it; I remember the rustle of her dress along the stone floor. When she opened it, a voice I recognised – a worshipper – outside: 'The Reverend had better come down the Obelisk,' he yelled. 'I think folk are about to burn it down!'

We rushed through the morning, all panicked breaths, brows sweating. As we turned onto St George's Circus, I saw a small crowd, and above it, bobbing on a tide like an unrowed boat, a male effigy hanging from the noose. A slow horror crept over my body. The effigy was supposed to be me. I felt such a sick terror. I wanted to flee. *Start again, John Church. Just turn and run and say, fuck you all, and start again, John Church. You were Nothing before; you can start over; make yourself Something again. You are not even truly John Church. Even that is not your real name. Erase yourself before others erase you; recreate yourself in your own image before others recreate you as they see fit.*

A hand touched my shoulder. It was the worshipper who had come to alert me. Beyond him was Mrs Hunter, her face wide with alarmed wonder. 'Ain't you going to do nothing, Reverend?' the man yelled, a kind of moral challenge, when I was spent with moral challenges. But what can one do in the proximity of violence?

Hearing the voice, someone on the edge of the crowd turned and pointed at me: 'There he is!' More people started to turn. One man rushed at me, kicking and shouting at me, calling me a degenerate, a pervert, a seducer. He was a rough sort, around my age, whose face I recognised, but I could not think from where. He lunged at me and I pushed him down, kicked him hard in the side, so that he writhed on the floor, glaring up at me in this strange self-pitying shame. He seemed startled by my retaliation, the shame of being punched out by a Sodomite.

He got up and flew at me like a demon. Before I had a chance to stop him, I felt some hard blow against my skull. I saw the stone he had clenched inside his palm fall to the ground, bouncing away from his attack on me. I tasted warm, salty blood in my mouth. I collapsed to my knees. He started spitting in my face then he pushed me down and started stamping on my head. All I remember was the dazing, ringing hammer-blow of his heel, *bang, bang, bang* against my skull.

*

For a while, I was in a sleeping half-world, of black shadows, of mysterious miasmas, of flashes of colour. A dry tongue, a ripped throat, my head aching like I can never describe, the slow, gradual knitting of a body – a consciousness – back together. By the time I had recovered at Mrs Hunter's, she had had her windows put in twice. She told me how they had brought me, unconscious and bleeding, back to her house, and that the Patrol had arrested the man who had attacked me. His name was Webster. I realised who he was from our fight years before: William Webster's brother!

★

On the Friday, Mrs Hunter asked me to leave. On the Saturday, I moved into the Obelisk, to sleep among the destitute. Was this my lowest point? Can you credit how far I had fallen? I had money to take private rooms somewhere, but what landlord would rent to me now, knowing at any moment the mob would burn the place down. At least at the chapel I could muster the protection of my remaining worshippers – and the street folk who saw me only as the man who had brought them kindness.

★

Shall I tell you of the pamphlets that fell like snow over every single street, hymning my made-up name: John Church. As briefly as a magnolia flower, I became the most famous man in London. (*Fuck you, Prince Regent! Fuck you, Lord Byron!*) But let me tell you also how the most successful pamphlets of all were written by those who meant only to do me harm, so my fame was worth nothing but a knife at the throat. In their stories, I was not the hero. I was the villain: the debaucher, the sinner, the perpetrator of a crime. The editor of the *Weekly Dispatch*, they said, was as pleased as punch. His circulation went through the roof.

★

My final descent into hell came on a Sunday, during the bible meditation. As we were all trawling through some verse or

251

other (because somehow, my congregation, in the face of my potential public martyrdom, insisted on the continuation of my ministry – like Gethsemane on the bottom of the Kennington Road!), one of my congregation burst into the chapel, with such force that all of us within jumped and squealed. He slammed and bolted the door behind him. 'The Patrol is here to arrest you, Reverend Church!'

The group drew breath and then started to crash around in panic. Any mood of pious defiance – all Meshach, Shadrach and Abednego – suddenly evaporated. People started groaning as one, some saying we should resist, others that they should run. My heart was pounding in my chest, I could feel my own panic rising. Now there was hammering at the bolted door. 'Open up! We have come for the criminal John Church!' a voice yelled, brutal, from outside.

A woman shouted to her husband: 'We must protect the Prophet!' At the beginning of this story, I told you: I am not a prophet. That was why the husband replied: 'Wife, perhaps we should leave instead.'

Feet started battering the chapel door, then bodies hurled themselves against it. Within, people were screaming. The bolt broke and the door burst open, slamming backwards. A torrent of men stormed in, Patrol officers all dressed in black and brass, swinging coshes, blowing whistles. One rushed at me and knocked me to the ground. I hit the stone floor of the Obelisk. I saw a black boot raised in the air, coming crashing down on my body.

'John Church, we arrest you for the foul crime of sodomy.'

I heard the sharp gasps of my congregation. 'Against whom?' I cried.

'There are several accusations.'

'*Several* . . . ?' one of my worshippers said, shocked.

'Tell me!' I cried. 'I have a right to know.'

'The first accuser is Adam Foreman.'

'And the other?'

The Patrol officer stood above me; his face was hellish. 'A man has accused you of assaulting him many years ago. He has come to court to accuse you.'

'*Who?*' I cried.

The Patrol officer was looking at me, so blankly amoral. 'William Webster.'

'AN EPISTLE FROM THE DEVIL
TO HIS FRIEND AND FOLLOWER JOHN CHURCH'
(Published during these events)

We are hypocrites both,
To deceive nothing loth,
   In short we're just form'd for each other;
   Then come Johnny, do,
Or I must come for you, –
   O, come to Old Nick, your dear brother.

You shall be treated well,
Dearest John, in hell,
   You on sulphur and brimstone shall feast;
   We'll with fires keep you warm,
And do all things to charm,
   As befits so illustrious a guest.

In hell, John, you'll meet
Your friends from Vere-Street,
   Which quite cosy and handy will be;
   For their chaplain in hell
You may be, John, as well
   As on earth you us'd one time, be.

FROM 'THE INFAMOUS LIFE AND TRIAL OF JOHN CHURCH' (ANON.)
(Published during these events)

The reader may probably have some curiosity to know what sort of a preacher this person is. I have gone to hear him; and I pity his poor deluded followers. He does indeed deliver himself in a full, clear, articulate tone of voice; but to criticise his style, or analyse the substance of his discourse, would be a fruitless labour: it would be like dissecting a cobweb. Unmeaning rhapsodies, and unconnected sentences, through which the faintest gleam of morality is not to be traced, must, from their evanescent nature, set the powers of recollection at defiance; they even escape from the lash of one's contempt. In his countenance there is none of that dignified mildness, none of that subdued expression of piety which one often observes in Christian preachers whose habits of life are conformable to their precepts. His manner is forward and imposing; and his eyes are continually employed in staring at some person among his auditors.

FROM 'THE TRIAL AND CONVICTION
OF JOHN CHURCH'
(Published after these events)

Some, perhaps, may think that too much severity appears in our obser-
vations against the Prisoner – but, can this be the case? Can any man
feel too indignant at the conduct of such miscreants? – We cordially
agree with the learned Counsel for the Prisoner, that if a wish would
sweep such characters from the creation, that wish would be imme-
diately expressed by every true British heart. – Are we too severe?
Remember the conduct of the Almighty, who sent fire and brimstone
from Heaven, and consumed the GUILTY Inhabitants of Sodom and
Gomorrah, lest their filthy bodies should pollute the grave.

Chapter Seventeen

or

A Radical Love

It was a hot day in August, the day my trial commenced. I had kept my freedom on account of my worshippers at the Obelisk miraculously raising my bail. Many allegations swirled in the press, centred on rumours about my role at Vere Street and my relationships with William Webster and Adam Foreman. I was charged with 'assault'. Of course, there was no assault. 'Assault' is the name Normal people give to love between Sodomites. There is an irony in it, I suppose, a terrible one, given that we are the ones who end up dead.

That first day, London's air was thick and soupy. I walked with my lawyer and a few members from the Obelisk. We arrived at the court, breaking through enormous crowds, some waving meat-cleavers in the air, more effigies (of me, hanging in a homemade noose). Around the entrance, a tide of protestors, wearing wooden crosses around their necks, said that I should be burned to death. A man stood bearing the legend 'JOHN CHURCH, INCARNATE DEVIL'. To my surprise, the man was Mr Linehan. When I made eye contact with him, he pointed his finger at me and started to yell not words you might expect – faggot, filth, sinner, Sodomite – but *deceiver*. 'Deceiver!' he shouted at me. *'Deceiver! Deceiver!'*

The courtroom was full: bodies pressed together, the air hot with febrile anticipation. The Vere Street scandal had flickered spectacularly back into life in London, with the capture of me, the last and perhaps the most egregious of its actors. I was the one who had married Hepburn and White. Although the charge against me was not for marrying men, the 'accusation' was widely recounted and hotly revived interest in the story, now three years old.

I looked up at the gallery above the courtroom. Then I saw them seated together in a dark corner. It was Leonora, and with her Sally, finally free from prison. They were dressed as men, huddled closely. Sally wore a short beard now – to conceal both her identity and her femininity, I supposed – and Leonora a hat which she did not remove. They gazed at me, directly, piercingly, allowing me to see them. It was then I realised the awful truth. They had come to perform the duty.

The courtroom was a deep, large space, panelled in dark wood. Through high windows, sunlight fell and captured the swirl and swarm of a billion particles of ancient dust, just as I had noticed walking through the molly house on my first visit there. I was made to sit in a caged box, a spectacle for the surging crowd of onlookers.

The judge and the other officers of the court filed in. I placed my hand on a bible and pleaded not guilty to the charges of sodomy. I looked around, picking out further faces, sitting with the prosecution. First I saw Adam Foreman. Then beyond him – sitting there like he had travelled through time – I could hardly believe it – William Webster. His brother was at his side.

William and I gazed at each other for a few seconds. Neither one of us dared to smile. He looked the same. A little heavier, a few years older, but then again: *who is not?* His eyes studied mine. Once upon a time, we had been so very deeply in love. What were we now, after all these years? Strangers, perhaps; but not quite. I should have felt red with rage in that moment, to see him there, betraying me, yet I did not; or at least I do not remember so doing. I felt glad to see him, to know that he was still alive.

The judge started going through the papers. He sighed repeatedly then summoned over both lawyers. There was some tense discussion. Momentarily, my lawyer looked at me with a glint in his eye; I did not understand. The judge sat back and cleared his throat, then he pointed at William Webster, although he had not yet taken the stand. 'You, man,' he said. 'Stand up.' William slowly rose to his feet. 'Is it true to say that you are an unwilling prosecutor?'

I saw my former love's confusion.

'I beg pardon, sir?'

'Is it true to say that you have not brought this case of assault on the basis of your own complaint, but have been coerced here by others?'

'I – I would not have come on my own account, Your Honour.'

I felt relief to hear it. The judge breathed out. 'So why did you come?'

'I came because the hack from the paper said I had to, and if I would not, he would start a case against me in my own district and accuse me there, though I have done nothing wrong.'

The judge raised his eyebrows and stared at the man I knew to be the editor of the *Weekly Dispatch*, who had done men like me such harm in recent times. He had helped himself to a prominent position among the Crown's lawyers.

'I see,' went the judge. He smacked his gavel. 'I see no point in continuing this part of the case. The period of time since the alleged assault and the unwillingness of the witness are as such to make any possible conviction untenable, and I will not indulge the law to drive up the circulation of newspapers on account of threats and insinuation.' The editor of the *Weekly Dispatch* squinted with discomfort; a rat exposed to the light. 'The witness is dismissed.'

There were gasps of surprise around the room. Could English justice sometimes *defend* sin? William's brother ran to the front of the court and began to shout insults at the judge, saying over and over that faggots should burn in hell and what about his family's honour, which was 'besmirched'. 'Besmirched!' he kept yelling. *'Besmirched!'* I watched William blink heavily, every time he yelled the word. The brother was bundled away by the court officers, leaving just William and me standing in the tumult, only fifteen feet apart, me inside the humiliating cage.

'I cannot believe it,' I said, 'after all this time.'

His eyes were on me, then roved around, and returned to mine. 'I would not have come unless they threatened me.'

'Thank you for not speaking against me.' He said nothing, just kept staring hazily at me. 'Do you still believe in our ideas?' I asked him, in part to show that I myself had kept the faith.

'Our ideas?'

'About the goodness of men. About how tolerance and love are inevitable. It has been a difficult path, William, but I have kept my beliefs in that revolution that is coming.' Leaning forwards, I put my hands up to the caged screen around the box in which I sat. I slid my hands up the bars. His eyes focused on me. I wondered if he might come with me now, back to Southwark. I could show him everything I had built, he would admire it, wander around the Obelisk, imagine its pews full every Sunday. Perhaps he would ask me if he could stay, and help me, assist me in some way. Maybe we would even fall back in love; truly, *who knows*? 'I have a chapel, and a large congregation, and my ideas are admired all over London. I wanted you to know what I have achieved. It is a great success . . . despite all this. Would you come and see it one day, William?'

He was just gazing at me, and then he spoke in a cold, clipped way. 'Good God, John, you never change.'

I did not understand. 'What do you mean?'

'Your ideas?' His voice now dripped disdain. 'They were my ideas! You have just stolen them and claimed them as your own.'

'How can you say such lies, William?' I asked, appalled. 'Perhaps we worked on them together, but you used to come to the shop on the Tottenham Court Road, and I told you them on my breaks, when we ate our luncheons in the sun. Do you not remember that?'

'No,' he said, and I *knew* he was lying. 'I remember coming into your shop and your eyes lighting up, and you asking me to meet you again. I remember you pursuing me, suddenly obsessed with me. I remember you persuading me to give up my job to become a preacher in London, with you, until I no longer knew what kind of person I was, or had ever been.'

'Stop it, William,' I said. 'Stop lying.'

'I remember your rages. I remember shaking in anticipation of what new madness each day would bring. I remember you telling me we had to become preachers, though I was afraid of how we would survive. I remember having no money, you spending money we did not have. I remember you not listening to me, what I wanted, not listening to what I needed.'

I knew I could not say the thing I wanted to say just then: *but we were in love.* I was just staring at him, in such horror. 'I never . . . never meant to frighten anyone, William. My rage . . . sometimes I just need to speak. I just need to defend myself.'

'You defend yourself by destroying others, though, John.'

He looked like he was going to weep. I grabbed the bars of the cage. 'I would never have hurt you.'

He let out a frustrated, almost tearful gasp from his chest; I could not make sense of any of it. 'You – you destroyed my mind. You pushed and pushed me, and when I did not do what you said, you barracked and abused me.'

Now I found my anger. 'Destroyed *your* mind? Your leaving broke me into pieces.'

Hearing our voices rise, a court officer got to his feet resentfully. 'Come on!' he growled, pushing William away. I stood up, still grabbing at the bars of my cage.

But as the officer moved him off, William swung around as if to launch himself at me. 'I had to get away from you, John!'

'Liar! Your brother came and forced you to leave because some ne'er-do-well wrote to him, and I was so destroyed, William. I was utterly broken by it, that was how deeply I felt.'

He stopped struggling to escape the court officer's grasp, and allowed himself to be pushed away. As he left, he just gave this sad, long look: 'John, it was me who wrote to my brother.'

'Liar!' I was yelling. 'Liar! *Liar!*'

And then he was gone. I suppose I must have started shouting, or hitting the bars of the cage, or spitting at him, because the court officers were yelling at me to sit down and shut up. The officers were striking the bars of my cage with their truncheons, slicing the skin of my knuckles still wrapped around them, but I felt nothing, not a single scratch. My rage always saves me from pain.

*

That afternoon, Adam Foreman took the stand. The courtroom, noisy and greedy for my next hurdle, having failed to get me before, was irritably called to silence. I lifted my eyes again to the gallery to see my friends, but they were no longer there. The Crown's barrister asked Adam Foreman his age.

'I shall be twenty the first day of December next.'

He had told me he was older. 'Do you know the defendant, John Church?'

'Yes, by sight.'

Another lie. The sight by which I knew Adam Foreman was

every inch of his naked skin, mapped with my eyes, tongue and fingertips.

'How long have you known him?'

'About two or three years.'

No, it was a year, at most. He was making it sound like I was seducing boys; I realised then that was what they had told him to say, so that prejudices might be confirmed. (*Who doesn't like their prejudices confirmed?*) They asked questions about if he knew me as a preacher, where Adam lived, how we met. They asked questions about a particular night, the September before, almost a year back (*so not two or three years*):

'Now, at what time did you retire to rest?'

'Near one o'clock.'

They did not ask: *Isn't that rather late, didn't you lie awake for hours, naked on your bed, waiting for a man to come to your unlocked door and fuck you till your pussy ached?* 'Did you go to sleep?' they asked instead.

'Yes, I went directly to bed.'

'After you had been asleep, did anything happen to you?'

A pause. 'Yes.'

'State what it was.'

'I had not been asleep more than half an hour, before I was awoken by someone putting his hands under the bedclothes, and laying hold of my private parts.'

This was another lie. My nature is impulsive, I admit that. My nature is hot and quick to excess. But this was not how our relationship had started at all. It started with weeks of long looks, his towards me, whispered suggestions, bedroom doors left unlocked. I wondered if this was just malice on his part, for me ending the relationship, or whether he was being paid, or made too afraid not to speak.

★

My trial broke over the weekend. When I left the courtroom, the crowd made my supporters and me walk through a nuptial arch of sticks and cleavers that they tapped on our heads and backs to make us think they might kill us at their whim. Friday night, I went to the Obelisk to preach but the danger was so great, with constant protests and threats. Some of the congregation stayed away, and some were encouraged even more to come, with the wonderful promise of my martyrdom.

I did not sleep on that night, and my exhaustion haunted – and deceived – me. Released from the tension of court, on the Saturday I felt as if I had fallen into a torpor. The muscles under my eyes twitched, my arms and legs hung heavy like corpse-limbs. By the time of the trial, my face had become well known in London, at least enough for people to point me out and go, 'That's him, that's *him*.'

On the Saturday night, exhausted, I slept like the dead, so that on the Sunday, I wanted to go out. It was humid, thundery, so I waited for the heat to break and for the heavy rain to come. Pulling on my greatcoat, I slipped quietly out into the heavy grey atmosphere, avoiding any human contact. I wanted no one else to look me in the eye, and laugh, and say that they were going to cut my throat, faggot. So I became a mouse, scurrying along skirting boards, as fast as I could, one gap in space to another.

I walked towards the river, thinking I would like to stand there in the rain, looking out at the Thames. (No, I was not thinking of doing anything foolish.) But halfway through the Borough, I found myself on the end of Mint Street, where Ned had lived, what seemed so long ago. Gazing down its wet, black cobbles, my emotions unexpectedly overwhelmed me. I suppose I must have walked past there many times in the last few years, yet just then my hurts seemed so unbearable.

I walked up the street to the front of what was once his home. Some curiosity made me want to see it again, in case I had imagined everything that had happened between us. As I stood there, it stopped raining, and people who were sheltering began to emerge to get their day's business done. Just as I thought I might have to scurry home, the door of his former house opened. A small child, an African boy, jumped out and started splashing delightedly in the new puddles in the street. He was perhaps eighteen months old with glittering, saucer-round eyes and pretty hair spiralling into soft curls high above his head. His spirit was so joyful and unencumbered by experience of life. He hopped foot to foot, clapping, in the sheer thrill of stamping through water. From the open door, I heard his unseen father's voice calling to him to take care.

I watched the child in his sweet innocence only a second or two longer, in that time far before all the things of adulthood come in to poison and derange us. The little boy, with his beautiful eyes, looked up at me and grinned for all the world to see his own cheeky magnificence. In that moment, he reminded me of myself at the age I was found alone, wandering in the street: here is a child, a *tabula rasa*. What will his life do to him? There is no way at this early point to find out, but I was that same toddler, riotous with life, alone in the street, shouting his name to no one, or to the mother who had just coldly abandoned him. Who does that to their child, and more importantly, why? Then I heard the father's voice speaking to me: 'What are you doing here, John?'

I looked up at him and said his name: 'Ned . . .'

I swear to you – *I swear to you* – in that moment, I had not even imagined I would see him here. He had left Mint Street, gone away, the landlady said. The last I saw of him was that awful day on Drury Lane. Now he looked almost exactly the same. Despite all the harm and the hurt, he was still so entrancingly beautiful. His eyes passing over mine were as sensitive and liquid and thoughtful as they had ever been. His lips pursed and released, in the shock of seeing me, no doubt. In that moment, all the hatred I had felt towards him in the last years entirely vanished. I felt only happy to see him. He was alive. He looked unharmed. He had not changed. He briefly knelt down to speak to the little boy. 'Go to Mama.'

The child turned around to look at a mother who was not there. 'Mama?'

'Yes, go to Mama.'

Mama? I wondered. 'Mama, Mama!' the child cried with the same joyousness.

Then I heard a second voice, female: 'Ned, why is *he* here? What does he want?' It was Lydia Caesar standing on his doorstep. She rushed out onto the pavement to scoop up the child. 'What does he want?' With the boy squirming in her arms, she walked towards Ned and me, so that we were all standing in the middle of the street. The boy's hand reached out and brushed his father's shoulder with his fingertips: 'Papa, pick up! Papa, pick up!'

With a sick, shuddering horror, I realised the truth: Ned had married Lydia Caesar and this child was theirs. I remembered that day on Drury Lane, when she had revealed that he was staying there; had they been lovers then, or perhaps all along? Was that why the Caesars had stopped coming to the Obelisk? Maybe Ned had told them to avoid me, that I was mad, that I was 'harassing' him. The lies he had told, the newspapers he had told them to, told anyone who would listen, all to cover up the truth that, once upon a time, we had been lovers – and in love.

But then I realised the most awful thing, which killed all that: this story was not about me and him, it was about him and her. I was swallowed up not in this story I have been telling myself, but in some narrative of man meets woman, just a bit-part player, easily erased from future versions. So, this, I thought, is the end of the story, and it's not even my story. Was this history not even mine, a narrative always belonging to someone else?

I remembered then that night in the tavern on Fleet Street, when Lydia preached – excellently – to her abolitionist crowd about how English people in the future will insist Africans stop talking about Slavery. She had said: 'We will say, "You used to make us sit behind a curtain at your dinners," and he will say, "Stop lying." He will say: "You are free now, why can't you be happy?" He will say: "You are free now, why can't you accept that the past is the past? You are free now, why can't you just let go of what we did to you?"'

I understood now that she was right. One day, all this will not exist. It will have changed, and two men will walk in the street unmolested, and then someone like me will say: *Do you remember when people like you used to hang people like us for entertainment outside Newgate Prison?* And you will reply: *No.* And we will say: *All right, maybe it was not you who did it, but it was someone like you, and one day, you could change your mind about us, or someone like us, and bring back the violence and the hate.* And you will say: *No, no, I never believed anything different to what I believe today.* What will happen then, to us, to what was done to us, to our histories? And then one day, when someone says that they need to protect women or children from people like us, and say the same old lies, told again, over and over, again and again, they will fix us with mean, hard, critical eyes and say: *You have your freedom now, by our permission, so why can't you shut your mouths, faggots?*

'May your . . . husband and I speak alone, Miss Caesar?' I asked. Of course, I knew she was no longer Miss Caesar; she was someone else now.

'I don't think I want to leave my husband here, with you,' she said. The child was wriggling in her arms, laughing, burbling to himself and to her.

'It's all right,' I heard Ned say. He was smiling at Lydia, and I could see that he loved her; how cruel it felt that he should so obviously love her. 'Just take the baby and wait at the end of the street.' I could remember that night in Hampstead, when I had got upset and he had calmed me down. Now he spoke to her like that. 'I won't be two minutes.' Now his tenderness and care was for her.

She turned, walking away, her little son's voice, happy and exquisite, on the wet air as he continued to wriggle in her arms. We watched her go. When she was at the end of the street, I turned to look at him. 'I only have one question, Ned. Let me ask it and I'll go.'

'All right,' he said. Always, that damned, neutral *all right*.

'How could you sell the letters? They have done me such harm. Even if you did not love me any more, even if you hated what I wrote, you must have known that selling the letters would destroy me.'

His eyes flickered as if he was looking for Lydia and their son. 'That hack from the *Weekly Dispatch* found me. He said I had to give him the letters or he would call the Patrol on me, name me in his newspaper. I could not risk that.'

'Who told them about you?'

'The Cooks, the Gees, does it matter?'

I suppose it did not. 'How did they find you, though?'

'I am an African named Ned. There are not a thousand of us in London.'

There was something I did not yet understand. 'So why didn't they ask you to come to court?'

'O, John, you truly do not get it, do you? What good would an African be to them in an English courtroom? I would do more harm to their case than good. Now I am just a name in a newspaper story, an English name, any virginal English boy, on whom the reader can paint any portrait they like.'

Like Adam Foreman, I thought. 'When did you move back here?' I asked, a second, uninvited question.

'When my son was born. I had stayed in touch with my old landlady and . . .' He paused, unsure what to say next. '. . . things had died down, she knew Lydia and I had a child, and she asked me to move back. She wanted a family to move in. She was sick of drunken bachelors.' He was about to say something else but then stopped himself. 'I don't have anything to say to you, John. There is nothing left to say.'

'There is always something left to say.'

'You've asked me your question, now go, John. Let's part on good terms.'

'Good terms, Ned? How are these good terms?'

'You sent me all those letters, John,' he cried. 'You turned up at my door.' He laughed again, just as darkly. 'It was too . . .' *Don't say 'crazy'*, I was thinking, *don't say 'crazy'*. 'It was too hard, John.'

I felt stalled by him saying that, the lack of hostility, the sadness in his voice. I could only respond with honesty.

'I want you to know, Ned, that I loved you very much. I want you to know that I loved you sincerely. Don't ever doubt that, even if you doubt everything else.' He looked at me then, and I saw the emotion in his eyes, making him doubt whatever he had been telling himself about me the last two years. 'That time we spent together in my rooms on The Cut, weren't they the happiest time? You sleeping in my arms, in my bed, waking in the morning, your lips against my skin . . .'

Suddenly his eyes went quite pink. 'Please, John, I cannot talk about it . . .'

I saw the love that was in him; the love that was surely for me. 'Can't what, Ned? Can't even admit what you truly felt for me? Can't admit what we had?'

He blinked and turned harder. 'Stop it, John! What we had wasn't just that, it was everything else too, the lies, the manipulation, not respecting my wishes, my limits, making me go to Vere Street, even involving me in Vere Street—'

I had to stop him talking. I did not want him to lie like William Webster! 'You were the one who said you were on a journey, and I was helping you with that!'

'Do you think Vere Street was my journey, John?' He now pointed towards his wife and child down the street. '*They* are my journey! Vere Street was your journey, John, perhaps. But they are mine. *This* life was what my journey was towards.' He had started speaking sharply, without mercy, with irritation: 'You should go away, John. I don't want to see you again. I don't want you to come here ever again.'

I was astonished by his cruelty; he had not been that person before; had his own failures and compromises poisoned him so; had Lydia pumped arsenic into his veins? I had to reach him, to get him past any hatred planted in him. 'My whole life, I was waiting for love, Ned. My whole life, I was waiting for someone to show goodness to me. Maybe that's why I came to believe in the innate goodness of human beings. Love is everything, Ned, and you cannot know what I would do to protect you, like you asked me to.'

He seemed bemused by this. 'I never asked you to protect me.'

'Yes,' I said. 'Yes, you did. The night I walked you to Mint Street and you let me inside your room. I told you I would always protect you. Have you forgotten?' It was an oath. He was gazing at me, at first with confusion but then suspicion.

'I don't think I did,' he said. It was then I heard the drone. Why did he deny it? How could he? If only he knew what I had had to do because of that oath I swore.

'Yes, Ned!' I insisted. 'Yes, you made me say I would protect you and that was what I have done!'

His eyes grew troubled. 'What did you do, John?' I could hardly bring myself to say. Now that he had denied what he had invoked in me, how could I explain? His lips pursed, that little movement of his mouth, so serious, a sign of his intelligence and thoughtfulness; how I always loved it. 'What did you do, John?'

There comes a time in life when we must tell the truth, I suppose, or at least stop dealing in omissions. This is a list of my omissions: I did not admit the existence of my wife; I told William that I was a virgin, when in fact, the horrors of my childhood were filled with rape and drove me to rent on the streets; I told Ned I had read a novel I had not; I did not tell Ned about the duty on the first day that we met; I did not tell Ned I was taking him to Vere Street, or about the last coach back from Hampstead; I did not tell you about the letters. If I have missed anything out, sincerely, I'll apologise, but let me be clear: *there is one omission about which I have not told you, and it is the worst thing.*

I looked straight into his eyes. 'It was me who told the Patrol about Vere Street. It was me who exposed the molly house, and I did it to protect you.' I saw his eyes flashing shock, horror, disgust, but suddenly I was entirely unafraid. 'Mr Linehan, from my chapel, saw us that night, after we kissed in the dark. But it was several weeks before the Patrol came to the chapel. He reported us.'

His eyes were running around the ground, wide with shock, and still I felt unafraid; I am not ashamed to love and I cannot be made to feel ashamed. 'They said that they would arrest you, prosecute you, pillory or hang us, you, unless I helped them break the molly house, Ned.' I took a breath. 'I cannot tell you, Ned, what that happening began in my life. I have blamed you for breaking me apart when you left me, but my breaking down started then. I am subject to wild impulses, foolish decisions, and perhaps that is part of why I told them. Maybe I could have fronted it out, but I remembered only – I was driven mad by my remembering – your request that I protect you. So I went back to the Patrol and told them everything, gave names, addresses, I did it all to protect you, Ned. I told them everything. I protected you, Ned, to save you, from the scaffold.'

The strangest sensation of peace came over me. It felt like a victory. I had shown him that I loved him so much that I would destroy the world for him. Nothing he could say, nothing Lydia could do for him, no lie he could tell about me, could ever match what I had done for him.

This next part is addressed to you, the reader. I have told you, told myself, that there were no more lies, but here we are, here it is: the deepest lie of all. When I was telling you, telling myself, this story, this narrative of which I felt I could be in control, I lied so that the story could be told. But people tell lies so that stories – histories – make sense to them all the time. History is all omissions and distortions of the truth. Why is it any different for me? My own history, I see it now, is just one long act of omission. *Scrub out my name, my experience, from its pages. Wipe me clean away.*

Look, I know you might never forgive me for what I have just told you. But if at this stage, you still crave redemption for me, still look for something of me you can save, let me tell you this. I regret nothing. After the lies that have been told about me, men like me, I have proven to myself that I am capable of the greatest, most expansive love. Know this further: I would do it all again. I would not change a thing.

His lips parted. 'Do you remember the first day we went for a walk, John?'

'Of course. We met at the Obelisk and walked across the river.'

'Do you remember how you asked me if I believed in what you believed, in the radical possibilities of love, the innateness of men's goodness, the inevitability of tolerance?'

'Yes. You talked about moral philosophy.'

'Did I? How I must have wanted to impress you.' He gave a grim, tight laugh.

'You said you did not agree with me, but you thought I was asking important questions.'

He nodded. 'But do you remember what the questions were?'

'No, not any more.'

'I said the questions were, who is a radical, and what makes them so? What is demanded of a radical, of radicals who spend their time demanding things? And I said the most important question is – is a person radical simply because they say they are, or is it because of their actions and behaviours?'

'Yes, I remember now.'

'I used to think, John – I used to think, can't he see, can't he see what people are truly like? Is he so innocent that he cannot see what people are truly like? People like to say they're good but that's all they're doing: saying it. They're just praising themselves, that they're kind, that they're tolerant, but where is the evidence they are? All I see is the same old hate. I used to think, he's so innocent, he's just going to end up disappointed and hurt when he realises the truth. And it made me worry for you, because I cared for you so much.' A horrible pain passed over his face. 'No, John, that is not true. I was in love with you. I was falling in love with you so fast and hard, faster and harder than I had even known was possible before.' He took a long breath. 'But now . . .'

'But now?' I asked, astonished by his confession of his feelings, after everything.

'But now I see the truth, John Church . . .' His eyes were suddenly on me so very merciless. 'You are just like all those others who pose as radicals, but do so only to enforce your own beliefs, protect your own egos, flatter your own vanities, without asking what does it mean to be radical, what does it require of you?'

273

'Stop it, Ned,' I said, wanting him only to go back to admitting his love for me.

'I see now that you built this fantasy of the radical possibilities of love, but you did it to deceive—'

'Whom did I deceive?' I cried.

'Yourself, John. *Yourself.*' I was, for the last time, amazed. 'You killed your friends, John. You killed your friends and yet you still pretend that you are a good man, still you pretend you act out of goodness, out of . . . out of *love*. But you're not a good man, you're the worst of men because yours is the worst hypocrisy of all: the person who does terrible things and then calls them good. Don't say you did these things to protect me, John Church! You did them to save yourself!'

'Shut up!' I yelled.

'You're far worse than those radicals in Hampstead! You have caused such harm to people who loved you, and all you can do is invite the world to admire you. You are the worst of people, John Church, and yet you insist you are the best.'

I felt such unadulterated, poisoned, poisonous rage then. *Let it fly*, I thought. *Let it protect me, my rage. Let it do its worst, and I'll regret nothing, of course.* I lunged at him, struck him hard in the face. He tumbled backwards, dazed by the blow. I kept raining blows down on him. '*I am* a good man!' I was yelling. '*I am* a good man! I am a good man . . .'

Ned was on the ground, rolling around, clutching his nose; it wasn't bleeding. There was a shout; I turned. Lydia was running back towards us, setting her son down at a distance. She was telling me to get away from them. Her – their – little son was starting to cry. I looked at this child, not two years old, crying in the street. I had once been that child, but it was my actions now making this child cry. Lydia ran right up to me, without a flicker of fear. She started pushing me, yelling at me, ready to fight me with all the boldness of any man.

'Get away, Reverend Church! Get away, and never come back, Reverend Church! Leave us alone! Damned priests, why don't you let people alone, and stop with all your violence and mischief?'

I was staring down at the street, its cobbles, my eyes burning, gazing at the patterns in the dust the rain had made. And in that moment, I pictured in their beautiful little child the child I had once been, before I was even named John Church, a child whose mother had (deliberately) let go of his hand in the London crowd, a happy child singing and clapping in the street, full of his own native joy, being let go of into the misery of a loveless life.

Back at the start I said that love is not for every child. I said that that's what the clever orphan knows. But this clever orphan has learned something else. That love is everything. That love can never be a source of shame. Yes, I am excessive. Yes, I am impulsive. So what if I'm extreme? It's like Mr Sellis said to me, that day I finally understood what I had to do with Ned: love is a radical thing that requires radical thinking, and radical action.

So hear this, before you judge me: I regret nothing. If even now you want to spare me a few sentences, a paragraph perhaps, to explain my history, you can shove it.

I told you: I regret nothing!

Afterword

This is a true story. Its chronology of events is largely as described. However, for the sake of clarity, I have significantly simplified the trial process, which actually took place over two actions, including a libel action brought by Church, separated by some time distance. Church was sentenced to two years in prison for 'assaulting' Adam Foreman at his second trial. All the characters connected to Vere Street were real people: Sally Fox, Black-Eyed Leonora, Miss Sweet Lips, Richard Oakden, James Mann, Tommy White and John Hepburn, Philip Kett, and James Cook and his wife, whose own name is not recorded. I have speculated some crossover between the masculine identities recorded in the legal record and the names of 'queens' widely reported in the press. Ned's name solely exists in the intense letters sent to him by John Church, also later published in the press. We know nothing else about Ned's life or identity.

The scandal around the Duke of Cumberland and his servant, Sellis, was real but suppressed; journalists went to prison for covering it. Sellis either committed suicide or was murdered in the Duke's palace apartment. The near-simultaneous suicide of a royal servant named Tranter, and the existence at Vere Street of a molly named the Duchess of Gloucester, a royal servant, is factual. Cumberland, Queen Victoria's uncle, lived a long life of great privilege, eventually becoming King of Hanover.

John Church was married to a Miss Elliott, whom he met at radical religious meetings. She died around 1813, before certainly the second of his trials and possibly the first, by implication, of alcoholism. The Gees, their landlords on The Cut, took part in the press campaign against Church, as did the Cooks, who almost certainly attempted to blackmail him and others; the Gees noted Mrs Church's heavy drinking and the couple's arguing. The Caesars and Mr Linehan are inventions. Almost all locations are real. The slum Clare Market was demolished in the early twentieth century.

John Church survived prison and returned to the preacher's life, publishing an autobiography, *A Child of Peculiar Providence*, in 1823. He disappears from history's pages soon after. The date and manner of his death are unknown. Like him, the men of the Vere Street scandal faded into obscurity. The moral panic about gay men in British society of which 'the Vere Street Coterie' was an early part continued into the second half of the twentieth century.

This novel was written during the Covid pandemic, amid widespread media commentary that society should and had compassionately come together to cope and deal with the crisis. Hearing this over and over again, I could not help but think of the gay men and trans people of my youth, who died in such huge numbers during the Aids crisis, and the abuse, neglect and hatred they faced from that same society. This book is written in remembrance of them.

Acknowledgements

First and foremost, thank you to Rictor Norton, whose work was so useful in researching this novel; in particular, his book *Mother Clap's Molly House: Gay Subculture in England, 1700–1830*.

I also want to acknowledge the following writers' work in helping me see how this book might work: Chinua Achebe, *An Image of Africa* and 'Africa's Tarnished Name'; Robert Aldrich and Garry Wotherspoon (eds), *Who's Who in Gay and Lesbian History*, where I first heard of John Church; Louis Crompton, *Homosexuality and Civilisation*; Peter Fryer, *Staying Power: The History of Black People in Britain*; Iain McCalman, *Radical Underworld: Prophets, Revolutionaries, and Pornographers in London*; Toni Morrison, *Playing in the Dark: Whiteness and the Literary Imagination*; Graham Robb, *Strangers: Homosexual Love in the Nineteenth Century*; Michael Taylor, *The Interest: How the British Establishment Resisted the Abolition of Slavery*; Chris White (ed.), *Nineteenth-Century Writings on Homosexuality*; and Jerry White, *London in the Eighteenth Century* and *London in the Nineteenth Century*.

Lastly, thank you to the following people: my editor Anna Argenio, my agent Veronique Baxter, Adi Bloom, Alix Christie, Tammy Cohen, Emma Flint, Keith Jarrett, Stephen Kolawole, Marianne Levy and Zahid Mukhtar.

About the Author

Neil Blackmore is the author of five novels. His work has been acclaimed for its radical redrawing of the historical fiction form and the parameters of queer historical fiction. His third novel, *The Intoxicating Mr Lavelle*, was shortlisted for the Polari Prize for LGBTQ+ Fiction. *The Dangerous Kingdom of Love*, his fourth, was memorably described as 'like Hilary Mantel on acid' and chosen as one of *The Times*' Best Historical Fiction Novels. He lives in London.